THE GOING BACK PORTAL

Connie Lacy

Wild Falls Publishing

~ ~ ~

Atlanta, GA

ISBN-13: 978-0-9996084-7-0

Published by Wild Falls Publishing
PO Box 29452
Atlanta, GA 30359

For all the good guys in my life

~

Also by Connie Lacy

The Time Telephone
A Daffodil for Angie
VisionSight: a Novel
The Shade Ring, Book 1 of The Shade Ring Trilogy
Albedo Effect, Book 2 of The Shade Ring Trilogy
Aerosol Sky, Book 3 of The Shade Ring Trilogy
Shade Ring Trilogy: Books 1 – 3 (ebook box set)

1

There was no denying Nana did sometimes resemble an old Indian woman. She certainly had the high cheek bones and brown eyes. But I stopped believing her tall tales when I was twelve. Not wanting to hurt her feelings, I humored her when she said she was one sixteenth Cherokee. Or one thirty-second. Or maybe one sixty-fourth. Her story changed from one telling to the next.

Still, she and I were close. BFFs, you might say. But as I left work that Friday on my way to dinner at Nana's house, Mallory Cleveland, the know-it-all reporter I worked with, gave me no end of grief. As usual.

"When was the last time you had a date?" she said. "I swear, you're sacrificing your love life for your grandma."

In no mood to admit my "love life" was pretty much non-existent, I scooted out the door, not bothering to reply. It's possible my job was part of the problem. Being a producer for an investigative reporter made me skeptical of any guy who came on to me. Not that there were many.

It only took a little over an hour to drive from Atlanta to Athens. But when I arrived at the familiar brick ranch with the pretty blue hydrangeas out front, only Jeannette's car was in the carport.

I pulled out my phone.

"Nana, where are you?"

"We're at the country cottage, sweetie. Where are you?"

"At your house."

"Why didn't you tell me you were coming?"

I almost blurted that she's the one who invited me for dinner – in Athens – but bit my tongue.

"How about I drive on over?" I said. "I can have supper with you and Jeannette."

"That would be splendid!" She held the phone away from her mouth. "Jeannette! Kathryn's coming for dinner!"

The highway to rural Madison County wound through areas barely touched by the twenty-first century. There were fields, pastures, chicken houses and the occasional rickety outhouse. And my favorite – the circle of ancient oaks surrounding a crumbling chimney, evidence that a farmhouse once stood on that hill where a family had carved out a living.

The red Georgia clay alongside the road was mostly covered with weeds that rippled in my rearview as I zoomed by. Once I crossed the Broad River, I was so far out in the country, it was like driving on a winding road to a bygone era.

Nana's cottage was pale aqua with white shutters. Tall red cannas bordered the front porch and a quaint white picket fence enclosed the small yard. Warm golden light spilled from the windows as I pulled into the gravel driveway. I was relieved I'd made it before dark, having a tendency to get lost in this backwoods area once the sun went down. GPS didn't always know when a road might turn into an abandoned cowpath.

I could hear Gracie, Nana's little Maltese-Poodle, yapping loud enough to wake the dead as I walked up the flagstone path. She quieted down when she saw my face, giving way to a squeal of delight from Nana like it had been a year since my last visit rather than a week.

"Kathryn!" she gushed. "What a pleasant surprise! I didn't know you were coming. You're just in time!"

She hugged me and kissed my cheek as I wondered if she remembered our phone conversation half an hour before.

"Smells heavenly," I said, breathing in the aroma of fresh-baked bread. I turned to Jeannette as she set a bottle of wine on the table.

"You know how to text, right?" she said.

I gave her a guilty look as Gracie sidled up, cuteness personified, angling for a scratch behind the ears. Which I dutifully supplied.

"Hope I didn't put you to too much trouble," I said, giving Jeannette a guilty look.

She reminded me of an attractive middle-aged black actress who regularly picked up Oscar nominations. Her eyes exuded intelligence and humor. She was much more than a live-in companion for Nana and we were lucky to have her.

"Homemade bread was our project today," she said. "I heated up some soup to go with it and Edie tossed a salad. Nothing fancy."

Nana could hardly wait till we were seated to tell me about a new neighbor. Which surprised me considering how remote the cottage was.

"She's a Cherokee Indian woman," she explained. "Hardly more than a girl, really. She and her husband live in a little house deep in the woods. It's down the hill behind my cottage, beside the river. And they have a cute little baby!"

I squinted at Jeannette for confirmation. She responded with a tiny shrug.

"But she has a terrible limp," Nana continued. "One leg is shorter than the other."

"A Cherokee family is living on your property?"

"I don't mind. They're nice people. But they're poor. I don't think they even have running water. She was washing laundry in the river."

"When did you visit her?" I asked, unable to hide my concern.

"Last Sunday when we were here."

"How do you know they're Cherokee Indians?"

"She told me so. She also used some words I didn't understand when she was talking to the baby."

"Maybe they were habla-ing Español?" Jeannette said.

"She wasn't speaking Spanish," Nana replied. "I know what Español sounds like."

"Did you walk down to the river with her?" I asked Jeannette.

"She was puttering around outside while I ran the vacuum," she replied. "I gave her a small basket and suggested she pick some plums from those old bushes at the edge of the yard."

Now it was *her* turn to look guilty.

I took a sip of wine as I imagined Nana in the woods by herself. What if those people were on meth? Or strung out on opioids? What if they followed her home and broke into the cottage looking for something to steal? Even if they were regular folks camping in the forest, what if a wild animal attacked her? I knew for a fact that black bears roamed the rural areas of northeast Georgia. Sometimes they even showed up in the Atlanta suburbs.

"Goodness, I was fine," Nana protested, apparently reading my thoughts. "It's just that my grandmother's been on my mind lately, and I remembered there were some old fig bushes where her house used to be. I thought it would be fun to make fig preserves like Grandma used to make."

Jeannette looked at the ceiling in a Lord-help-me kind of way.

"I know some people think it's old-fashioned," Nana said, "but the neighborly thing to do is for all three of us to pay Forest Water a visit."

"Forest Water?"

"Isn't that a lovely name? We can walk down there right now so I can introduce you."

She pushed her chair back from the table and stood up as though we should follow her out the door.

"It's almost dark, Nana. How about we go in the morning?"

She eyed the front window, noticing dusk had settled, then sat down again.

"Did I ever tell you about that passenger who put his hand on my fanny on a flight to Madrid?" she said suddenly. "He squeezed my derriere and gave me such a lecherous grin! The nerve! Of course, times were different back then. If I had a nickel for every time a man touched my behind while I was a stewardess, I could've bought myself a week at a ski resort in the Swiss Alps! Not to mention all the times I was propositioned."

"You were one hot babe!" I teased.

She fluffed her hair like an old movie star in reply.

"And the uniforms we wore," she said. "They were baby blue with matching pillbox hats. So pretty. But we had to watch what we ate. Couldn't gain a pound or they'd fire us. Too bad I had to retire so young. Stewardesses couldn't gain weight, they couldn't be married and they couldn't be over thirty!"

"Unbridled sexism," I muttered.

When we finished eating, the three of us cleared the table, Nana having moved on to regaling us with stories about her second career as an elementary school teacher.

"That's the best age," she said. "I don't like it when they get all hormone-y."

She chuckled as she headed off to brush her teeth, her little black furball trotting along behind.

"I take it she invited you to dinner and forgot to tell me," Jeannette whispered.

"Yeah. She said to come to the Athens house."

"You're sure you have my cell number?" she said.

"You're right. My fault. I'll keep you posted from now on. But, honestly, I'm not sure this cottage is the best place for her, isolated as it is."

"That's above my pay grade," she replied, loading bowls into the dishwasher.

"I need to call my mom. I keep telling her she should come for a visit and she keeps saying she will when she can find the time."

Jeannette knew how I felt about my mother's absence. It would be one thing if she were a few states away. Moving to Hong Kong meant she was on the other side of the world. I was pretty much on my own handling whatever came up. Well, me and Jeannette.

After coffee and a bowl of oatmeal the next morning, the three of us set off through the woods. The early June foliage was beginning to darken from brilliant spring green to the deeper verdant green of summer.

A jeering squawk drew our eyes to a branch above us and we watched as a stunning blue jay dive-bombed a smaller brown bird.

"Blue Jays may be pretty," said Nana, "but they're too much like school yard bullies for my taste."

Jeannette and I both laughed. Nana was not amused.

I'd only come this way a couple of times when I was growing up and didn't remember how far it was. Which alarmed me once again that she'd walked it by herself. It was a twenty-five minute hike before we finally heard the rush of the Broad River.

We found ourselves in a sizable clearing, now in the process of being gradually erased as saplings stretched toward the sun. The land sloped sharply toward the riverbank with noticeable terracing where I assumed crops had once been planted. On a hill to the right, rotten boards littered the ground. But there were no people and no building in sight.

"This is where Grandma lived," Nana said. "The house sat right here." She gestured toward the dark lumber. "She died when I was ten. Nobody wanted the house because it didn't have electricity this far from the road, so they hauled off most of the wood. After a while, the trail got overgrown and you could hardly find it anymore."

A fleeting expression of sadness crossed her face.

"This way," she said, perking up as she moved carefully beyond the blackened planks.

Instead of following, we watched as she made her way gingerly around a patch of sun-dappled fig bushes as tall as she was.

Nana looked every bit of her eighty-four years, with short white hair, a lovely wrinkled face, glasses that were only a decade out of fashion, and liver spots on her bony hands.

"Yoo-hoo!" she sang out. "Forest Water, where are you?"

Jeannette and I exchanged a concerned glance before turning toward the river so Nana wouldn't hear us.

"Edie was talking about her new Cherokee friends while you were in the shower this morning," Jeannette said. "She thinks we should take them a chicken casserole to welcome them to the neighborhood."

"I think my mother's going to have to find time in her busy schedule to fly home, whether she likes it or not," I whispered.

My eyes settled on the river as it flowed over rocky shoals mid-stream. Muddy from recent rains, the current was swift, flanked by a wall of green on the opposite bank, untouched by modern development. One of the last free-flowing rivers in Georgia, the water shimmered in the morning sun.

"Mom always says I'm exaggerating. I'm sending her an email right now."

I tapped away on my phone as Jeannette meandered along the riverbank, taking in the view. Engrossed in laying out my concerns in the email, I nearly dropped my phone when a high-pitched scream shattered the tranquility of the abandoned farmstead. I spun around to see Nana stumbling toward me, her eyes filled with anguish.

"Nana, are you all right?"

"Oh dear, oh dear!" she cried, opening her hand to reveal a half-eaten fig. "He slapped her." She looked behind her as though expecting someone to be there.

"Who slapped..."

"A horrible, horrible man," she said, voice quivering. "We've got to help her."

"Are you talking about the Cherokee woman?"

"We should call the police!" she said.

"Everything's going to be all right," I said, then turned to Jeannette as she hurried toward us. "You take her back to the house. She might like a cup of tea."

"You come too, Kathryn," Nana said. "He might be dangerous."

"I've got my pepper spray," I lied. "I'll join you in a few minutes."

She handed me the mangled fig as Jeannette took her arm. I watched them retreat slowly up the hill, disappearing into the trees. By the look in her eyes, Jeannette was thinking the same thing I was. Nana hadn't been tested yet for Alzheimer's, but the time had come. One of the symptoms was delusions.

That call to my mother would have to be sooner, rather than later.

I moved closer to where Nana had her episode. Fig trees had apparently been planted along the perimeter of the old house. You could see the outline by where they still grew.

A short distance away were more bushes with big, fuzzy leaves and dark fruit about the size of a golf ball. I walked over to take a look and discovered the same thing. The bushes defined the outer edge of a smaller structure that once stood here – this one about the size of a metal shed for storing a lawn mower. The flat area between the two buildings must've been a garden. Squinting in the sunshine, I could make out the eroded furrows.

A light breeze rustled the leaves above me. Together with the whoosh of the river, it was like phantom voices whispering in my ear. Which made the hairs stand up on my arms. No wonder Nana was having delusions. I could almost feel a presence, myself.

I studied the outline of the smaller building. Along the back, a rusted hinge lay half buried in leaves and pine straw next to several smooth river rocks. Nudging the ground cover with my toe, I discovered small animal bones, colored beads and feathers. There must've been a door here. I was about to drop the half-eaten fig and step inside the boundary when it occurred to me that Nana was chewing it when she had her hallucination or whatever it was. Opening my hand, my eyes took in the pink, seedy flesh inside thick brownish-purple skin. Could the fruit have triggered it?

Determined to find out, I popped it in my mouth and crossed the invisible threshold. An old-timey sweet flavor hit my taste buds as a loud buzzing filled my ears. I closed my eyes, my head swimming. When I opened them, I was inside a small hut. Staring at me was a pair of intense dark eyes belonging to a young woman seated on what looked like an Indian blanket, nursing a baby.

2

She was younger than me with lustrous black hair plaited into a thick braid hanging down the front of a simple grey farm dress. There was an angry red welt on one cheek and a sheen of sweat on her face. In her arms she cradled a plump, dark-haired baby at her breast.

Unconventionally beautiful, her piercing eyes transfixed me.

I tried to imagine how I appeared to her. My brown hair was loose on my shoulders and I suddenly felt naked in my tan shorts, white top and hiking sandals.

Why couldn't this little shack be seen from outside? I'd read about scientists developing real-life invisibility cloaks. But it wasn't logical that such a device would be draped over a primitive wooden hut in the Georgia countryside.

Just as I was about to speak, a man's voice shouted in the distance causing us both to tense. She lifted a shawl folded beside her, tossing it to me, gesturing for me to cover myself with it.

"If you don't come out, I'm coming in!" the man thundered.

She raised her hand warning me to be silent. It took a great deal of effort for her to rise from the blanket and step outside, still holding the baby protectively in her arms. A severe limp caused her to rock from side to side. Nana was right – one of her legs was shorter than the other. Much shorter.

Her words were too soft for me to make out, but his reply was not.

"You gonna do your wifely duty, you understand me? I'm tired of you hiding in that damn shack."

She replied with a calm voice.

"One more night!" he said. "You better be back in my bed tomorrow night, y'hear? You're my squaw and don't you forget it." There was grumbling as he walked away.

She waited a moment before re-entering the hut, holding her hand up again, cautioning me to hold my tongue. She spoke gently to the baby in a language I didn't understand.

Lowering herself slowly onto the blanket, she observed me for a moment before speaking, her voice low.

"You must leave. It is not safe."

She spoke precisely, as though she were a foreigner who learned English in a classroom. But there was no trace of an accent. Her manner was that of a young woman wise beyond her years.

"Are you Forest Water?" I whispered.

She nodded, a hint of surprise in her expression.

"Was that your husband?" I said.

Her answer was a tired sigh.

"Were you visited by a white-haired woman a few minutes ago?"

"I warned Old Grandmother to stay away. You must also."

"But..."

She laid the baby on the blanket, got to her feet and pushed a narrow door open at the back of the hut where I'd first entered. She slipped outside, returning with a fig in her hand.

"You must eat this and travel through the doorway," she said, placing it in my hand.

"I have so many questions."

She locked eyes with me as though trying to look into my soul. Having apparently come to a decision, she squatted beside the blanket, folding it back to reveal a layer of pine straw. Scraping the pine straw aside exposed the lid of a large metal box. She lifted the heavy lid and pulled out a leather pouch. From the pouch, she withdrew a book, opened it and ripped a handful of blank pages from the back. She stuffed the loose pages back inside the pouch, returned it to the box, closed the lid and covered it with the pine straw and blanket. Then she handed me the book.

"You must go," she whispered, eyes blazing.

"But..."

She gestured for me to put the fig in my mouth as she tugged the shawl from my shoulders.

I reluctantly placed the fruit between my teeth and passed through the small doorway.

Dizziness overwhelmed me as the buzzing in my ears returned, momentarily blocking out all other sound. I found myself standing in the clearing, the fig half-chewed in my mouth. I whirled around to discover the hut no longer existed. My muscles felt as though I'd run a marathon. Not willing to trust my wobbly legs, I remained motionless, dazed by what had just happened.

There were two possibilities – the figs contained some kind of psychedelic substance, causing me to have the same hallucination Nana had, possibly by virtue of power of suggestion. Or I had traveled back in time. Which was so freaky that my skin tingled. In my business, skepticism was ingrained. I wasn't easily taken in by a ruse. What I thought had happened could not possibly be the truth.

I looked all around the clearing for the young woman who called herself Forest Water. Then, to be sure the shack didn't still exist, I walked back and forth over the spot where it had been. There was nothing there.

Then I remembered the book. It was solid in my hands, the brown leather smooth to the touch. The book was real. The place was real. And as much as the rational part of my brain rebelled against the idea, I knew I had somehow visited the past.

Suddenly impatient to know the story of the mysterious dark-haired beauty, I made my way to a large rock on the riverbank. I untied the strap holding the book closed and opened it with care. So many words, perhaps written with a fountain pen or a quill, the letters sometimes puddled with excess ink, sometimes as thin as a strand of hair. The ink was black, the paper a cream color and rough to the touch. But the words were not in English. I had no idea what language or alphabet I was looking at. Some of the letters were familiar, but many looked like Arabic or Greek.

Carefully flipping the pages, I discovered the entire book was written in this foreign language. Completely inaccessible to me. I had to talk with Nana.

When I reached the cottage, she was sitting in her aqua armchair, Gracie in her lap, Jeannette seated across from her on the couch. They were having cinnamon muffins and a cup of tea. On the surface, it was a peaceful scene, but the air in the room was charged.

I fixed myself a cup and took a seat at the other end of the sofa from Jeannette. I tried to act casual but it was a challenge.

"So, Nana, tell me more about your neighbors."

"We've got to find a way to help her."

"Tell me about your first visit," I said, sipping my tea.

She stroked Gracie's fur as she talked.

"I've been having dreams about my grandmother lately. In the dreams she's trying to tell me something as she cooks figs like she did when I was a little girl. I can almost smell them cooking, the dreams are that vivid. It made me wish I could make some preserves like she used to make. So I walked down to the river to see if those old fig trees might still bear fruit after all these years. And sure enough, there were some ripe ones. I ate one, then another. I was on my third fig when I found myself inside a little wooden shed. I heard a woman singing and followed the sound through a door and around a house to the riverbank. There was this pretty black-haired girl washing clothes in the river with a chubby baby in a strange baby carrier leaning against a tree. I think I spooked her because the girl looked at me like I was a ghost."

Nana paused, her features pinched in concentration.

"I told her I was picking figs, holding up my little basket, and I said I hoped that was okay. Then it occurred to me I should introduce myself. I told her my name was Edie and she said her name was Forest Water. I said 'what a lovely name.'

And she told me her baby's Cherokee name was Butterfly. I was excited to find out they were Cherokee Indians. She let me kiss the baby on her soft cheek. And then she led me back to the hut. Once we were inside, she opened a small back door, giving me a fig to eat as I left."

Nana stared into space, a faraway look in her eyes.

"And then you visited again this morning?" I said.

"It was awful."

"You said there was a man."

"A terrible man. He yelled at her and slapped her across the face! Knocked her to the ground!" She looked from me to Jeannette. "Then he spotted me and yelled ugly things, told me to get off his property. I wanted to help, but Forest Water called out for me to leave. I should've given him what for! I'm so ashamed."

She hugged Gracie close.

"I don't think there was anything you could've done," I said.

"I should've tried."

I crossed the room to give her a hug. "Everything's going to be all right."

I was bluffing. My experience as a member of an investigative news team had prepared me for many things. This wasn't one of them.

"We've got to help her," she insisted. "We have to call the police!"

She had no clue she'd traveled to the past. She assumed those people were some poor neighbors without modern conveniences.

"Don't worry," I said. "I'll get in touch with someone."

"What's that book you've got?" Jeannette asked, obviously trying to distract her.

"I found it in a box by the river."

"What kind of book is it?" said Nana.

"Not sure yet. It's written in a foreign language. I'm taking it back to Atlanta so an expert can help me figure it out."

No way I was telling them I met Forest Water too. Or that I heard her husband threaten her. Or that she gave me the book. Jeannette would think Nana wasn't the only one suffering delusions.

Pulling my phone out, it only took a moment to find what I was looking for. It came back to me as I read. A man named Sequoyah created a Cherokee alphabet back in the early 1800s. Looking at a few examples, I was convinced the mysterious book was written using the Cherokee Syllabary. Now all I had to do was find someone to translate it.

I was slammed all week with a story the Channel Seven Watchdog Team was working on. We got a phone tip from a teenage girl about her high school drama teacher. She claimed the guy offered her and a girlfriend private acting tutorials for twenty bucks, then spiked their drinks with something that knocked them out before having sex with them.

After running it by the station lawyers, I did preliminary phone interviews, then Mallory did on-camera interviews. We shot the girls in silhouette, their faces in shadow, disguising their voices. It was left up to me to do an on-camera interview with a psychologist who specialized in sexual predators and domestic violence.

Tawdry is the word that came to mind. To be honest, I found it hard to believe, even when the girls showed us the lurid video snippets they said the guy texted them. I couldn't help but think they'd hooked up with a boy at school who was now humiliating them for fun. How could they fall for a porno ruse like that? I mean, coaching them – with a camera recording it all – on how to do a nude sex scene so they could learn how to audition for movies? Please!

The honchos decided we would go undercover to get our own video, along with proof he was drugging the girls. Mallory insisted it would have to be me, not her.

"Even if he doesn't watch our newscasts, my face is plastered on billboards all over the city," she argued. "He'd recognize me right away."

Which was true. She was our station's star investigative reporter. Then again, I wasn't exactly the ideal candidate either.

"I'm twenty-nine years old, Mallory. Pretty sure I can't pass for a teenager."

"You don't look that old. Not most of the time anyway."

I gave her a look. But I had to admit even if the teacher didn't know who Mallory was, the odds of her passing for a high school girl were slim to none. Besides being smart and tenacious, she was a striking black woman with a capital W.

"Once we get you dolled up with the right clothes and make-up," she said, "he won't know the difference."

When I went into TV news, I never guessed one of the occupational hazards would be playing dress-ups while impersonating a teenager.

But that's exactly what I did Tuesday evening at a makeshift theater with about thirty folding chairs. That's where Ed Hobbs was directing a play so bad, having my teeth cleaned would've been more fun. Dressed in black leggings, a bare-shouldered top, a dishwater blonde wig with bangs and a hidden camera in my Boho glasses, it's possible I might've fooled the casual observer. I hung around afterwards, pretending to be a starry-eyed high schooler desperate to break into the movies.

Ed Hobbs looked like the kind of teddy bear next-door neighbor you'd trust to feed your cat while you were out of town. Pushing forty, pale and soft around the edges like a guy who spent too much time playing video games, he seemed to believe me when I said a girlfriend told me she'd heard about his one-on-one training. He said, as luck would have it, he had a cancellation the following night.

When I showed up at his house the next evening wearing the wig and spy glasses and a shorts outfit Mallory chose for me, my hidden camera was already recording. Hobbs had a polite, business-like manner, which made me wonder again if our teenage sources might be stretching the truth.

"So, you want to break into film?" he said, guiding me to a large bedroom.

It smelled like a freshly cleaned motel room. There was a queen-sized bed, a small couch, a lamp table, two cameras mounted on tripods, directional track lighting hanging from the ceiling and black curtains over the windows.

"Yeah," I said, deciding short answers might be best so I wouldn't give myself away.

"I happen to know auditions will be announced in a couple of weeks for several parts in an indie movie shooting here soon. They'll want you to do a bedroom scene where the guy seduces the girl. Have you ever done a scene like that?"

Which made me giggle at the ridiculousness of the whole set-up. Could be, our informants were on the up and up.

"It's normal to be nervous," he said, his voice all soothing and fatherly. "I've got just the thing to help you relax." He opened the closet door to reveal a small refrigerator. "Let's see, I've got beer, wine, and bottled mojitos and margaritas."

"A margarita maybe?"

"Coming right up!"

With his back to me, he opened a bottle and filled a red plastic party cup, delivering it with a big smile. When he returned to the fridge to get himself a beer, I poured some of my drink into an empty water bottle hidden in my purse. Then I took a tiny sip so my breath would smell right.

After chugging half his beer, he proceeded to pull the covers down on the bed, then fiddled with the cameras.

I strolled toward the sofa, surreptitiously pouring more of the margarita into my bottle.

"Okay," he said. "I think we're ready. Cameras are rolling. Did you bring the twenty dollars?"

Rather than speak, I slid the crisp bill from my pocket and set it on the table.

"Thanks," he said. "You can leave your purse there too."

I zipped it as I set it down and moved tentatively toward the bed, holding my half-empty cup, aware his cameras had recorded me forking over the money. Smart. He videotaped every girl paying him for his services.

"Finish your drink," he said. "Then we'll get started. We'll watch the footage afterwards and I'll give you pointers on how to improve your performance."

I gave him a deer in the headlights stare, keeping the hidden camera in my glasses trained on him.

"Believe me, you'll feel much more relaxed and unselfconscious once you've finished your margarita," he said. "Bottoms up!"

I lifted the cup to my mouth and pretended to drink.

"It's best to remove all your clothes since that's what they'll want you to do at the audition," he said. "You'll need to feel comfortable doing the scene undressed."

He sounded almost like a nurse giving you directions before the doctor comes in to examine you, never using the words nude or naked.

"I think I'd rather keep my clothes on," I said.

"I have to tell you, a lot of the girls who complete my tutorial thank me for my thoroughness. They say it really helps them relax when they get to those auditions. And, believe me, there's plenty of competition. Beautiful girls willing to show their stuff, willing to get into character." He downed the rest of his beer.

Slick. That's what he was. Slick.

"Actually," I said, "I'm not feeling too good."

"You'll feel better once you lie down." He patted the bed reassuringly. "We'll go slow."

Hurrying to the table, I set my drink down and retrieved my purse. "I've gotta go."

I rushed down the hallway, across the living room and bounded out the front door. Racing across the lawn, I climbed into my car and locked the doors as I cranked the engine. In my haste to get away from Mr. Sleaze, I actually peeled a wheel.

Mallory was disappointed I didn't crawl into bed with him so we could have that video for our report too.

"Easy for you to say," I replied, not wanting to admit I was scared to death all alone with a professional pervert.

"I know all about predators," she replied. "My sister was married to one. And they've got to be stopped. Which is why I wanted as much video as possible."

She eased off once we learned the drink he fixed me contained a strong dose of a popular date-rape drug that would've knocked me out for sure. That, plus the footage of him handing me the drink and encouraging me to empty my cup before joining him on the bed was enough, along with the video from the girls and their interviews. Before we asked Hobbs to talk with us on camera, the lawyers would have to do their thing.

When Saturday finally arrived, I met with Dr. Eric Murray, an Associate Professor of History at the University of Georgia with a specialty in Southeastern Indians, and more specifically, Cherokee Indians.

I found a number of translation services when I searched online but wanted a more personal touch. Someone I could speak with face to face. I didn't like the idea of sending the book – or even the scanned pages – off to some anonymous translator. The mysterious black-haired Forest Water entrusted me with what I assumed was her story. I wasn't about to betray her faith in me. So, after reading several of Dr. Murray's blog posts and sampling two of his books, I thought he might be a good choice. Especially since he seemed to actually care about the Cherokee.

We agreed to meet at Jittery Joe's coffee shop just off the UGA campus. I got there first and, after ordering coffee and a

Danish, laid claim to a small table by the front window. As I settled in, a man in black spandex bicycle shorts and a form-fitting iridescent yellow and blue jersey breezed through the door, looking straight at me.

"Ms. Spears, I'm Eric Murray," he said, extending his hand.

"How did you...?"

"Found your picture online."

"You must be an accomplished Googler. So much for maintaining my anonymity."

I avoided being on camera in my job, which helped when I needed to be incognito, as with the unpleasant story we were currently working on. Sometimes my voice could be heard asking questions or there might be a shot of me from behind, but the station made a point of keeping my face off the air. I even used a picture of my tabby cat as my profile picture on social media and made sure my privacy settings were as tight as possible.

He paid for a cup of coffee and a cinnamon bun, then sat across from me, the total opposite of what I expected. He was a little older than me, about six feet, dark hair, not exactly leading man handsome, but with character actor good looks. Looking every bit the avid bicyclist, he didn't reek of sweat, so he must not have ridden far, or the strong aroma of coffee masked his scent.

"First things first," he said. "Call me Eric."

"And you can call me Kathryn."

"Deal. Now tell me what you're hoping I can translate. You said it might be right up my alley?"

"I think it may be a diary. Possibly written by a Cherokee woman."

"Written in the Cherokee Syllabary?"

"I think so."

"How'd you come into possession of it?"

He took a bite of his cinnamon bun.

"Found it in a box on an abandoned homestead along the Broad River. On my grandmother's property."

"Any idea when it dates from?"

"I'm hoping you can tell me."

He sipped his coffee, watching me as I retrieved a sturdy shoebox from beneath my chair and set it on the table. His eyebrows shot up as I opened the lid.

He promptly removed the coffee mugs, plates and silverware from the table, setting them by the trash can. He held his finger up, indicating he'd return in a moment, then ducked into the men's room.

"I washed my hands," he said as he rejoined me a moment later.

Carefully lifting the book, he held it gingerly with both hands.

"Doesn't look overly worn," he said, but he was obviously intrigued. He slowly opened the cover. "It's definitely the Cherokee Syllabary. Interesting, there's not much sign of age. No yellowing, no fraying. I don't see any indication of fungus in the paper."

He couldn't take his eyes off the pages. While he read, I wandered up to the counter and got a second cup of coffee. I stood and sipped, watching him as he silently mouthed some of the words to himself. After a few minutes, I sat down again, pulling my chair away from the table and holding my coffee in my lap.

"The narrative reads like it's from the era of the Trail of Tears," he said. "If that's true, she might've attended one of the mission schools where they taught the Syllabary. That could be of historical interest. The question is: is it authentic? I'd want an expert to examine the paper and ink. It doesn't look modern, but there are ways people can fake it. Although, in this case, I don't know what the motive might be. Unless, of course, you're the counterfeiter and this is a ruse to meet me."

There was mischief in his eyes and a slight twitching at the corners of his mouth.

"I'll have you know I thought you were a dry, middle-aged academic when I emailed you."

He let loose with a big laugh. "Touché!" he said, returning the book to the shoebox like he was handling a bomb.

"So, I was right. It's a journal."

"It appears to be a woman's story about how her family was forced off their land and rounded up with other Cherokees for removal to the west. She talks about her mother arranging her marriage to a white man so she wouldn't have to make that long trek to Oklahoma, apparently because of some kind of physical infirmity."

I took a deep breath, anxious to know everything in the diary.

"Interesting you found it in Madison County," he continued. "By the time of the Trail of Tears, most Cherokee lived in north Georgia. But at one time the Broad River was the dividing line between the Cherokee and Creek Indians. Some Cherokees may have still lived in that area on family farms."

"So you'll do the translation?"

"I need to get confirmation the manuscript is authentic. If it's a fake, it's rather well done. The antiquated language, the style of the script, the leather cover. If it's for real, I might be interested in writing about it. By the way, her name was Amadahy."

"Ama...?"

He pronounced it slowly for me. "Ah-ma-dah-hee. That means Forest Water in Tsalagi."

Which sent a little shiver down my spine.

"Tsalagi?" I said.

"That means Cherokee. The language and the people. It's a word the white man got from the Creek Indians who used it to refer to the Cherokee people. The Cherokee called themselves Aniyunwiya – the Principal People."

He pulled out his phone, filling in a receipt form for the diary, and emailed it to me on the spot. Then he closed the shoebox and tucked it under his arm as he rose to leave.

"You can't carry it on your bicycle," I said.

"Don't worry. The bike's on the back of my car. I'm driving to a park to join a group ride. I'll drop the book off at my condo first."

We said our good-byes and he drove away, leaving me with knots in my stomach. I should've felt some relief, I suppose, but a sliver of dread lodged in my gut. I had a feeling the translation wouldn't cheer me up.

Dr. Murray – Eric – said he'd keep me posted. I was pleased we hit it off. Made me feel more comfortable letting him take the manuscript, as he called it.

I cranked my Camry and took off toward the Loop, but when I got to the interchange, I veered east, not west toward

Atlanta. I felt like I was being pulled back to Madison County. I called Jeannette and offered to bring barbecue.

"Good," she said. "That'll distract her for a while. She's chomping at the bit to go down to the river."

We had a nice lunch at the kitchen table. But as soon as Nana lay down for her afternoon nap, I was out the back door.

"Don't let her follow me," I whispered to Jeannette.

"Why are you going down there again?"

"I wanna poke around."

"You know her mind is playing tricks on her. And if you keep talking about it, it's not going to help."

"Mother emailed me she'll fly home soon, but she couldn't give me an exact timetable yet," I said, hoping that would satisfy her.

By the time I reached the riverbank, I'd worked up a sweat with the temperature hovering in the low nineties. I lifted my hair off my neck, fanning myself with my other hand as I took in the view from the shade of a tall hickory tree close to the water's edge. I waited a few minutes before making my way to where the little hut used to be. My mouth was dry as I walked nervously around the fig bushes. My plan had been to find out what was in the book before taking any action. But I couldn't ignore the sense of urgency inside me.

My hands balled into fists as I got into position. Before I could change my mind, I plucked a fig from the bush, biting into it as I walked through what I'd come to think of as the time portal.

The shack was like an oven. An empty oven that smelled like cornbread. I held my breath, afraid to move, waiting till the buzzing in my ears and the dizziness eased. Then a shriek split the silence. It was a woman's voice. And there was the sudden wailing of a baby and a man's voice shouting. Then a different woman's voice saying something and a woman crying.

Without thinking I reached for the door but caught myself. Looking down at my outfit – khaki capris, a pale green top and sandals – there was no way I could pass myself off as a traveler stopping to drink from the river.

"I told you!" the man shouted, but I couldn't understand the rest of his words.

The baby's bawling grew louder and there was that unfamiliar woman's voice saying something.

I couldn't hide here and do nothing. Glancing about, I saw the shawl I'd covered myself with the last time and wrapped it around me. I pushed the front door open a fraction of an inch, but only the garden was visible. I nudged it a tiny bit more. What I saw was an unsettling tableau. A man towered over Amadahy while a young black woman in a long brown dress stood a few feet away holding Amadahy's baby in her arms. Nana's description hadn't prepared me for the sight of this barbarian with the ragged beard.

"I ain't eatin' no cold cornbread!" He lunged at her, shoving what looked like half a loaf of cornbread in her face, causing her to lose her balance and fall to the ground.

The baby reached out for her mother, trying to escape the other woman's arms.

"Make her shut up!" the man barked.

The woman struggled mightily to maintain her grip on the thrashing child while Amadahy pulled herself to a sitting position, brushing crumbs from her eyes.

"Cooking a bunch a food in the morning to eat *cold* the rest of the day might be the Cherokee way," he yelled, "but it ain't my way!"

Amadahy rose with difficulty. As she did so, her eyes were drawn to the hut, looking straight at me. She instantly averted her gaze but fear was obvious in the set of her jaw.

Hardly breathing, I gently drew the door closed. Any notion I'd had of intervening in the volatile situation completely evaporated. It dawned on me I might make things much worse. I removed the shawl and folded it, realizing I needed to leave immediately. But as I set it down, I knocked a cup from its nail on the wall. It landed with a clank on a blackened pot.

The voices in the yard changed and I heard heavy footfalls approaching. I leapt out the back door, grabbed a fig from the bush and stepped back inside long enough to pop it in my mouth. As I bit down, I fled through the doorway.

My ears filled with buzzing as I found myself standing on the edge of the clearing. The hut was gone. Only then did it occur to me that I might be in danger from that brute.

It was a challenge focusing at work on Monday. Our first order of business was requesting an interview with Ed Hobbs. Usually, it would've fallen to me to place the call. But since I was the one who recorded the incriminating video, we decided Mallory would reach out instead. I sat in a chair by her desk so I could hear the conversation and take notes. She told him we were doing a story about his private tutorials while drugging and filming underage victims.

"We tested the drink you served one of your clients and confirmed it contained Rohypnol," she said.

There was silence on the other end. Then the connection dropped.

We got to work writing our story. That afternoon we met with the station attorney who went over our script with a fine-toothed comb before we put our report together. A decision was made to air the story the following evening, which meant another hectic day editing the package and letting the lawyer eyeball it mid-afternoon before demanding last minute tweaks. Mallory had to re-record one of her standups and a couple of sections of the voice-over. But she was ready to do her live shot for the five o'clock show, looking as cool as a chilled Roma tomato in her signature red dress, which, of course, accentuated her feminine charms.

But once the report was broadcast, we couldn't relax for a minute. The rest of the week was a frenzy of follow-up reports. Police got a search warrant and confiscated Hobbs' computers and smartphone, and charges were filed. We did a slew of interviews and reports covering reaction from the school board, parents and students. A dozen more girls came forward, admitting they'd been suckered by that degenerate, worried sick he'd release those embarrassing videos.

Despite my fatigue, I awoke before dawn Saturday morning, eager to drive to Athens. As promised, Eric had some pages ready for me. We met again at Jittery Joe's, which seemed appropriate since I'd already chugged two cups of coffee before I got there, and had ordered what would be my third as he sauntered through the door.

"We think it's the genuine article," he said, his misgivings of the week before now replaced with unabashed enthusiasm. "Although the manuscript is amazingly well preserved."

That's the first thing out of his mouth, even before he got his coffee, and before we sat down at the same window table where we'd talked the first time. Today, he was dressed in navy deck shorts and a button-up shirt. Not the colorful I've-got-something-better-to-do cycling togs.

"Tragic story," he said, placing the shoebox on the table. "The part I translated covers events of 1838 as the Cherokees were rounded up and marched west, and continuing into 1839. I scanned it so I could return the journal to you. My first few pages of translation are in here too," He patted the shoebox. "I'll also email them to you."

Tucking a wayward strand of hair behind my ear, I decided not to ask him to tell me more. I needed to read it for myself. In private.

"Amadahy was very likely full-blooded Cherokee," he continued. "Quite a riveting first-person narrative."

I reached across the table, lifting the box to my chest, and rose from my chair.

Surprise mixed with disappointment washed over his face as he stood too. My guess is he wanted to talk about the diary with me. But there was no way I could engage in small talk when I was anxious to start reading.

"I translated it into Standard English rather than trying to recreate the Cherokee speech pattern," he said. "I added the month and year in parentheses for you. I was so fascinated by the story, I spent a lot more time on it than I planned to."

He gave a small shrug.

"Which means a lot to me," I said.

It was obvious he was giving me and my project extra attention. And the way he looked at me, I wasn't sure which he was more interested in.

"I have to get back to Atlanta," I added, anxious to leave.

"Right, well, I'll email you more pages as I translate them."

"S'gi," I said, pleased I'd looked up the Eastern Cherokee word for 'thank you.'

"Hawa," he replied.

It was all I could do to drive home, dying to find out what was in those pages. As soon as I walked into my apartment, I kicked off my shoes, fixed a glass of iced tea and planted myself on the sofa. My silly cat, Pixie, meowed and nestled close beside me, purring softly as I lifted the translated pages from the shoebox.

Amadahy's Journal – Part 1 (May 1838)

I do not blame my mother. Neither do I blame my father. I do not blame Selu, the Corn Mother. Nor Selu's husband, Kana'ti, the hunter. I blame the white man who came from afar, forcing the Aniyunwiya from our Ancient Soil. I blame the white man for using trickery to rob us of our birthright and push our people toward the Darkening Land where Death awaits. I blame the white man for telling us we are sinners, when, in truth, it is they who are sinners.

My mother believed the chiefs of the Cherokee Nation when they said white leaders in Washington City would let us stay on our Ancestral Land. But then she had a dream that soldiers would break down our door and take everyone away. So she and her sisters prepared for the journey. Old Noon Day said our family would receive land in the west.

But my mother said I must stay behind. She judged I could not walk beyond the Great Mississippi River with my disfigurement. I begged her to let me go, but her mind was firm, like a mother hawk pushing her baby from the nest, forcing it to fly.

One morning during the Planting Moon, she helped me onto the back of the mule and took me to call on the young white man who bought land along the Broad River where our family had lived for generations. He was not like the white men who would place their hard shoes upon the neck of the Cherokee. Learning that the land he purchased had once belonged to our family, and that we had been forced to leave so white settlers could take it, he came to our new home to speak of his regret. Mother told me that she saw a glimmer of desire in his eyes when he came to visit us that day, watching me translate English to Tsalagi and Tsalagi to English. She said his face grew red like a brilliant sunrise. His name was Isham Barnes.

When we arrived, he wiped his hands on his overalls and pushed his unruly hair from his sturdy face. He was like a nervous squirrel, motionless, not sure which way to run. I slid from the mule and stood beside Agitsi as she spoke in our tongue. She nodded her head when she finished speaking, the signal for me to say her words in his language. But my mouth would not open.

I looked into her eyes – the eyes that held the wisdom of our grandmothers – shaken by her speech. She told me to say to Isham Barnes that I was sixteen years old – of marriageable age – and would make a good wife for him. She told him my bad leg did not keep me from being a strong woman who could work in the garden and the field. She said I could already cook, grind corn and do all manner of women's work.

She nodded again, more forcefully, flicking her eyes at Isham Barnes.

So I turned her words into English, staring at his dusty shoes, feeling the heat in my cheeks like a rock warmed by the sun on a summer afternoon.

When he did not reply, Mother spoke again. "Behold with your own eyes – Forest Water is a beautiful maiden with smooth skin and a well-formed body. My daughter can read and write in your language and our language after going to the white man's Mission

School. She also learned much from her grandmother who had Great Powers as a Medicine Woman and Conjuror. She will bear you many healthy children. But her crippled leg will not allow her to make the long journey our people must undertake. It would be best for her to remain here on our Ancient Soil with a white husband so your leaders will not force her to march."

As I translated, the words stuck in my throat like dry cornmeal. When I finished, Isham Barnes looked at my mother, then at me, then at my mother and then at me again, his mouth opening and closing like a fish in the river.

"The soldiers will come very soon," Mother said. "We can make her ready for the ceremony by the time the sun reaches its zenith."

I translated.

His Adam's apple bobbed as he swallowed.

I always dreamed of choosing my husband as my mother and her sisters did. I thought of Standing Together – Degataga – the boy who caught my eye at the Green Corn Ceremony. Of how I thought one day we might become man and wife. It was a great sorrow for Mother to give me away to a white man I did not know. But I understood I would cause my family many hardships on the long journey. I could not walk far without pain and I moved slowly. Although it made my heart heavy, I knew there was wisdom in her plan.

Mother looked Isham Barnes directly in the eye. He replied by raising his chin as if he were no longer the fearful squirrel, then locked eyes with me as though trying to see the bottom of a deep lake.

"Would you be my wife of your own free will?" he said, his voice soft as rabbit fur.

I looked upon his features before answering. He had bushy eyebrows, thick wavy brown hair and a square jaw. He did not have the grace of a Cherokee man. But he had dignity and kindness in his eyes. I trusted Mother's instinct.

"Yes."

Upon returning home for the last time, I bathed in the stream and dressed for the wedding ceremony in my blue gingham dress.

Isham Barnes arrived on his chestnut horse as our shadows began to lengthen, freshly scrubbed, his hair damp. He wore a clean shirt and the dirt had been wiped from his brown shoes.

It was a hasty ceremony – he had no venison, I had only a small sack of corn. Mother's eyes darted toward the trail again and again. I tried to be strong, but tears fell from my eyes when she hugged me good-bye. I embraced my little sisters and brother, fearing I would never see them again.

That is when we heard thundering hooves in the distance. Mother squeezed my new husband's arm.

"Flee into the woods!" she cried. "It has begun!"

"What has begun?" he asked when I translated her words.

"Go now!" she commanded. "They will take Amadahy!"

I spoke her words in English, watching as comprehension dawned in his eyes.

Picking me up like I was a child, he ran to his horse, lifting me onto the saddle. He grabbed the reins and swung up behind me, digging his heels into the horse's flanks. We galloped toward the trees, but a gunshot rang out and horses pounded close behind us, men's voices shouting for us to stop. Two men overtook us, threatening to shoot.

"I'm a white man," Isham Barnes cried. "And this is my wife."

"If you're a white man, why'd you run?" said the man wearing a brown hat.

"I believe he's trying to keep this here pretty squaw for hisself," the one with hair like straw said, followed by coarse laughter.

"You're right, Johnny. But he can't keep her to hisself now." He put his hand on my arm.

My new husband knocked it away, shuddering with anger.

The man called Johnny waved his pistol. "Climb down before I shoot your head off."

"I'm trying to protect my bride," my husband said.

Johnny scratched his ear just before the other white soldier clubbed Isham Barnes from behind with the butt of his gun. My new husband crumpled and fell from the saddle, knocking me off as well. We both landed hard on the ground, the horse bolting toward the trees. Johnny shouted to the other man to give chase.

I scrambled to pull my dress over my legs, then leaned over Isham Barnes, noticing blood on the back of his head. He was unconscious but breathing.

"Get up, little Injun," Johnny said, his voice making me wish I had poison mushrooms to feed him. "You're coming with us."

He trailed behind me as I walked toward the house.

"Ain't never seen nobody walk funny like that," he said. "Looks like you need to cut about five inches off that left leg to even things up."

Besides the two men who chased us, there were six other men on horseback, some with long muskets. The leader was tall with no hair on top of his head, his stained hat resting on the horn of his saddle.

"You are hereby evicted from this land, which is now the property of the state of Georgia," he crowed, reminding me of a swaggering rooster.

They forced my aunts, my younger sisters and my brother to stand in the yard, allowing Mother to go inside to get what she could carry in a bundle. Then some of the white men went into the house, filling their saddle bags with our belongings.

"Where's Doyle?" the bald man asked.

"Chasing down a horse," Johnny replied.

"We're moving out, with or without him." The leader put on his wide-brimmed hat and turned his horse. "Let's march!"

We moved toward the trail, the soldiers mounted on horses while my family walked like a small herd of cattle being led to slaughter. The men laughed, watching me rock from side to side. I stared straight ahead as though my ears did not hear.

Their laughter soon faded and their leader ordered me to "get a move on." I walked faster, but as the sun lowered in the west, pain coursed through my hips and back.

Mother whispered that I should ask the smelly white bald man if I could ride a horse behind one of the men. She said I should also ask how far we were traveling. But I remained silent.

Then she ordered me to ask if the children could have some water. I translated her request.

"When we come to a stream, ya'll can drink," Johnny replied. He pulled his canteen from his saddle bag, drank and wiped his mouth with the back of his hand, looking down at me as he did so. "I might consider giving them young'uns a drink if you promise me a roll in the hay when we make camp for the night."

My eyes sought the ground to avoid revealing the fire burning inside me.

Our day's journey ended along a small creek as the sun set. We quenched our thirst from the stream and Mother shared cornbread filled with beans she had made that morning. She took none herself.

I refused also, letting the others take my portion. I had listened intently as we walked, hearing bits of the white men's conversation. I told Mother what I had learned. That we would walk four days to a fort where we would join others of the Cherokee Nation to be held in what the white men called a stockade. There we would wait until our people were marched west. I did not tell her everything the white men said, fearing she might be killed trying to protect me.

When it was time to sleep, we were each tied to a tree, our hands behind us. A half moon and the stars shone down through the branches. I pretended to sleep, waiting with dread. I did not have to wait long.

Johnny came quietly, whispering that I should remain silent if I did not want my family to suffer. He untied me and led me into the woods until we were far enough away so the others would not hear. He pushed me to the ground and stood over me, unhitching his pants. I fought the urge to scream as he laughed quietly in the dark.

A sudden thud made me jump. He fell forward, landing on the ground beside me. I raised my arm to protect myself, seeing the shadow of another man where Johnny had stood a moment before.

"Don't be afraid. It's me, your husband."

Isham Barnes moved swiftly, tying Johnny's hands behind his back and binding his feet. He tied a bandanna over his mouth to keep him from calling out.

Without a word, he helped me to stand, then hoisted me on his back and carried me silently through the trees. When we reached his horse, he lifted me onto the saddle, climbing up behind me. We moved slowly through the woods until we reached a small trail, then he urged his mount to a gallop. We rode all night, stopping three times to rest the horse. When we paused at a small stream, we spoke in hushed tones.

"Did they hurt you?" he whispered beside me as we cupped our hands to drink.

"No." I did not wish to speak further about the evil white men. "And your head?"

"I'm all right. Found my horse in the woods."

"A soldier went to search but did not come back."

"Those men ain't soldiers. They're farmers and ne'er-do-wells called by the government to serve as militiamen to round up the Cherokee in these parts. The one who knocked me out waited for his family and they done moved into your mama's house."

We remounted and continued on our way.

"You were brave to come for me," I said.

"You're my wife," he said softly in my ear, his arms wrapped around me.

We listened for riders behind us, but none followed. We reached his homestead as the sun rose in the east, a ghostly mist rising from the river as though we were in a sacred place.

I was shy and so was he. We were still dressed in our wedding clothes but now they were soiled and torn, our bodies stinking of many hours on the road.

We ate dried fish, then bathed in the river – first me, then him. After I cleaned the back of his head, he led me inside the house. Mother gave me guidance before the ceremony, but uncertainty and fatigue weighed on me as he folded the quilt down on the big bed in the corner.

He cleared his throat before speaking, keeping his voice low.

"You sleep on the bed. I'll sleep on a blanket on the floor."

Confusion must have shown on my face.

"We're both dog-tired," he said. "And we ain't really got acquainted yet."

And so it was for three nights, me on the bed, Isham Barnes on the floor.

He was not what I expected a husband to be. He worked alongside me in the field doing woman's work. He said where he came from it was man's work. He also helped hoe the garden, which was always a Cherokee woman's chore. He fed the chickens every morning and gathered the eggs. He picked a basket of figs for me to cook from the fig bushes around the old women's hut. He did not know my grandmother planted them long ago and tended them, using her potions, herbs and totems before this land was taken from us.

When he snuffed the candle on the fourth night, he did not lie on the floor. He crawled into bed beside me after bathing in the river by starlight. In the darkness he spoke his heart to me.

"I know you didn't wanna marry me," he said. "But when you and your mama showed up and she offered you to be my wife, I hid my jubilation so I wouldn't scare you. Because I wanted you real bad. I'll be a good husband, Forest Water."

When he put his mouth on mine, I could feel his hunger. But his hands were gentle on my body and he moved like a spring rain, slowly watering the soil so corn will grow and flowers will bloom. He whispered my name like a prayer. And I was thankful for Mother's wisdom.

It was during the Green Corn Moon that news arrived with Old Noon Day as he fled north to the Mountains of Blue Smoke. He said my family was locked inside a large pen at Fort Scudder with hundreds of men, women and children of the Cherokee Nation. He said many among the Principal People were dying of sickness and bad water.

In the autumn, a white trapper stopped to water his horse and feed his stomach at our table, telling us that many wagons had departed from the fort. But he said few people rode in the wagons, most of them forced to walk.

Isham held me close that night as we lay together, not for pleasure, but for comfort. He kissed my forehead and caressed my hair, loose on my shoulders, as I imagined my family walking many weeks to settle in a strange place far from our home.

Upon learning more about Cherokee ways, he repaired the women's hut. He also dug a hole in the floor and hid a metal box his grandfather brought home from the white man's War for Independence for keeping special belongings. Once it was buried and covered with a blanket, he gave me a diary he traded for in town and two bottles of ink.

"You can write about your people and your life," he said. "Many years from now our grandchildren can read your words."

His gift gave me great pleasure.

When frost painted the leaves with silver, he said he must hunt for game farther from our land. I did not speak my thoughts that we could survive the winter trapping small game nearby and using Cherokee fish weirs. I saw that he needed to prove his manhood to me now that he knew farming was done by women among my people. But leaving me alone was a burden on his mind so he traded with a neighbor to send his slave, Ginny, to help me.

On the morning of his leaving, he mounted his horse as I stood wrapped in my shawl trying to be strong. He looked at me and suddenly dismounted, setting his hands on my shoulders.

"I love you, Forest Water," he whispered, and kissed my mouth.

He rode into the forest, twisting in the saddle to wave at me before the trees swallowed him. I was not afraid. But the house and the land were empty without him, like a stream during the dry time.

Ginny was taller than me, lean and graceful like a young doe, with skin the color of fresh acorns. I was thankful to have her help. She was surprised to learn I was Cherokee, saying she didn't know Indians lived so close. She asked many questions about my life, my family, my husband. She was taken from her family when she was sold from the plantation at eight years of age. She was sixteen now, same as me.

We shook the persimmon trees near the river and picked up the ripe fruit before the raccoons, squirrels and deer could eat them. We set most of them out to dry in the sun. Then I taught her how to make persimmon sweet bread, giving her a loaf and keeping two for my husband's return. On the second day, we gathered hickory nuts beneath the golden branches, breaking them open with a hammer, then grinding them into meal for making bread and stew. Working together reminded me of my mother sharing chores with her sisters, as is the custom among my people.

I slept alone in our bed for three nights with a knife under the ticking. The sun was high the following day when Isham emerged from the trees, dragging a buck behind him on two poles, three rabbits hanging from his saddle.

When he stopped at the edge of the yard, he dismounted and walked toward me without speaking. He wrapped his arms around me, raising me from the ground, burying his face in my hair.

Together, we skinned and butchered the deer, hanging it in the smokehouse for the night. Then we washed quickly in the icy river and hurried to the house where a blaze in the fireplace warmed us.

Eating corn and beans with persimmon sweet bread, our eyes were drawn to each other. When we lay together on the bed, he breathed my name as we beheld each other in the flickering firelight.

I kissed him and his body grew firm with desire.

"I love you also, Isham Barnes," I whispered.

Our passion burst forth like a trout leaping from the river, its scales sparkling in the sunlight.

Early in the Snow Moon, I vomited after rising one morning and knew I was with child. Isham smiled like a small boy when I told him he would soon be a father, gently rubbing his hand across my flat belly.

We were fortunate companions, happy working together and lying together at night, our bodies entwined under the quilts. I had not expected such deep feelings to grow between us. But it made my heart soar to be with a man whose eyes looked upon me with strong affection, a man who treated me with respect and tenderness, a man whose calloused hands brought me such pleasure.

My body was strong as the baby grew inside me. The movements were like those of a happy foal prancing in the grass beside its mother.

Isham sent for Ginny when my time came. Our baby was born as the sun set late during the Nut Moon (September 1839). A big baby girl. We named her Betsey Kamama Barnes. Isham chose the name Betsey in honor of his mother. I chose the Cherokee name Kamama – Butterfly. I had never seen a man love a baby like he did.

But one day as I dug sweet potatoes in Harvest Time Month, a shadow fell on the garden in front of me, sending a chill through my body. That is when Isham's brother arrived at our house on foot, saying his horse had been stolen. They had the same father but different mothers, and Jonah was ten years older. Both had thick brown hair, but they did not look like brothers in any other way. Jonah was like a tall, jagged rock. I did not like the way his hard eyes rested on me. And his words at our table held no warmth.

"You've got a nice farm here, little brother," he said, scratching his dirty beard, crumbs of food dropping upon his shirt. "And a nice little Injun wife."

I lowered my eyes to hide my distaste.

For two nights he slept in our small barn.

"I do not trust your brother," I said to Isham as we lay quietly in our bed, Betsey asleep between us.

"You got good instincts," he said. "I'll talk to him tomorrow, give him a little money so he'll be on his way."

But the next morning, as he finished his eggs and coffee and rose to tend the fish traps, I was seized with dread.

"Isham!" I cried, the baby at my breast. "I am afraid."

"Of what?"

"That you are in danger."

He returned to me and kissed me lightly on the mouth, stroking the baby's soft hair.

"I can take care of myself," he said. He patted me on the cheek, his eyes full of love, and walked out the door.

I finished nursing Betsey and cleaned the pan and plates before gathering clothing in a basket. I packed the baby on her cradle board, strapped her on my back and headed to the river to do the washing. The sun peeked above the trees, breaking the morning chill.

When I reached the riverbank, I set the basket on a large rock and placed Betsey in the sun so she could sleep. Then I stepped into the shallows to begin my work. But there was something dark floating in the water mid-stream. I shaded my eyes with my hand.

Summoning my strength, I waded through cold, chest-deep water to the shoals where a carcass was trapped in the swirling current. It was the size of a bear. But I recognized the overalls and *the thick brown hair before I turned the body over to see the sightless eyes of my dead husband.*

I buried my face in my hands after reading that final sentence. Unlike Eric, who thought he was translating a journal of a woman buried long ago, I'd met Amadahy. I'd heard Jonah's callous voice.

Dementia or not, Nana was right. We had to help.

Translation of the diary had to shift into high gear. I needed more pages. Fast.

Eric answered his phone with surprise in his voice. When I told him I needed the entire translation ASAP, he hesitated before answering.

"Even though it's summer semester, I do have a couple of classes to teach."

"Of course."

"Plus, I have a deadline for an article I'm writing for publication."

"I'll double your fee."

"You'd think someone's life was at stake," he said, amusement in his voice.

I had to persuade him without revealing the truth. Because if I told him the truth, he'd categorize me as a nutjob. And I wouldn't blame him. Which meant he wouldn't take me or the manuscript seriously. "It's really important to me."

Momentary silence.

"I can only work so fast," he said. "It's not like doing your multiplication tables. It's more like solving a complicated equation where you have to think about each step, evaluate and check your conclusions."

I sighed.

"I'll do it," he said. "On one condition."

"Condition?"

"That you have dinner with me tonight."

Any other time, I would've jumped at the opportunity. I didn't get invited out often. And when I did, it was someone I wasn't interested in. But all I could think about right now was Amadahy. Still, I was asking him to push everything aside and focus on my project. I couldn't exactly claim I was too busy.

"I'll drive to Atlanta and pick you up at six-thirty," he said. "I'll have you home by nine-thirty. Promise."

⁓

"How about popping over to Piccadilly Cafeteria for liver and onions?" Eric said as we pulled away from my apartment.

As I struggled to come up with a tactful reply, wondering what in the world I'd gotten myself into, he busted out laughing.

"God, the look on your face!" he cried. "Priceless!" And he laughed some more.

"Okay, so that's a test, right?" I said, rolling my eyes. "You begin every first date that way."

"I couldn't resist."

We ended up at a tapas restaurant with rooftop seating where he'd made a reservation. I didn't usually go to trendy places and was taken off guard when I spotted the too-famous-to-go-undercover Mallory Cleveland. I knew she had a lot of connections, but was surprised to see her with Reggie Edwards, a state senator rumored to have his sights set on the governor's office. They stopped by our table long enough to make quick introductions and for Mallory to give Eric an appreciative once-over. She winked at me as they followed the maître-d' to their table. Which made me blush thinking about the Monday morning third degree I'd have to endure.

"Glad I'm not them," Eric said when they were out of earshot. "Look at everyone gawking."

"Look closely," I said. "They're both eating it up."

"You may have a point."

When our waiter arrived, Eric ordered fourteen or fifteen little dishes, from chickpea pancakes to smoked carrots, accompanied by some good sangria.

I steered the conversation in his direction as Spanish guitar music played in the background.

"Tell me why you specialized in Cherokee Indian studies."

"Believe it or not, I have some Cherokee blood."

I examined him, looking for some telltale sign. He had dark hair and light brown eyes. But he looked like an American of northern European extraction.

"Yeah," he said, "I don't fit the image. My dad used to say our family had Cherokee ancestry way back. My reaction was always – yeah, right, Dad."

"Sounds familiar."

"You know, there's a label for that. It's called Cherokee Grandmother Syndrome. A lot of Americans suffer from it. But when I was a senior in high school, I saw an ad for a DNA test kit. My dad split the cost with me. And guess what – the results showed I'm about one percent Native American. Who knew my dad wasn't just blowing smoke!"

We shared a laugh.

"I was enthralled," he continued. "I immersed myself in Cherokee culture in college and post-graduate studies. Along the way I discovered some test results aren't always accurate, especially back in the late nineties. So I worked with a genealogist to trace my family tree."

"And?"

"Apparently Dad was right. My great-great-grandma had a family Bible that said her grandmother was half Cherokee."

"Wow."

"My half Cherokee ancestor was born in 1846, not long after the Trail of Tears.

"Fascinating."

"And my test results also say I've got some African DNA. Not bragging or anything, but I'm what you might call fashionably multiracial."

He grinned and took a bite of potato tortilla.

"My grandmother thinks we've got Cherokee ancestry too," I said.

"But you don't believe her?"

"I think she may have a case of that Cherokee Grandmother Syndrome you mentioned, along with early Alzheimer's. Why are so many of us Native American wannabes?"

Our second round of sangrias arrived and I realized how relaxed I was, sitting across the table from him.

"One theory is that claiming indigenous ancestors absolves us of guilt," he said, his voice buzzing with energy. "You know, if my fifth great-grandmother was Cherokee, then you can't blame me for stealing their land and forcing them on that deadly march."

"I don't think Nana has a guilty conscience."

"Some folks might think it makes them more interesting, more exotic, more American. Although there was a lot of intermarrying going on back then, so you never know. And, of course, there was the shameful reality of white men forcing themselves on women of color."

Then he asked me about my job, like he thought it was the most intriguing profession in the entire world. But I had the feeling he wasn't trying to flatter me. That he was the kind of guy who was interested in all kinds of things, including being a producer for an investigative news team at a local TV station.

When his phone dinged, he waved our server over to order dessert.

"I have to have her home by nine-thirty or she turns into a field mouse or something," he told the waiter.

My cue to roll my eyes. Again.

We wrapped up with small bowls of cappuccino gelato and managed to pull up in front of my apartment at nine twenty-five.

"I've got five minutes to escort you to your door and say good-night," he said, keeping a straight face.

Without a doubt, he was attractive and fun to talk to. But programming his phone to keep him on schedule? Really?

I turned to thank him for dinner as I pulled my key from my handbag.

"Better five minutes too soon than a minute too late," he said. "A variation on William Shakespeare."

"Just out of curiosity, are you always Mr. Punctuality?"

"Not on your life! I'm trying to impress you. I also have to rush home to work on an important translation project I'm doing for a hard-nosed boss."

Before I could think of a witty comeback, he trotted down the sidewalk and jumped in his car.

"A deal's a deal!" he called out, cranking the engine and pulling away with a jaunty dink of the horn.

Pixie greeted me with a loud meow as I stepped inside.

"It's only nine-thirty," I said.

Another meow.

"Yes, I like him."

She purred and rubbed against my leg.

"You don't have to be jealous."

As I picked her up, my phone rang. It was Nana.

"You're up late," I said.

"I can't stop thinking about Forest Water. Did you call the authorities?"

"Yes," I lied. "Someone's going to visit them soon. Can you tell me a little bit more about the man you saw?"

"His eyes were mean as a barbed wire fence as Grandma used to say. And he had a messy beard that needed trimming. When he slapped her, he looked like he wanted to hit me too. But she told him I didn't understand. She called me Old Grandmother."

"Tell you what – when I come over tomorrow, I'll go check on her."

"I wish you would."

Late the next morning, after coffee and muffins with Nana and Jeannette, I announced I was walking down to the river to look for more artifacts.

"And check on my neighbor," Nana said.

"Definitely," I replied, feeling a little deceitful toward Jeannette who gave me a slightly exasperated look.

I grabbed my backpack and headed into the woods, walking so fast I nearly tripped over a rock about halfway down the hill. I was wearing khaki capris and a white summer tank top which would work nicely as undergarments for the outfit I'd packed. It was an ankle-length, long-sleeved dress I'd worn for a crowd scene in a high school production of *Les Miserables* that was rotting in the back of my closet. Made of dark grey cloth, I thought it would help me fit in. I slipped on a pair of black flats – the best I could do on short notice. If anyone saw me, at least I wouldn't look like a woman in her underwear. There were butterflies in my stomach as I prepared to go undercover to the nineteenth century.

Leaving my backpack on a rock, I used a rubber band to pull my hair into a ponytail, then twisted it into a small bun.

A ripe fig in my hand, I hesitated at the doorway, afraid of what I'd find on the other side. My dad was a doctor and I remembered him talking about the Hippocratic Oath. Before he died in a car wreck when I was fifteen, he used to talk about the importance of doing no harm. If you couldn't cure someone, at the very least, you shouldn't hurt them in the process of treating them. I wanted to help Amadahy, but I had to remember – if that wasn't possible, I must do no harm.

I bit into the fig and stepped over the bones, beads and feathers.

Once the buzzing subsided, all I could hear was my own angsty breathing. Standing inside the empty hut, I composed myself. There was the distant murmur of the river and the chatter of a squirrel. But no voices.

Easing through the shack's front door, there was no sign of anyone. I paused beside the well-tended garden where green cornstalks gleamed in the sunshine, with bean vines climbing the stalks and squash plants meandering in the rows.

As I took a tentative step, I heard singing. It was a woman's voice in the distance, off to my left where the trees abutted the clearing. I moved with as much stealth as I could manage, careful where I planted my feet, trying not to step on a twig, remembering all the movies I'd seen where that mistake brought down the wrath of the bad guys. The closer I got to the trees, the better I could hear the woman's haunting voice singing softly in a language I didn't understand.

With the baby sleeping peacefully strapped to her mother's back, Amadahy squatted by a bush at the tree line, her hands moving back and forth to a basket beside her. The word bucolic came to mind.

Before I took another step, she turned with a start, cutting short her melancholy song.

I'm not sure who was more alarmed – her, at seeing me once again, or me, upon noticing she had an ugly black eye.

"You must go home," she whispered, dropping a small bunch of herbs into her handwoven basket.

"You're the one in danger. You should leave him. Take your baby and run away."

She shook her head stubbornly.

"You can't let him do that to you," I said.

"I cannot abandon my land." She slipped the handle of the basket over her arm as she rose, then gestured for me to follow her.

"Who's this trespassing on my farm?" Jonah called out from behind us, causing the baby to awaken in alarm.

There was something about his gravelly voice that brought to mind bare knuckle fighting. I couldn't help but flinch.

Amadahy turned to face him as he drew close enough for the stench of his body to reach us.

"She is lost," she said.

"Something shady going on here. What's your name?" He rared back, looking down his nose at me.

"Kathryn."

"Well, Kathryn, you're interrupting my woman here from important wifely duties. She's gathering special Injun medicine plants so she can birth me some baby boys. Which is what I need to run this here farm – some big, strapping sons. And the sooner, the better. So you skedaddle on outta here and let her get back to work. Understand?"

My head nodded but my mouth apparently wasn't on the same circuit.

"I'm curious about how your wife got that black eye."

Amadahy tensed beside me. "I hit my face on the door," she said.

"Now, why would you go and tell a lie?" Jonah said, then turned to me. "I walloped her when she got outta line."

"But why would you hit your wife?" My mouth seemed to have a mind of its own.

"You must be simple. A man's got a right to beat his wife if she don't act right."

"But you can't…"

"You telling me what I can't do?"

"She is from far away," Amadahy said. "She does not understand our ways."

"You want me to beat you again?" he said, grabbing her by the wrist, causing the baby to cry.

"You savage swine!" I blurted.

He let go of her and turned his fury on me – swinging his arm in a mighty arc, his big grimy hand striking my face so hard, it knocked me backwards. I yelped in pain, covering my cheek with my palm, eyes stinging.

"Ain't nobody gonna talk to me like that," he said, reaching for me, a malicious glint in his eyes.

I dodged his grasp, racing along the edge of the garden. But how was I supposed to pick and eat a fig while navigating the time gate with Jonah panting and cussing right behind me? I'd never make it. I streaked by the hut, across the yard and past the outhouse. He was gaining on me and I was quite literally running out of options. Hearing the river in the distance, I poured on the speed, adrenaline pumping. I didn't slow down when I reached the riverbank, taking a leaping dive into the water, praying I wouldn't land on a submerged rock. I sank below the surface as I was swept downstream.

Escaping that monster's clutches didn't mean I was safe. While I was a decent swimmer, the current was swift. Complicating matters, my long dress and shoes dragged me down. I held my breath, trying to pull the zipper down the back of the dress. But it was stuck and I struggled to surface again, sputtering and gulping air as I raised my mouth above water. I almost kicked the shoes off, but realized my city-girl feet wouldn't last long if I had to find my way back barefoot. I curled my toes, doing my best to keep them on.

The Broad River of Amadahy's time was a far cry from the Broad River of my time. There was more water and it flowed faster. Now I feared it might be the death of me.

I was tiring and needed to extricate myself from the current. Rather than fight it, I had to use it. I did a modified breast stroke, keeping my head above water as I aimed for the right bank. Bit by bit, I edged closer. Then my foot touched bottom. But the current was still powerful enough to push me along, so I used my foot like a pole, touching bottom and thrusting my body toward the trees again and again, until I reached the riverbank.

Dragging myself from the water, I collapsed on the ground, lying on my back, eyes closed, chest heaving. But I couldn't rest. I needed to get back to my own time.

When my breathing returned to normal, I stood on shaky legs, hugging the riverbank as I set off for the farm. I had no idea how far I'd traveled downriver. At least I'd managed not to lose my shoes, which I was grateful for. But they were waterlogged and my dress was heavy and clung to my legs. Still, I didn't want to remove it in case someone saw me.

I stumbled along the bank, making brief detours into the trees because of thick underbrush. My wet clothing helped keep me cool in the midday heat, but it gradually dried out. I stopped from time to time to cup my hands and drink from the river, splashing water on my head. It was slow going, but I didn't dare stray inland and become lost in the woods.

My wild trip downstream had only taken a matter of minutes, but the return journey by foot took ever so much longer. The sun rose higher and higher as I staggered along, trying to avoid the tall grasses that scratched my ankles. Then, in the distance, I spotted the shoals mid-stream I'd noticed the first time I came with Nana and Jeannette, realizing now that was where Amadahy must've found Isham's body.

I ducked into the trees, listening and watching. The intense fear in the pit of my stomach was new to me. This was the first time I'd ever feared for my life.

Moving slowly, I stopped every ten feet or so to listen and scan my surroundings. I wanted to emerge from the trees directly behind the shack so nobody would see me. The closer I got, the louder every sound became. My breathing, the swishing of my tattered skirt, the squishing of my ruined shoes. At last, I arrived at the edge of the forest, squatting behind a large pine tree. My skin prickled as my eyes darted this way and that. The last fifty feet would be across open ground – no trees or bushes to hide behind.

I was disconcerted by the sound of a baby crying. Then Jonah's voice shouting. They were in the house. I couldn't make out the words.

It dawned on me I should make a break for it while they were occupied. Oh, but I hated leaving Amadahy and her tiny daughter behind. For a split second, I imagined myself sneaking inside and hitting that ogre on his thick skull with a frying pan. Although if I dared to enter the house, I knew *he* wouldn't be the one who got hurt.

Lowering my head, I ran like a cat fleeing a vicious dog. I'd almost reached the small back door when their voices suddenly grew louder. They were outside now and it sounded like they were heading my way.

"Don't tell me no more that I ain't allowed!" he shouted. "I'm the man of the house!"

The baby's crying grew louder.

Yanking a fig off the bush, I stepped inside, immediately swinging around to exit the same way. There was a sound at the hut's front door, Jonah's voice roaring just beyond. Cramming the whole fig in my mouth, I bit down and charged through the portal.

I nearly choked on the grainy fruit, scared witless that he was right behind me. But the shack was gone. His voice was silent. I was back in my own time. Leaning forward, I planted my hands on my knees to hold me up, allowing my heart to stop pounding in my chest.

My backpack was right where I left it. I pulled off the dress, removed my ruined black shoes and stuffed them in the bag, slipping my hiking sandals on. The bun I'd fashioned was long gone, my hair snarled about my face. Because my muscles were sore, the normally easy walk back to Nana's made me droop. I didn't sit down to rest, though, knowing she would be worried.

"Don't be alarmed," I called out as I stepped through the back door of the cottage. "I'm okay."

"Kathryn!" Nana cried. "What happened to your face?"

"Don't worry, I'm fine," I said, rubbing my sore cheek.

"You look like you've just been voted off the tribe on *Survivor*." Jeannette shook her head, looking me up and down.

"I took an unexpected swim in the river."

"I was worried about you," Nana said. "Afraid that bad man might've hurt you."

"I'm a mess," I said, "Gotta go home, take a shower, put some anti-biotic cream on my scratches."

"You need a power wash," said Jeannette, wrinkling her nose.

"Love you, Nana." I kissed her cheek, keen to make my getaway.

"I'll walk you out," she replied.

She didn't speak until we were nearly to my car.

"Is she okay?" she whispered.

"Yes," I lied.

"And the baby?"

"She's fine too."

"Thank heavens."

"Don't worry."

"The police should arrest him," she said. "I cannot abide a man hurting a woman."

"Me neither, Nana. Me neither." I sat carefully in the driver's seat, my aching body complaining with every movement. "I'll take care of it."

Waiting till I reached the first stop sign, I texted Eric.

"Don't suppose you've got any more pages translated?"

My phone rang almost instantly.

"I got a few more translated today," he said. "I was going to email you tonight."

"I know I'm being pushy. It's kind of a weird situation."

"I'll send you what I've got. It's pretty dramatic stuff. Picks up right where the last pages left off in the fall of 1839."

"Thank you."

"You sound exhausted," he said.

"I'm fine. And thanks again for last night."

Setting the phone on the seat beside me, I pulled over and waited. I didn't have to wait long.

Amadahy's Journal – Part 2 (October 1839)

Pulling his body from the water took all my strength. Once on the riverbank, I searched for a wound, but found none. As weakness spread through my limbs, I wished only to lie upon the ground with my baby in my arms. But I could not.

I saddled the horse and attached the pole sled, then dragged Isham's body onto the sled, tucking a shovel beside him. With Betsey on my back, I stood on my sitting rock to haul myself onto the horse. I rode slowly all the way to my family burial ground. Isham Barnes was not born a Cherokee, but he was a Good Husband to me and the father of my child. I chose to bury him where I would one day rest beside him.

First, I dug the grave. Then I wrapped him in cloth and lowered his body into the earth facing west toward the Darkening Land. After covering him with dirt, I hauled rocks from the stream that ran alongside the meadow, building a small mound to protect him from animals.

With no Medicine Man or Beloved Woman to perform the death rituals, I sang the song of lamentation, calling out Isham's name over and over.

Betsey joined me, crying out in sorrow for her dead father. I nursed her and we returned to our empty home. After tending to the horse, I immersed myself seven times in the river, facing east, then west each time, as is the Cherokee custom.

When the sun set behind the trees, I had no strength left to purify the house. Neither did I have the desire to remove the smell of my husband and the objects he used – his razor, his comb, his clothing. My eyes overflowed with tears as I lay on our bed with only Little Butterfly beside me. My husband was dead. My mother and my family were far away. I prayed to the Great Spirit that my family would return. I called out to Selu, the Corn Mother, for strong medicine to help me.

When I awoke the next morning, Jonah stood in the center of the room watching me. He walked to the table, looking for food.

"Where's my brother?" he said, eyeing the empty fry pan.

My voice remained silent.

"I didn't see him in the barn or by the river," he said. "He gone into town?"

I scooped Betsey into my arms and crossed to the hearth, laying her on a quilt. Adding a log to the embers, I used the poker to build a new fire with dried bark.

"Gone hunting?" he said.

I shook my head.

"Where is he, woman?"

My eyes met his and I knew the truth. Bad Brother killed Good Brother, like the story the Missionaries told from the white man's Bible.

"I do not know," I said, unwrapping day-old bread and setting it on the table.

I carried my little daughter to the riverbank, nursing her there, waiting until Jonah ate before returning to the house. Later, I told him I could run the farm alone until Isham returned. But he would not leave, demanding food every day, watching me work the field and the garden, watching me haul water.

After three moons, he rode into town, returning with a piece of paper.

"Since Isham ain't coming back, the judge done ruled that he's dead." He flashed the paper at me.

"He will return." I lowered my eyes so he could not look into them.

"He ain't coming back and you know it."

I kissed my baby's soft head.

"I did this for your sake," Bad Brother said. "Cause if you ain't married to a white man, they'll send you out yonder where all the Injuns live now. Ain't exactly a good place, from all I hear. And I happen to know a feller name Johnny who told me you was s'posed to go with your family when they rounded 'em up, but you snuck off in the middle of the night. I'm making you a damn good offer.

We get hitched and you don't have to march way out to the Oklahoma Territory with that bum leg of yours. Pretty sure you'd never make it."

Betsey held tight to my fingers.

"Not many men want a woman looks like you," he said. "But I don't mind much. Your face is pretty enough. And you got a fine body, 'cept for that leg. You tend the field and garden, do the cooking and birth me some sons, we'll do all right. That way, I don't have to tell the sheriff you're living here against the law."

I held my head high but did not speak.

"Isham was my brother. He married a squaw who ain't legally got a right to this here land. So it's mine now."

The next day, we rode into town on Isham's horse with Betsey strapped to my back. It was a bitter cold winter day and wind whipped my face. After the small-eyed judge spoke the words of marriage, I watched Jonah make his mark on the paper. Then I took the quill pen, dipped it in ink and signed the paper with the Cherokee Syllabary. Instead of signing Amadahy – Forest Water – I signed Immokalee – Tumbling Water. Thus, I did not marry him since I did not sign my true name.

In bed that night, Jonah was rough and uncaring. He did not shave his beard nor wash his unclean body. He would not let me answer Betsey's cries from her basket on the floor. From that night, she was not allowed to sleep with me.

When he left the house the next morning, I cleaned myself before removing all his belongings and setting them in a pile outside the front door. It is the Cherokee custom when a woman divorces her husband.

I now had only Little Butterfly to warm my soul. Sadness filled my spirit that Kamama would not remember her father's tender *love. That she would only remember the evil man who stole his place in our home. Bad Brother destroyed the harmony and balance in our lives, taking his own brother's life, forcing me to serve his needs, shouting at my daughter and making her cry. I tried to teach her to ignore his cruel voice, telling her I would soon return to hold her close.*

This is when I began to write in the diary Isham gave me, saying he believed I would have much to say. I hide it in the strong box he buried inside the menstrual hut.

While carefully applying makeup before work the next morning, I decided to talk with the psychologist I interviewed for our report on the high school teacher. Dr. Vargas knew his stuff.

I sent a tactfully worded email, asking him if he could spare me a few minutes by phone to discuss a friend of mine in an abusive relationship. We'd given him some valuable free PR on our primetime newscasts. Hopefully, he'd be okay doling out a little pro bono advice. I wouldn't mention any names. Or that I was referring to a woman who lived nearly two centuries ago.

Coffee in hand, I strode into the newsroom, bracing myself for Mallory's needling. People were already staring at me. She must've blabbed about my date Saturday night as soon as she walked in the door.

When I reached our office, I found her sipping her daily cappuccino, engrossed in a video report on her laptop.

"You've got to see this," she mumbled, eyes trained on the monitor.

"See what?"

Looking up, she narrowed her eyes like I was an interloper into the rarified domain of the investigative news team.

"God, not you too!" She cried.

"What?"

"That slap mark on your face."

"I don't have a slap mark on my face."

"Jesus, Kathryn! I know a slap mark when I see one. You've also got a bruise on your arm."

I twisted around to view my reflection in her private mirror. In my bathroom at home, three coats of Erase, a layer of foundation and face powder seemed to have done the trick. Not under the intense newsroom lights.

"Not a slap mark, Mallory. I hiked down to the river behind my grandmother's house yesterday and had a run-in with a tree. As for the bruise on my arm, I've probably got several other bruises – and scratches too – because I fell into the water and went for an unexpected body surfing expedition."

She rose from her chair and stood close in front of me, inspecting my face.

"Remember last year when I interviewed that county commissioner's wife who accused him of hitting her?" she said.

She was way too close, so I scooted over to my desk to put some distance between us.

"Her face looked a lot like yours," she continued. "Anyone can see that's a handprint."

"It's not a handprint! I'm not even in a relationship with a man."

"Oh, right! That fine college professor I met Saturday night appeared to be a man."

"Eric?"

"Very much a man."

"Well, I'm not in a relationship with him."

"I saw the way he looked at you," she said, giving me googly eyes.

"Please!"

"Bottom line – Saturday evening your face was normal, now it's not. Don't forget I've been through this with my sister. I can spot domestic abuse a mile away."

"I appreciate your concern, but the fact is, I managed to do this all by myself yesterday impersonating a klutz!"

That's when my phone rang. It was Dr. Vargas. I said hello as I made my escape to the hallway.

I've always hated lying. Unless it's a little white lie to avoid hurting someone's feelings. Like when Nana bakes me brownies and I don't want them in my apartment because they're a huge temptation. I ooh and ahh, give her a thank-you hug, then deliver them to the break room at work. Okay, I eat one, then take them to work. Or when it's something as important as saving Amadahy from a certain Stone Age tyrant. I was making it up as I went along with Dr. Vargas.

"Yes, I told her she should leave him, but she says she can't do that. I think it's the financial side of it. She doesn't want to give up the property and she doesn't have any money. Plus, she's got a baby to take care of and no family to lean on. Are there techniques, you know, for re-education?"

"Ms. Spears, I wish I could tell you there's a quick fix – medication that could be administered, a class the abuser could take. But you're talking about having to psychoanalyze each man, find out what kind of upbringing he had, what kind of influences he had, what kind of abuse he, himself, might have suffered, whether his father or some other adult in his life abused women, thus setting an example. The list goes on and on. As much as I'd like to give you a twelve-step program to rehabilitate this guy, it's challenging even when a professional works with someone like him. Can you convince him to see a counselor? If not myself, then someone else who specializes in treating abusers? I could give you a list of practitioners. There are support groups too. For him, and for her."

"I..."

"Tell you what – I can email you some resources for your friend."

And that's how we left it. With me feeling like a totally inept dumwad.

It was after ten and I was in my pajamas when the doorbell rang. I couldn't imagine who might be at my door this time of night. Putting my robe and slippers on, I looked through the peephole and was baffled when I saw two police officers standing on my front porch – a man and a woman.

"Is something wrong?" I said as soon as I opened the door, thinking there might be some kind of emergency in my apartment complex.

"Kathryn Spears?" the woman officer said.

"Yes?"

"I'm Officer Rimes," she said, "and this is Officer Williams. May we come in for a moment?"

"What's this about?"

"We're just checking up on you. We got a report that your boyfriend may have hit you."

My mouth fell open.

"I think you must have the wrong apartment," I said. "First, I don't have a boyfriend. And, second, as you can see, nobody has beaten me up."

"May we step inside for a moment?" she repeated.

I moved out of the way and reluctantly ushered them into the living room. They didn't bother to hide their interest in my cheek, now devoid of makeup and obviously bruised. So I gave them my spiel.

"I went hiking yesterday and stumbled into a tree. Which made me lose my balance and fall into the river. The current was strong and I ended up taking a very uncomfortable swim before finally making my way back to the riverbank. No one hit me."

I wasn't about to admit what really happened. If anyone went looking for Jonah Barnes, they'd think I was lying since nobody lived on that plot of land anymore. I guess I could've claimed some hiker or vagrant hit me, but they'd want a description and there was the possibility some poor man might actually be arrested. Jeez!

The self-assured Officer Rimes did the talking while Officer Williams, a stocky guy with a tattoo peeking out from under his sleeve, took notes.

"Ms. Spears," she began.

"Who called the police, I'd like to know," I butted in. "If it was my co-worker, I'm gonna be pissed. She knows good and well I would never in a million years tolerate any kind of violence."

"She was worried about you," she said, her voice filled with concern. "She said she called a psychologist you interviewed for a report your station did recently and he said he talked with you about a friend being abused."

I could feel the heat rising in my face.

"That's a very common ploy by women," Officer Rimes continued. "Appealing for help by describing her own abuse like it's a friend she's talking about."

"You know what? I *was* talking about a friend. A friend I'm very worried about. And, by the way, I thought psychologists and psychiatrists and doctors were supposed to have rules about privacy. You know, patient confidentiality?"

"Are you a patient?"

I grunted under my breath in frustration.

"No offense, but are we through?" I said, trying my best to maintain a modicum of civility with these poor officers who were only doing their jobs.

"No, actually," she replied. "Dr. Eric Murray is currently being interviewed by Athens police about what may have transpired over the weekend to leave you with a bruised face."

"He's being interviewed?" My voice was shrill.

"As we speak. Now, the question is – and consider carefully before you answer – do you want to press charges?"

"As a matter of fact, I do want to press charges! I want to press charges against the tree that I ran into and I want to press charges against the Broad River, specifically the section in Madison County behind my grandmother's cottage, for causing all these bruises and scratches all over my body!"

I yanked my front door open and gestured with a flourish for them to leave.

"Thank you for checking on me," I said.

Officer Rimes handed me her card on their way out.

"In case you change your mind," she said.

They headed for their cruiser, which was parked right in front of my apartment so everyone would know who they came to see.

Mallory was going to get it. She was going to get it so bad. I had half a mind to drive over to her expensive Ansley Park home and let her have it with both barrels. I was steaming!

But then I thought of Eric. What must he think of me? He's the one I needed to focus on. To apologize for my stupid, buttinsky reporter friend!

I found my phone, clicked on his number and listened as it rang and rang, then rolled over to voice mail. I hung up. He was probably still being grilled by the cops.

"Dammit!" I screamed.

Besides being understandably upset, he was probably also deciding at this very moment to stop translating the diary, figuring I was a bona fide kook.

What if I drove over to his place? He lived somewhere in Athens. Sitting on my bed, I used my laptop to search for his address. Only took a couple of minutes.

An hour later, I rang his doorbell, looking down at myself in alarm. I was still in my PJs, robe and yellow bunny slippers. I could only imagine what his neighbors would think.

No answer. I rang again. Still, no answer.

Had they hauled him down to the police station? Was he sitting in a little room, a bright light hanging from the ceiling as a tough investigator interrogated him? I rang again, then knocked on his door.

A moment later, I walked back down the steps, considering whether to drive to the police station. The door opened behind me. Turning around, the first thing I noticed was the frown on Eric's face. The second thing I noticed was his bare feet, pajama shorts and white wife-beater T-shirt. Naturally.

"You do look like someone slapped you around," he said.

"I'm sorry. It was a total misunderstanding."

He opened the door wider, waving me in.

We sat on opposite sides of the booth in his blue and white kitchen, small glasses of orange juice and a granola bar between us. Like we were kids having a sleepover and sneaking into the kitchen in the middle of the night for a snack. He tore the wrapper off, breaking it in two, half for him and half for me. Despite the peculiar circumstances, somehow it felt natural sharing a granola bar in our jammies.

"That does look like a handprint on your face," he said, then took a bite.

"Mallory jumped to conclusions. She shouldn't have called the cops. And she sure as hell shouldn't have blamed you."

"But I can understand where she was coming from. At least she cares enough about you to…"

"She was completely off base!"

"Where's the bruise on your arm?" he said.

"Listen, here's what happened. I stumbled as I ran down the path from my grandmother's cottage to the river, and I fell, you know, fell headlong into this big tree. I didn't realize I was so close to the riverbank as I staggered around holding my face, and I landed in the river. The current carried me a good way downstream before I was able to make it to shore again. I've got bruises and scratches all over me. Haven't you ever fallen and banged yourself up?"

"Yep. Plenty of bruises and scratches from cycling. But I've never had a handprint on my face."

"It's not a handprint!"

"Why do I not believe you?" he said, downing the rest of his juice.

I closed my eyes, imagining what would happen if I told him the truth. But there was no way I could do that.

"You really don't strike me – pardon the pun – as the type of woman who would…"

"I'm not!"

I pulled my robe tighter around me, marching toward the front door, Eric trailing behind me.

"This has something to do with that Cherokee woman, doesn't it?" he said.

I faced him, trying to come up with a believable reply.

"It does," he said. "I can see it in your eyes. But you don't want to betray a confidence."

What was I supposed to say?

"Jonah," he said. "He's the one who slapped you."

He was getting too close for comfort. I opened the door, not wanting him to read my thoughts.

"So the journal is a fake," he said.

"It's not a fake." I replied, trotting down the front steps.

"But it wasn't written in the eighteen hundreds."

He followed me to my car as a man and a woman walked by, taking note of our pajamas, probably assuming we were a married couple having a spat.

My car chirped as I unlocked it.

"I guess I was right to be skeptical when we first met," he said.

There was no harshness in his voice. No anger. In fact, his voice was sympathetic even though he didn't understand at all. Which made me realize how much I really liked him. How much I wished we could continue seeing each other. He made me laugh. He listened. He cared. We had chemistry. The kind of chemistry I'd dreamed of. But now it was over before we ever really got started.

"You're too nice," I said. It would be much easier to drive away if he lashed out and accused me of deception.

"I'm guessing something's going on that's not of your making."

"You have no idea."

"But I do have an open mind. And an open door."

He smiled, pointing at the front door of his condo standing wide open.

I remembered thinking Nana was off her elderly rocker until I took a bite of that fig and walked through the invisible portal. Explaining wouldn't work.

"I'll pick you up at seven tomorrow evening," I said.

Tuesday mornings were usually busy. Especially for the investigative unit. But I closed our office door when I arrived and waited for Mallory to give me her attention. She was the picture of innocence.

"You know who I hung out with last night?" I said.

She shrugged, nonchalant as you please.

"Two police officers," I said, "who were convinced I was the victim of domestic violence. Because a certain well-known TV reporter called them and told them so."

"Listen, Kathryn," she said, "we can't have a member of the Watchdog Team going out in public with bruises on her face. It would kill our credibility. I also can't sit by and allow a friend and co-worker to be victimized. Not gonna happen. So if you're expecting an apology, forget it. You'll just have to pray to the Lord for an attitude adjustment."

"I was not beaten up by a man!"

"Bullshit. And everyone knows it."

Then she returned to her laptop like she had more important things to do than listen to me deny the truth. I was on the verge of getting really steamed but decided I might do the same thing if she denied a slap mark was a slap mark on *her* face.

"Okay, Mallory, I get it that dealing with your sister has made you skeptical. But you can rest assured I would never let a man hit me."

It was obvious she didn't believe me, but she zipped her lip.

It was five till seven when I arrived at Eric's condo. Per my instructions, he was dressed comfortably in khaki shorts and a green T-shirt.

With the weather getting hotter now that it was the middle of June, I was dressed similarly, my hair pulled into a ponytail to keep it off my neck. We looked like a couple of summer camp counselors.

He had way more restraint than I would've had if the tables had been turned, not asking once where we were going. He enjoyed the scenery, eyeing me occasionally, no doubt noticing my fingers tapping nervously on the steering wheel as I questioned my sanity.

I pulled off the road a short distance from Nana's cottage, parking behind a couple of scrub oaks. We cut across a field where cotton used to grow, now abandoned to tall grasses.

Sneaking past the house, we took the path to the river. When we reached the clearing, I led the way to where the hut used to be, pointing at the vague outline on the ground. Then I picked two figs from the bush and handed him one.

"Okay, I know this is going to sound strange, but you have to eat the fig as you step across the boundary. Right here." I pointed to the spot. "I'll go first. You follow me."

The look on his face told me he was asking himself if he was the butt of an elaborate joke.

"You have to be quiet," I said. "And it's going to be kind of strange. Ready?"

He fingered the fig in his hand.

"Okay, let's do it." I put mine in my mouth.

Stepping forward, I found myself inside the shack. A few seconds later, Eric appeared behind me, gasping. I forgot to warn him about the buzzing and dizziness.

After confirming the hut was empty, I turned to look at him. His eyes were so wide, he looked like a little boy who'd been given a puppy for his birthday. He surveyed the interior, taking in the blanket on the floor, the bird feathers tucked here and there along the walls, the cooking pot beside a small firepit, a handwoven basket.

From outside, we heard an off-key male voice singing loudly nearby. I realized it was Jonah belting out an exceedingly drunken version of *Yankee Doodle*.

Eric gave me a confused look as the singing came to an abrupt halt and Jonah shouted.

"Come on over here, woman!"

"I must get my Indian medicine," we heard Amadahy reply.

"Hurry up! Soon's I'm done with this bottle, you and me going inside."

His singing resumed, even rowdier than before.

I motioned to Eric that we should leave. We were turning to go when the front door of the hut swung open and

Amadahy appeared. Seeing us, she swiftly stepped inside, pulling the door shut behind her.

She gave Eric an inquisitive glance, taking note of his bare legs, then looked at me like I was an apparition.

"Bad Brother said you drowned," she whispered.

"I can swim."

"Do you bring a gun?" she said, her eyes fixed on Eric.

He was thunderstruck, face to face with the woman whose words he was translating. He struggled to make his voice work.

"A gun?" he whispered.

"No, we don't have a gun," I said.

"You must leave," she said.

I tugged Eric toward the back door, plucking a fig for each of us from the bush.

"Same procedure as before," I whispered.

As soon as we were outside, he did a one-eighty, looking for the hut that no longer existed. Mouth open, he shook his head repeatedly, searching all around for any kind of structure. He was almost panting in his excitement as though he'd just won a cycling Gran Prix.

Lightning bugs blinked on and off in the deepening shadows as he scanned the clearing with fresh eyes, wandering around the space where the shack, the house and the garden used to exist. He returned to the portal and squatted down, touching the river rocks, the rusted hinge, the small bones, feathers and beads partially concealed under the pine straw. He plucked a fig from the tree and turned it this way and that in his hand, then put it to his nose and sniffed.

The sun had set and I suggested we get going before it got too dark to see. Neither of us spoke.

It was a quarter till nine when we emerged from the trees. We drove back to his condo in silence. He seemed to be in a state of shock.

When we arrived, he invited me in. No granola bar and orange juice this time. He poured us each a big glass of red wine and set a can of mixed nuts on the coffee table. Gesturing me toward the blue sofa, he settled into a matching chair.

He took a large swallow of wine and gave me a dumbfounded look.

"If I'm not mistaken," he said, "we traveled back in time. I cannot believe those words just came out of my mouth."

"I know."

"You were right about one thing. If you'd tried to explain, I would've thought you were..."

"A nutcase."

He chuckled, turning his wine glass up again.

"Figs," he said.

"Not any figs."

"Yeah, I remember she said her grandmother was a medicine woman and conjuror who grew figs using some kind of magic. And the taste. I swear those figs tasted like the past."

He was right. They had a subtle flavor. Not like the fruit I was used to eating.

"It's incredible – I got to see an actual Cherokee menstrual hut," he said, like an archaeologist might sound after discovering an unknown ancient civilization. "Cherokee women used to spend time together in those huts. It was a women-only environment that helped nurture their sisterhood, you might say. Traditionally, menstruation and childbirth were associated with spiritual power."

"Spiritual power?"

"Yeah," he said. "Men knew better than to mess with women. Cherokees viewed bodily fluids as powerful, especially blood."

"Obviously, Jonah doesn't have a clue."

He twirled his glass, lost in thought.

"Now you know why I'm in such a hurry for the translation," I said.

"No kidding. So the drunk dude who couldn't carry a tune was Jonah?"

"Yep."

"And he's the one who left the handprint on your face."

"Correct."

"And why did she ask if I had a gun? Did she think you brought me along to kill him?"

"The thought did cross my mind."

"So," he said, "we're the only ones who know?"

"My grandmother knows. She just doesn't know she knows. She's the one who told me about Amadahy. But she doesn't understand they're in the past. She thinks they're her neighbors. She wants me to call the police and have Jonah arrested."

"Wow."

"The thing is, she's right. Amadahy does need protection. I told her last time I visited she should take the baby and run away. But she says she's got to stay on the land. I talked with a psychologist, trying to figure out whether a man like Jonah could change his stripes. But the psychologist says it's tough even with face to face counseling. And he says Jonah would have to want to participate. Fat chance of that."

"I'll shift into high gear on the translation," he said.

⁓

Next morning there was an email from Eric time-stamped two fourteen a.m. with more translated pages. I lay back down on the bed, ignoring my full bladder and my empty stomach, and opened the file. As I read, Pixie wandered in, snuggling against me.

Amadahy's Journal – Part 3 (May 1840)

On a warm day in Planting Month, as Bad Brother worked the fish traps and I picked early squash in the garden, Betsey on my back, I heard the familiar croak of a treefrog. I answered with my own whistle and trill of the cardinal, familiar to him from our childhood.

He emerged from the trees dressed in deerskin leggings, a Cherokee shirt and moccasins, his long black hair on his shoulders, a bone-handled knife tucked into the skin belt at his waist. It was traditional Cherokee garb, not white man's clothing like many among the Aniyunwiya wore to please our oppressors.

Degataga – Standing Together – was a member of the Wolf Clan and one year older than me. I had not seen him since the Green Corn Ceremony of my fifteenth year.

"Old Noon Day said you and your family marched west," I said, speaking to him in Tsalagi.

"I slipped away under cover of darkness with my cousin. We joined other Cherokee in the Mountains of Blue Smoke."

I remembered well his courage in stickball, his boldness speaking his thoughts. I also remembered dreaming of him, imposing and graceful in the Cherokee way. But that was in the Time Before.

"Old Noon Day told me the white man you were forced to marry is dead," he said.

"I was not forced. He was a good husband, not like other white men. Now his brother claims the farm, calling me his wife."

Before I could speak more, Jonah arrived like an angry skunk, threatening to spray an attacker to scare him away.

I switched to English.

"This is my cousin, Standing Together," I explained. "He is also a member of the Paint Clan." I did not reveal his real clan, wanting Bad Brother to believe we were kin.

Always shrewd, Degataga did not display surprise at my deception, understanding at once that it was necessary.

"Ain't you s'posed to be out there in Injun Territory with the rest of the Cherokee?"

Degataga turned to me and said in our language that we should not let Bad Brother know he spoke English. He asked me to translate the words. I agreed it was better not to reveal too much. He asked me to tell Jonah he lived in the north now.

When I spoke his words, Jonah asked why he came.

Degataga replied that he was looking for farm work, which he was accustomed to doing.

Bad Brother spat dark tobacco juice on the ground at Degataga's feet, challenging him. But Degataga did not flinch.

"All right," Jonah said, wiping his mouth with the back of his hand. "Two bits for the week. Sleep in the barn and eat the leavings from our table."

I said the words in Cherokee.

I knew Jonah agreed to pay him because he did not like to work. I also sensed Degataga did not come to earn money. He knew I would need help with the woman's work during planting time.

The next day we toiled side by side planting corn, squash and beans in mounds – the traditional Cherokee way. It was then that Degataga spoke his feelings.

"You cannot remain married to the evil white man."

"We are not married."

I explained I did not sign my real name on the marriage paper and performed the Cherokee divorce ritual after the first night.

"As is the custom of the Aniyunwiya, you have the right to leave him if the marriage is diseased. You must not remain with such a man."

"It is my family's home. Our burial ground is here. When my family returns, I must be here waiting."

He looked hard into my eyes. "What if they do not return?"

I made no reply.

"Forest Water..." he said, pausing a long time before continuing. "I would not say these words so soon after your husband's death, but our lives have changed. Now we must kiss the boots of the white man. Washington City does not care about the Principal People. I must speak the words you are not ready to hear. Since I was a boy, I planned for you to be my wife. And then the removal came to pass. I was forced to march west to the Darkening Land. You were driven into marriage with a white man you did not know."

"His skin was white. His heart was like ours."

"And now he is dead and you are left with a man who has no heart. I have come to take you back with me. We can marry in the traditional way. I will be a good father to your daughter. The Wolf Clan is the protector clan. I will protect you."

"The Paint Clan is the clan of the medicine people. And I will use my grandmother's strong medicine to keep our land."

He studied me to read my mind, then set his jaw.

"I also thought you and I would one day marry," I said. "It was you I waited for at the Green Corn Ceremony. But we are no longer children. You are free to marry another."

When the sun traveled below the horizon and the night owls roosted in the trees, I heard Degataga's flute from the riverbank. A mournful song filled with unspoken words of love.

Eric's voice was thick with sleep when he answered my call the next morning.

"Kathryn?"

"Even her childhood sweetheart wants to save her from Jonah's clutches. But Amadahy told him the same thing she told me: she has to stay on her family's land, has to take care of the family burial ground. Has to wait for her family to return."

"Yeah, she…"

"So I'm thinking if she refuses to leave, I have to figure out how to defang that snake in the grass."

He yawned loudly.

"Or," I said, "if she's intent on staying, there's got to be a way to get Jonah to leave."

"Hm."

"But what would make him want to abandon that little farm where he's the big cheese dictator?"

"Um… well… I don't know. Gold maybe?"

"Gold?"

"I haven't even had my orange juice yet," he said, his voice husky. "Thinking out loud here."

"Yeah, we could lure him away with gold fever!"

"Ironic," he said, "that's one of the big reasons the Cherokee were forced out. The Georgia Gold Rush began in 1828 in Dahlonega. Then the land in north Georgia became so valuable, white leaders were only too happy to steal it from the Cherokee Nation."

"So we tempt him with gold nuggets," I said, "The California gold rush is about to happen, right?"

"A few years down the road."

"I like it."

"Now," he said, "can I go pee?"

"We'll never get this story done if you don't stop farting around on your phone!"

Mallory's sharp tone jolted me from my research. For the five years I'd worked as her producer, she'd relied on me to be a go-getter. Always the one to keep digging until we got the information we needed or the interview that was crucial to our report. But my mind was many miles and a couple of centuries from the newsroom.

She caught me checking websites where you could buy gold online. After doing some research and checking Nana's deed to the Madison County property, I figured I'd need enough gold to equal a hundred dollars in 1840 money. Gold was valued at about twenty-one dollars an ounce back then, but the price now was nearly thirteen hundred dollars a pop.

"Sorry," I said.

After sneaking a few minutes here and there, I placed my order shortly before lunch. Which meant I could focus on my work the rest of the day.

Waiting for delivery turned me into a bundle of nerves. But Friday evening when I signed for the package, there was no feeling of relief. Having them in my possession only increased my agitation.

To my admittedly untrained eye, the nuggets looked like they'd been dug out of a stream somewhere. Now the challenge was infecting that big, brainless bully with gold fever.

When I texted Eric to let him know, he called immediately, insisting I jump in the car and drive to Athens. He promised a home-cooked meal when I arrived for our strategy session. I tossed a change of clothes in a bag, figuring I'd spend the night at Nana's before we took the gold through the time gate in the morning.

Eagerness was written all over his face when he answered the door wearing a grey apron and brandishing a spatula, his hair a little mussed, looking like a sexy TV chef.

"Basmati rice, yellow squash and tofu stir fry with Vidalia onions and fresh garlic," he announced.

"Smells divine." I set my purse on the table in the foyer and followed him into the kitchen.

"Pour yourself a glass of wine while I finish up."

There was a bottle of red and a bottle of white on the table and two wine glasses. White plates with blue trim, cloth napkins and silverware were already laid out. I slid into the far side of the booth so I could watch him at the stove. Pouring myself a glass of red, I was curious whether he was responsible for the royal blue and white décor. It had a decidedly clean, masculine look.

Three minutes later, he set a big steaming bowl of rice and a matching bowl of stir fry on the table. He doffed the apron, sitting across from me and gestured for me to serve myself.

"So," he said, filling his glass, "where's the doubloons, matey?"

"I can't believe I bought five gold nuggets," I said, digging them out of my pocket and placing them on the table.

"Wow!"

One at a time, he picked them up, turning each one over in his hand, rubbing the gleaming metal, mugging like we were partners in crime.

"I've never held a piece of gold in my hand," he admitted.

"Yeah, feels weird."

"Must've cost you an arm and a leg," he said.

"My credit card actually groaned when I clicked the 'pay' button."

"Good one."

I wasn't used to being around a man who could cook. Actually, most of the women I knew couldn't cook either. Me included. I usually ate frozen dinners, cans of soup, the occasional bowl of cereal for supper. Nothing like this impressive meal made from scratch.

"Okay," I said. "I think I've died and gone to culinary heaven."

His signature laughter filled the room. "You're easy to please. It's only a quick stir fry."

I rolled my eyes with theatrical exaggeration, filling my mouth again.

"You have no idea," I said, rice dribbling from my lips.

He laughed again. Funny, how his laughter made me feel all comfy and warm inside.

Then we turned to our planning session. It was easy to talk big about luring Jonah to leave with the promise of striking it rich panning for gold. Quite another to make it happen.

"I think it'll have to be a man who does the talking," I said, turning serious. "Besides being a lowly woman in his eyes, he already hates my guts."

"How about we pose as a married couple?"

"I wish I hadn't provoked him."

"What did you say to him?"

"I called him a savage swine when I found Amadahy with a black eye. He said it was his right to beat his wife."

"And that's when he hit you."

I nodded.

"I've got it – I could apologize to him for my wayward wife's bad manners," he said, a twinkle in his eye. "I think the gold will soften his attitude. We could offer to buy the farm."

"Then we tell him where the gold came from."

"The California Gold Rush begins in 1848, which is only eight years later." He pulled his phone out and searched a moment. "Sutter's Mill, Coloma, California. The American River."

"So, we tell him someone paid us in gold nuggets who prospected for gold on the American River in Coloma, California. And lots of men are getting rich out there panning for gold."

"As for why we want to buy his homestead?"

"We're looking for a farm along the Broad River because..." but I couldn't think of a good reason.

"Because we like to eat cat fish."

"Har."

"Because we're kayaking enthusiasts," he joked.

"We could tell him we want to grow a crop that's water-intensive."

"As long as we don't use the expression water-intensive."

We finished our dinner, cleared the table and loaded the dishwasher, adjourning to the living room, which I now realized was also tastefully done in blue and white.

"You either have a decorator's flair or..." I said.

"Or I asked my sister to make my condo look sophisticated and masculine."

More laughter.

Which launched us into conversation about his family. We talked about the younger sister, a graphic artist with a talent for interior design, and his parents who moved to Savannah after the kids grew up because they liked the historic vibe. It was fun listening to him talk.

I was laughing again an hour later when I caught the expression on his face. There was fondness in his eyes. But more than that, there was desire. I could feel a blush rising.

"I should probably go," I said.

"Go?"

"Nana has a guest room."

Carefully setting my wine glass on the coffee table, I started toward the foyer.

"You've had too much wine to drive all the way to your grandmother's house," he said.

"I only had two glasses. Besides, she lives right here in Athens."

"Much too far," he said. Normally full of mischief, his eyes were full of invitation now.

He moved closer, resting his hands on my waist. I let out a long, shuddering breath as he leaned into me, kissing me lightly. It was the kind of kiss that made me ache for more. Oh, he tasted good. And when he pulled me close, I kissed him back. Rather passionately.

"I believe," he whispered, "I believe I've fallen for you."

Of its own accord, my hand came to rest on his cheek.

"Is it possible," he said, flicking his eyes toward the stairwell, "that we might…"

Kissing him softly in reply, I took his hand in mine and we ascended the stairs.

We made love as the bedside lamp filled the room with a warm glow. A feeling of belonging bloomed inside me as I lay in his arms as though I'd been waiting for him my whole life.

⁓

Before heading out of town the next morning, we stopped at a second-hand store. I found a long black skirt that was a little too big for me. Which, when I tucked a white blouse in and cinched up the waist with a cheap belt, created a passable nineteenth century outfit. Eric bought a pair of grey slacks, a white shirt and a cheap sport coat.

We refined our story on the drive over, deciding to stick as close to the truth as possible. We were Eric and Kathryn Murray. He was a college professor and I was his wife. We decided I shouldn't hold a job outside the home, although it rankled a bit.

As before, we cut across the field to avoid being seen, and into the woods, our anxiety level rising the closer we got to our destination.

"We don't have to do this," he said once we reached the clearing. "I mean, think about it, Amadahy's been dead for…"

"I know, I know."

"Even little Betsey…"

"…is long dead. I get it!" Although I didn't mean to sound so irritated.

He shifted from one foot to the other.

"You don't have to go," I said. "I realize it's a lot to ask."

"I'm all in."

"You're right – she's long since turned to dust. But I can't live with myself if I don't try to help her. You stay behind!"

"Not happening," he said. "It's the chance of a lifetime for a historian with a specialty in Southeastern Indians."

"Something to put in the bio for your next book?" And I gave him a smirk.

He grinned and yanked his polo shirt off, baring his bicyclist chest as if to remind me he was a real man.

After changing into our 1840s duds, we gave each other an approving once-over, although he looked nothing like my image of a nineteenth century man. He was apparently having similar thoughts.

"You look way too pretty and too independent to pass for a nineteenth century farm wife." He leaned in to give me a sweet kiss on the lips. "But there's no one else I'd rather travel through time with." Said with a mesmerizing look that made me tingle ever so slightly.

Once we were in place, we ate our figs, crossing the invisible doorway. When the buzzing and dizziness subsided, we realized no one was inside the hut. But I noticed a pair of women's shoes on the blanket. They were actually low-rise lace-up boots, the black leather scuffed and faded.

"Wait," I whispered, removing my own flimsy shoes, setting them to one side and slipping Amadahy's boots on my feet. Not a perfect fit, but they looked much more authentic than my ruined black ballet flats.

We exited through the rear door and hurried to the woods behind the hut, zigzagging through the trees until we reached the trail. Only then did we walk toward the small wooden house nestled by the river as though we'd come by foot from town. The sun was directly above us when we knocked on the door.

Amadahy opened it, Betsey on her hip.

"Who is it?" Jonah called out.

Her face betrayed her consternation.

"I said, who is it?" he barked.

We heard a chair scrape the floor, then heavy footfalls before Amadahy was unceremoniously pushed aside and Jonah's tall frame filled the doorway. He squinted as though he was shocked to see me.

"Figured you drowned in the river," he said, sounding like he wished it were true.

"I nearly did."

Then he looked hard at Eric, using a dirty fingernail to pick food from his yellowed teeth. "You her husband?"

"That's right," Eric said, putting on a touch of a southern accent. "I'm Eric Murray and this is my wife, Kathryn."

"We done met," Jonah said, hostility mixed with curiosity showing on his face.

"I want to apologize for my wife's behavior last time she was here," Eric said. "Sometimes she forgets herself."

Jonah's eyes were full of suspicion. "Why ya'll knocking on my door at dinnertime?"

"Well, Mr. Barnes," Eric said, "we heard you might be interested in selling your farm if the price is right."

"The price would have to be damn right," he said. "Come in the house so I can finish eating."

The house was one big room with a four-poster bed on the left. A rough wooden table and benches sat near the fireplace along the back wall. A cast iron Dutch oven rested on the floor in front of the hearth.

"Pour 'em some a that stew," Jonah said to Amadahy as he lowered himself onto the bench facing the door.

"No need," I said, overwhelmed by his body odor.

"You too good for my table?" he replied.

"Stew sounds great," Eric said. "That's very hospitable of you."

Jonah resumed eating, dipping a large spoon into his bowl and slurping loudly.

Amadahy gestured for us to sit on the bench across from him, then ladled stew into bowls, setting them in front of us along with a couple of spoons. Then she sat down on a stool at the end of the table closest to the fireplace. She held Betsey on her lap, mashing the stew on her plate before sharing it with the baby.

"Where ya'll from?" Jonah said between slurps.

"Atlanta," I said.

"Never heard of it."

"It's a little crossroads on the other side of Athens," Eric said.

"How come you interested in my property?"

"We want to grow some crops that need a lot of water," Eric said. "Planning on digging some irrigation ditches from the river to the fields."

"Irrigation ditches."

As Eric engaged the enemy, so to speak, I did my best to mind my manners as I ate the gamey stew. I could tell Jonah had already decided we were naïve city slickers. But his accurate perception might work to our advantage if he thought he could make money off of a couple of easy marks.

"We'd like to make you an offer," Eric said. "And I brought along a bottle of whiskey as a gift." He slid the bottle from the paper sack he was carrying and set it on the table.

Jonah belched as he eyed the whiskey. "How much you offering?"

"We've got some gold nuggets my brother gave me to pay off a debt he owed me."

Talk about eyes bugging out. We definitely had his attention.

"My brother's been very successful panning for gold in California," Eric continued. "Coloma, California on the American River near Sutter's Mill. You ever heard of Sutter's Mill?"

Jonah shook his head.

"My brother says there's a lot of gold in that river," Eric said.

"Let me see." Jonah pushed his empty bowl aside.

Eric reached in his pocket and pulled out four gold nuggets, placing them in the center of the table.

Our host snatched them, holding them up to the light. Suddenly, he placed one in his mouth and bit down. He did the same with the others, inspecting each one afterwards for bite marks before returning them to the table.

"The land is worth more," Amadahy said, taking Jonah – and us – by surprise.

She'd been listening intently as she fed the baby. We hadn't anticipated she might throw a monkey wrench into our little gambit.

"Reckon my squaw's right," Jonah said, the corner of his mouth curling slightly as he reached for the whiskey bottle.

"How many acres you have?" Eric said.

"A hundred," Jonah replied.

"Seventy-five cents an acre for one hundred acres comes to seventy-five dollars," Eric said. "Each of these four gold nuggets weighs about an ounce. Since the price of gold is about twenty-one dollars an ounce, all together, they're worth a little over eighty dollars. I'd say that's a fair price."

"This land is not for sale," Amadahy announced.

Jonah gave her a sidelong look, apparently a little conflicted about his "squaw" speaking out of turn. To his credit, he seemed to be weighing her comment's impact on bargaining with the greenhorns sitting across from him.

"You ain't considering the house," he said. "and the barn, the smokehouse, that shed out back. And it's right here on the Broad River. A dollar fifty an acre might be more like it."

"I'm not as dumb as I look, Mr. Barnes," Eric replied.

Jonah laughed out loud, showing off his gap-toothed mouth. Then he lifted the whiskey to his lips.

"A dollar an acre," Eric offered.

"Them four gold pieces ain't worth that much." Jonah wiped his mouth with the back of his hand.

"As it turns out, I was holding back another one to use for supplies," Eric said, reaching in his pocket to retrieve the last piece of gold, setting it on the table. "You'll find it's pure, like the others. That's exactly what's coming out of the American River. In fact, my brother says many of the nuggets are much larger than these. Men are getting rich out there in California pulling gold from the shallows."

Jonah bit into the fifth nugget, examining the bite marks as he'd done before. Meantime, Amadahy cleaned Betsey's mouth with a rag, casting suspicious eyes at Eric and me.

"Not for sale," she repeated.

This time Jonah glared at her. "Why don't you take Miz Murray outside for some womenfolk talk."

She paused for an instant before rising from her stool and placing the baby on her good hip. I followed her into the yard and toward the river, an uneasy feeling in the pit of my stomach as I watched her rock from side to side.

"Why?" she said.

"We're trying to help you," I whispered.

"You would help by taking my land?"

"We don't really want your land. We want you to have it."

The expression on her face made it clear she considered me a fool.

But before she could say another word, there was a shout and a thud from inside the house. I took off running, Amadahy trailing behind me. When I burst through the door, I saw Jonah standing over Eric, who was lying face down on the floor.

~10~

I screamed and rushed forward. But as I reached Eric's limp body, Jonah grabbed me. Betsey began to cry as Amadahy pleaded with him to let me go. He ignored her, man-handling me out the door and across the yard to the smokehouse. Once inside, he tied my hands behind me before shoving me onto the dirt floor. He left me there, locking the door behind him.

"Oh, Eric!" I cried. "Please don't be dead. You can't be dead!"

A tidal wave of guilt swept over me. I'd been only too happy to accept his offer of help, too quick to jump on his random comment about gold, never imagining in a million years that our plan would veer so horribly out of control. How naïve we'd been. Jonah was a dangerous man.

The dark shed reeked of smoked meat. And for a second, I imagined hanging from one of the meat hooks above me.

A man's voice outside startled me. I squirmed, trying to sit up, dreading what Jonah might do to me.

Twisting around as the door flew open, I watched him unceremoniously dump Eric's body beside the fire pit in the center of the small enclosure. He hurried out, locking the door again.

It took a moment, but through my tears I realized Eric's hands were tied behind his back. Why would Jonah shackle a dead man?

I scooted closer on my butt.

"Eric?" I whispered. "Eric?"

Because my hands were bound, I couldn't turn him over to see his face. Dragging myself around to the other side, I leaned close so I could feel his breath on my cheek. Thank God, he was breathing. His eyes were closed. No marks on his face. I scooted along the dirt floor until I could see the back of his head. There was dried blood in his hair. Jonah had attacked him from behind, knocking him unconscious.

His head needed cleaning, but, looking around the shed, I could see there was no water. Even if there had been, I couldn't use my hands.

"Eric? Can you hear me?" I gently kissed the side of his face.

Voices in the distance caused my muscles to tense. It infuriated me that we were so vulnerable. So helpless. The door rattled and I held my breath as Amadahy appeared, a bowl and a rag in her hand, little Betsey on her back.

She squatted beside him. When she set the bowl down, I could see it was half full of water. Without a word, she dipped the clean rag in the water, wringing it out before carefully washing the gash on his head. She repeated the procedure several times.

"Please help us," I said.

She got to her feet, fatigue showing in the way she moved. "I will return." She locked the door on her way out.

Sitting on the hard dirt in that dark, smelly shed, panic skittered just beneath the surface of my skin, like prickles of electricity that might short out my wiring at any moment. It was all my fault. For some reason, I'd considered myself immune to the danger in Amadahy's world. Even after Jonah slapped me and chased me to the river. I always thought I could escape through the time portal. How foolish I'd been.

Amadahy entered, the baby observing us over her mother's shoulder. She carried a gourd of water with an earthy odor. Kneeling beside him, she proceeded to dip a small cloth in the gourd and dab Eric's lips over and over.

"What's that?" I asked.

"Cherokee medicine."

At length, he licked his lips as she applied the concoction to his mouth. After several minutes, he moaned softly.

"Eric?" I said.

Grooves appeared between his brows like he was in pain while Amadahy continued touching the wet cloth to his lips.

I spoke to him again. "Wake up, Eric."

He slowly opened his eyes.

"Dark," he whispered.

"We're in the smokehouse," I explained.

"He's gonna smoke us and eat us?" he said, his voice weak.

Which told me he would be all right.

Amadahy rose to leave.

"Can't you untie us?" I pleaded.

"Hell, no, she can't untie you!" Jonah barged in holding the bottle of whiskey we'd given him in one hand and a rifle in the other. "She's going into town." He called after her as she walked out of the shed, "Don't dilly-dally neither!"

Then he nudged Eric with the toe of his shoe before examining the whiskey.

"Never seen a square bottle," he said. He sniffed it before taking a sip, then smacked his lips.

"What kind of whiskey?" he said.

"Jack Daniel's," I replied, remembering from Amadahy's journal that he was illiterate.

He took another swig and wiped his mouth with the back of his hand, holding the weapon in the crook of his arm. "Mighty nice of you."

If I'd been desperate before, the sight of that long barrel nudged me close to despair.

"Appreciate you bringing me them gold nuggets," he continued.

He raised the bottle again, taking a big gulp, then wheezed loudly with satisfaction.

"You know what I paid for this here land?" he said. "Not one penny. Inherited it from my dead brother. He bought it from the man who got it in the land lottery of 1832, once the Injuns was told they couldn't live here no more." He took a moment for another drink, then slowly sat down on the floor, leaning against the wall, holding the bottle in one hand and laying the gun across his lap.

"When the sun goes down, I got a woman to lay in my bed. And one day soon, she's gonna give me some sons to raise up. I can go to town anytime I want, have me some fun. Don't lack for much. Why would I traipse way out yonder, work myself to death panning for gold?"

He let loose with a big guffaw like the joke was on us. Which, unfortunately, was true.

After taking another drink, he continued gloating, a gleam in his eyes.

"I ain't ignorant. I know for a fact some folks don't never strike it rich." His eyes bugged out as he focused his attention on Eric. "What would I do with a bunch of money anyways? Already got me this here musket. Granpaw brought it home from the war. Still shoots good." He waved it around, giving me a fright. "Got me a horse, food to eat. Got me a hard-working woman, even if she walks like a lopsided hen."

He held the bottle up toward the light streaming in through the open door, then took a hefty swallow.

"Damn, this is good." He squeezed his eyes shut for a few seconds as the liquor slid down his throat. "So you see, offering me them gold nuggets was a waste of your time. But not a waste of mine. 'Cause them gold pieces is gonna come in right handy. I done hid 'em where nobody can find 'em."

"Mr. Barnes," I said. "Can you please untie us and let us go?"

"Let you go?"

"Yes, we'd really like to go home."

"Now, Miz Murray, why would I wanna do that? So you can go find the sheriff and tell him I robbed you?"

"The gold pieces are yours." Eric winced like it caused him pain to speak.

Jonah nodded so unsteadily, he looked like a bobblehead doll. Then he opened his mouth to speak, but hoisted the whiskey bottle to his lips again, gulping loudly. Then he ran his tongue over his rotten teeth.

"You know where I sent my squaw? Into town to fetch my friend Johnny." He let that bit of news sink in. "Johnny needs a woman for his whorehouse." He sniggered and took another taste.

"You've gotta be kidding," I said.

"Do I look like someone who wastes time on tomfoolery? As for you," he said, looking at Eric, "don't think Johnny's got any use for you."

I realized I was chewing my lower lip and forced myself to stop.

"Mr. Barnes," Eric said, "seems like those gold pieces would be enough to pay for our freedom. We promise not to go to the sheriff. He wouldn't believe us anyway."

Jonah scratched his armpit and took another drink. He set the bottle between his legs splayed out in front of him, moving the rifle to the ground beside him. Then he rested his head against the wall.

"We gonna wait on ole Johnny." His words slurred as his eyelids drooped.

Eric and I didn't move a muscle as we watched him drift off to sleep, his right hand resting on the gun. I had no doubt he'd pull the trigger if he heard so much as a peep out of us. We waited a few minutes until his breathing turned to quiet snores.

"I sure could use a drink," Eric said, keeping his voice low.

I held my breath, waiting for Jonah to respond, realizing Eric was raising a trial balloon. But the snoring continued. And his grip on the weapon relaxed.

Eric shifted his body and sat up slowly like he had a severe headache.

"If he wakes up, drop to the ground fast," he whispered.

We wriggled about, slowly getting our feet beneath us. When we were finally in a squatting position, trying our best to keep our balance with our hands tied behind us, I gave him a look to signal I was ready and we both struggled to stand up. He lost his balance but steadied himself as he came fully upright. We tip-toed toward the door, hoping against hope that Jonah wouldn't wake up.

Halfway through the doorway, there was a snort behind us. We jerked our heads around, fully expecting to be staring down the long barrel of his rifle, but Jonah only smacked his lips, eyes closed, his head lolling to the side.

We made a break for it then, bolting across the yard as fast as we could go with our hands bound behind us, me leading the way to the small back door of the hut. Once we reached the fig bush, I faced away from the bush so I could get my hands on the figs.

"You guide me," I whispered.

He told me to move my hands farther to the left, then a little lower, until I wrapped my fingers around a fig. I plucked it carefully from the branch.

"Okay," I said, "you bend over and put it between your teeth."

He leaned over behind me, taking the fig into his mouth. But as he bit down, we were jarred by an unmistakable bellowing.

"Inside the hut," I whispered, struggling to open the narrow door.

Eric stepped inside close behind me, still holding the fig between his teeth, terror in his eyes.

"Put your mouth on mine," I said. "Hold tight to the fig with your teeth. I'm going to bite off half of it."

If someone had walked in at that moment, he would've thought we were playing a kissing game with our hands tied behind our backs. But this was no game. It was a matter of life and death.

I put my lips on his and carefully sank my teeth into the fig as he gripped it tightly with his incisors. When I had half of it in my mouth, I gestured at the back door. We heard footfalls and Jonah's voice yelling behind us in a drunken rage as I led the way, chewing the fig as I stepped through the doorway.

"You ain't..."

But his voice was silenced as I lost my balance and fell to the ground. I held my breath, waiting. Three seconds later Eric materialized out of thin air, landing on top of me with a groan. From where we lay, the hut no longer existed.

"He shot me," he mumbled.

As gently as possible, I used my body to roll him off of me.

"Where?" I said.

"My back."

Raising myself above him, I scanned his shirt. There, on the right side about halfway up his back, was a splattering of blood.

I lay down behind him so we were back to back. As quickly as I could, I worked to untie the rope binding his wrists. It took what seemed like forever. Then I moved around in front of him with my hands behind me.

"Use your hands to untie me," I said.

He didn't move.

"You've got to do it before you pass out."

He was able to slowly draw his arms to the front so he could work on the rope binding my wrists. It took several minutes, but I finally felt the knot loosen. I sat up and twisted around, alarmed by the pallor of his face.

~11~

First, I retrieved my phone from the backpack I'd left by a tree. Then I took off my long skirt and ripped a strip of cloth from it. Balling it up, I pressed it against the wound, trying to stanch the flow of blood. Maintaining pressure with my left hand, I called 911 with my right, directing them to my grandmother's cottage. Then I called Jeannette, giving her a heads-up about what happened – leaving out some crucial details – and asked her to escort the rescue crew to the river.

I maintained pressure on Eric's wound for what seemed an eternity. I thought he'd drifted off to sleep, so I was surprised when he spoke.

"Hiking," he said, his voice alarmingly weak.

"Right."

A short time later two Emergency Medical Technicians arrived carrying a stretcher as they followed Jeannette down the path. Nana was close behind them, her face knotted with worry.

The EMTs knew what they were doing, quickly lifting Eric onto the stretcher, starting an IV and hurrying back the way they came. Jeannette led the way. Nana and I trailed behind.

"Did that horrible man shoot him?" she asked.

Nothing like getting right to the point. At least she waited until we were far enough behind that nobody would hear. I debated what to say, fearing she'd tell Jeannette or my mom.

"I didn't see who shot him."

She gave me a skeptical look.

"Is he your boyfriend?" she said.

"I guess you could call him that."

"You guess?"

I shrugged.

"Tell me about him," she said.

Boy, did I not want to talk. And there was a part of me that almost told her so. But she was my sweet Nana.

"His name is Eric Murray."

"I knew a Murray when I was a little girl. Can't remember his first name."

"He's an Associate Professor at UGA."

"Well, well. What department?"

"History." I didn't tell her what his specialty was. That would've led to a conversation I didn't want to have.

Nana chatted about one thing or another the whole way back to the house. It dawned on me as I climbed into my car that she was trying to keep my mind off the worst-case scenario. Which hit me hard me once I was alone. I broke the speed limit all the way to Athens.

When I arrived at the hospital, I checked in at the desk, then settled into the ER waiting room. It was then I noticed why my feet were killing me. I was still wearing Amadahy's lace-up boots, which were about a size too small.

I was surrounded by a motley collection of humanity, from the skinny, middle-aged woman with full-sleeve tattoos sitting across from me, to the preppy college kid in plaid shorts with a hematoma on his forehead the size of a plum. But I wasn't interested in their misery. Just my own.

Resting my head on the back of the chair, I braced myself for bad news. My nerves were frazzled. It was all my fault. Eric would never have been shot if it weren't for me.

While the tattooed lady suffered a coughing fit, the man at the check-in desk called my name. Knowing surgery should take a while, it was with shaky legs that I headed in his direction. I definitely shouldn't be summoned this quickly unless... but I couldn't go there.

He had no news to share, instead giving me directions to a room where I found Eric lying on his back, eyes closed. He was alive – that much was obvious. He was hooked up to an IV and had a cannula in his nose giving him extra oxygen. I moved to the bedside, standing helplessly beside him, afraid to touch him or say a word.

A woman doctor in blue scrubs breezed into the room.

"I'm Doctor Rao. Are you his wife?"

"We're not married."

"But you were with him when he was shot?"

"Yes. Is he..."

"He's all right. No surgery needed. There's no bullet."

I couldn't hide my confusion.

"Dr. Murray," she said, taking his wrist in her hand. "Can you wake up?"

Eric's eyes opened as though she were a hypnotist who'd counted to three and clapped her hands.

"Dr. Murray, how are you feeling?" she said, her voice a little louder than necessary.

He nodded in slow motion.

"You're going to be fine," she said. "You didn't need surgery because there's no bullet inside you. There's what appears to be a bullet hole on your back. But it's only about an inch deep."

"What?" he said.

"I've seen a lot of gunshot wounds," she said. "But I've never seen one like this. It's like the bullet started into your back and then said 'nope, not going in there!'" She chuckled at her little joke before continuing. "Is there any chance you were injured with some other type of weapon?"

"There was a gunshot," Eric said.

"Hm. Well, we cleaned the wound and stitched you up. You'll need to have the stitches removed in about ten days or so. We also found a small gash on the back of your head."

"Must've happened when I fell," he replied, impressing me with his quick thinking.

"Have you had a tetanus shot recently?"

"Don't know if I've ever had one."

"I'll order one for you."

She paused briefly at the door. "Oh, the police will be here soon to ask a few questions."

"The police?" he said.

"Anytime we get a gunshot wound, we're required to report it to the police. I'll stop by when the officers get here."

He asked for water as she left. I retrieved a cup from the nightstand and helped him drink.

He swallowed, looking disconcerted. "We were..."

"... hiking in the woods. I know."

"And we didn't see who shot me."

"Right."

He took another sip as the door opened and in walked two uniformed officers.

"Mr. Murray," the short one said. "I'm Officer Rodriguez and this is Officer Jackson. We understand you suffered a gunshot wound?"

Eric grimaced before replying. "I'm not sure."

Officer Jackson took notes while Officer Rodriguez asked questions.

"What do you mean, you're not sure?"

"We heard a gunshot, then I felt pain in my back, but the doctor says there's no bullet."

Rodriguez exchanged a look with his partner as I did my best to act natural.

"Where were you when this happened?"

"We were in the woods along the Broad River," Eric said.

"What section of the river?"

Eric looked at me, unsure how to answer.

"In Madison County," I said.

"Can you be more specific?"

"We were in the woods behind my grandmother's cottage. I can give you her address."

Officer Jackson held his notepad in front of me and handed me his pen so I could write it down.

"Where were you wounded?" Rodriguez asked.

"In the back."

"Did you see who shot you?"

"No."

Rodriguez turned to me. "Did you see who shot him?"

"No."

"Where were you in relation to Mr. Murray?"

"Pardon?"

"Behind him? Beside him?"

"I was in front of him."

"Mr. Murray, is that correct?"

"Yes," Eric replied. "Of course."

"What time did this occur?"

"Uh…" Eric looked at me.

"I'd guess it was around three," I said. "But I'm not sure."

"What were you doing at the time of the shooting?"

"Hiking," Eric and I both replied in unison.

"Did you notice anyone in the area beforehand?"

Eric paused for a second before responding. "No."

"You're not sure?" Officer Rodriguez said.

"My head's still a little muddled," Eric said.

Doctor Rao reappeared, greeting the officers as she took Eric's wrist in her hand, apparently checking his pulse.

"Doctor," Rodriguez said, "we understand no surgery was needed?"

"Correct," she replied. "There was no bullet."

"Did it pass through his body?"

"There's no exit wound."

Officer Jackson looked up from taking notes, a puzzled expression on his face.

"There's an entry wound but no exit wound," Rodriguez said. "And no bullet in his body?"

"That's right," Doctor Rao said.

"Any evidence of drugs?" Rodriguez asked.

"No," Dr. Rao replied, then turned her attention to Eric. "You can go home in the morning. The nurse will give you care instructions. Take it easy for a week or so, see your regular doctor for a follow-up. And you might want to stay out of those woods."

She gave a quick wave to the officers as she left.

"All right," Rodriguez said. "I think we're done here. We'll pass our report along to the Madison County Sheriff's office and the GBI. Don't know if anyone will contact you or not."

There was low whispering as soon as they reached the hallway.

⁓

Eric was tender the next day and had to move slowly, but he could walk without assistance. He was relieved to be home, but we were both still a little shell-shocked.

We sat together in his kitchen booth for coffee and a bagel we picked up on the way.

"I think I figured out the mystery of the bullet hole," I said, applying a thin scraping of butter to my bagel.

"What's your theory?"

"Jonah opened the door and fired the gun directly at you, right?"

"Right."

"The bullet hit you in the back, right?"

"Right."

"But the bullet struck you just as you were going through the time portal. So, in the split second you were still in 1840, the bullet pierced your skin. But as you fell through the doorway, the bullet no longer existed in our time. It continued on its trajectory in 1840, hurtling through the open door and landing in the woods." I took a bite of my bagel.

"Excellent deduction, Sherlock."

It was a light moment that most certainly stemmed from our desire to avoid the seriousness of what we'd experienced. Because there was nothing funny about Jonah stealing the gold, knocking Eric unconscious, threatening to sell me into sexual slavery and shooting to kill as we made our escape. Everything was suddenly more complicated. If that was possible. But neither of us wanted to delve deeper quite yet.

I didn't stay long, knowing he needed rest. Plus, I had to go by Nana's house. Jeannette had messaged me they were returning to the city after yesterday's events, asking if I could come over.

When I arrived, they were all three out of sorts – Nana, Jeannette and Gracie, who wouldn't stop barking even after I joined them on the screened porch with a glass of tea.

"Gracie, hush up!" Jeannette snapped.

"Come here, sweetie," Nana cooed, taking the pint-sized dog in her lap. "She doesn't like it here in the city."

"I'm sorry, Edie. I'm kind of jumpy today, Jeannette said, turning to me then. "How's your friend?"

I'd texted her with an update as I was leaving the hospital the night before, not wanting them to worry.

"He's home. Probably fast asleep by now. Doctor says he'll be fine."

"Isn't that amazing there was no bullet?" Nana said.

"Curious. That's what it is," Jeannette said. "Someone else might not be as fortunate. If there's an armed drug addict close to the cottage, I don't feel comfortable taking Edie over there."

"But we can't abandon Forest Water!" Nana objected.

"Believe I'll fix some lunch now," Jeannette said, taking her glass and disappearing into the kitchen, obviously biting her tongue.

"I don't understand it," Nana said. "Jeannette's concerned about *us* but why isn't she worried about Forest Water? She's the one in danger. You did talk with the police last night, didn't you?"

"Yes, they came to Eric's room and asked some questions."

"Good. They need to arrest that terrible man."

"In the meantime, you and Jeannette can stay here in Athens."

"Now that the police have been notified, I'm sure everything will be cleared up soon. Isn't that right, Gracie?" she said, giving the little dog an affectionate hug.

As I climbed into bed that night, my phone dinged. It was an email from Eric with a few more pages. I was surprised he had the strength to tackle it. But he said when he woke up from a long nap, he felt an urge to find out more about our Cherokee friend. He said this latest entry was about events in May of 1840, several weeks before any of our visits to the past.

I trotted downstairs to read it on my laptop, sitting in my usual spot on the couch. Pixie plopped down on the keyboard but I gently moved her to the cushion beside me and opened the file.

Amadahy's Journal – Part 4 Planting Month (May) 1840

Sorrow lived inside me after Degataga departed, like a sickness with no cure. He promised to return soon and asked me to ponder his offer of marriage, saying I would be like a slave owned by a cruel master if I stayed with Bad Brother.

The next day Jonah rode into town. I wished it to be a long absence, but he returned after only two days. When he dismounted, shouting for me to prepare a meal for him, I thought of Degataga's words. And when Bad Brother demanded I lay next to his unwashed body, Degataga's words filled my mind once again.

But he brought with him good news. He defeated Ginny's owner, Silas Wheeler, in a game he called Poker. Because Mr. Wheeler did not have money to pay the debt, Jonah agreed for Ginny to help me on the farm two days each week until the debt was paid.

She arrived on foot the next morning one hour after sunrise, telling me she would rather work alongside me than by herself at the Wheeler farm.

She helped me plant pumpkin seeds, watermelons and potatoes. She also helped with Betsey, making her laugh and singing her songs I did not know. We talked as sisters do, sharing stories and speaking of family.

"I ain't seen you since your first husband died," she said. "I sure am sorry. I liked Mister Isham better than Mister Jonah. Master says they brothers, but they don't seem like it to me."

I continued working, deciding it was best to remain silent. When she spoke again, it was about her family.

"I dream of seeing Mama again someday. My brothers, Lonnie and Nate, too. They grown men now."

Her eyes betrayed the same sorrow I felt when I thought of my own family.

"I been worried lately that Master gonna sell me away," she said. "He ain't got money like he used to. Nowadays, my supper is leftovers from their supper. And then he go gambling and drinking and spending money he ain't got. The missus, she right angry."

"We have food. You must eat before you return home."

"Tell you what – I'll cook supper for you. I'm a good cook. Wish I could stay here with you. I'd work hard and help with the baby. Master says you gonna be having more babies soon."

"I do not want to own you."

"I hope Master don't sell me to no plantation. I like to cook and sew and help with the babies. Don't wanna work the fields like Mama done."

"We have no money."

"I don't like when Master has his way with me, but I hear tell it's worse on the plantation. At least Master ain't mean and rough. He don't hit me and I ain't never had a lashing. Mama's back was striped something fierce."

My hands stilled.

"Course, what I really want..." she lowered her voice, looking around to be certain we were alone, "...is freedom."

"Yes," I said, understanding more than she knew.

Late in the afternoon, Jonah called out to me that he had catfish, fresh from the river, and wanted them fried for supper.

"I can fry catfish real good," Ginny said.

We washed up in the river and went inside. She wished to show us her skill. I changed Betsey and nursed her while Ginny worked.

When it was ready, she proved her words were not false boasting. Crispy catfish were piled on a big plate in the center of the table with fried potatoes.

I noticed the look in Jonah's eyes. That is when I saw what he saw – a young woman with a pleasing face and body that men would admire. But when I moved to the table and signaled for her to sit with us, he objected.

"Slaves don't sit with white folk," he said.

Ginny's smile faded away.

"I am not white," I said.

"But I am."

"I gotta go now, so I'll be home before dark," Ginny said.

Wrapping three pieces of fish in a clean rag, I followed her outside, forcing the food into her hands.

~12~

It was gridlock on the roads Monday morning, which was unfortunate since I was running late. When I hurried into the office without my morning cup of coffee, it was stress, not caffeine, that flowed through my veins. My plan was to check in, then run to the break room and get a mug of coffee from the Keurig machine. But the atmosphere in our workroom was like a powder keg with a lighted fuse.

"Last week it was a man's handprint on your face," Mallory said. "This week your boyfriend is shot in the back under, shall we say, suspicious circumstances? And you were there! Tell me again you're not in an abusive relationship."

I was blindsided. No other way to put it.

"Not that phony innocent face again," she said, clicking her pen over and over as she sat at her computer.

A part of me wanted to turn around and make tracks. Another part of me wanted to tell her to mind her own business. Then there was yet another part of me that wanted to know how she knew about the shooting. She read me like I had a flashing sign on my forehead.

"*Athens Observer*. A headshot of your esteemed college prof." Her voice oozed sarcasm. "And a quote with your grandmother."

"What?"

"I sent you the link for your convenience. And you better read it quick, because the boss is expecting you in his office pronto."

Turning on my heel, I threaded my way across the newsroom to the big shot's office, wishing I'd had my morning caffeine fix.

When he was asleep, Ray Powell probably didn't look the least bit imposing. But I'm not sure he ever slept. He was the watchdog of watchdogs, the control freak of control freaks, with a booming voice and a quick mind.

Because his door was open, I tapped on the doorframe instead. He motioned me to one of the leather chairs in front of his desk, leaning back and crossing his arms over his chest.

He was the first black news director at our TV station and proud of his achievements – the highest ratings for the six and eleven p.m. newscasts, second place and gaining on the competition with our revamped morning show. Plus, an investigative news team that won lots of awards. He was a pro. And he liked to surround himself with pros.

"All right, Kathryn, let's cut to the chase. Mallory thinks you're hiding some kind of violent relationship. She sent me a link to the Athens story this morning, which, I have to admit, sounds kind of dicey. She also filled me in on the slap mark on your face last week. And while I don't like poking my nose into my employees' private lives, if you're involved in domestic abuse, physical fights, drugs, or anything that reflects badly on our news department..."

"She's got it all wrong. I'm definitely not in a violent relationship. Definitely not doing any drugs or hanging out with anyone who does drugs."

"She also told me you talked with that psychologist you interviewed about a *friend* who's in an abusive relationship." He used air quotes around the word friend. "Which, I'm told, is often the way a victim reaches out for help."

"I'm not a victim, Ray. I'm not reaching out for help. Not for myself, anyway. Eric Murray would never hurt me. He wouldn't hurt a fire ant. We're not doing drugs. It's possible the woods behind my grandmother's cottage may not be safe anymore. That's why I'm insisting she stay at her Athens home for the time being. While I appreciate Mallory's concern, there's nothing to worry about."

His eyes bored into me.

"I'm telling the truth," I added. "I would never tolerate someone who hit me. Never!"

"I'll tell Mallory to cool it. But, hear me good – if there are any more unsavory reports, I may have to intervene. Bad PR doesn't help my news department. You follow me?"

He turned his attention to his phone before I finished nodding.

I read the story in the Athens paper while waiting for my K-cup to brew. Leaning on the counter in the break room, I scrolled on my phone, stunned the paper made such a big deal out of it. But then, it was a UGA associate professor who was shot in the back, and a producer for one of Atlanta's premiere investigative reporting teams was involved. Plus, they had Officer Rodriguez saying no bullet was found in Eric's body. Then there was the quote with Nana.

"I've been trying to get the police to do something about that bad man who lives down by the river behind my house for some time," Edie Crawford said.

Mrs. Crawford owns the wooded property where the alleged shooting took place. She called police Sunday afternoon to file a report after Dr. Murray was rushed to the Athens hospital.

Calls for comment to Dr. Murray and Mrs. Crawford's granddaughter, Kathryn Spears, were not returned.

Yeah, I had a couple of missed calls from numbers I didn't recognize. One of them left a message, which I never listened to, figuring it was one of those stupid recordings threatening me about a credit card or something. I was actually glad I hadn't been given the opportunity to comment. What would I have said?

Coffee in hand, I returned to the Watchdog Team office for a little tête-à-tête with Mallory. She was prickly as a rose bush. But we managed to call a truce after I tactfully reassured her she was dead wrong. Still, the comradery we'd shared in the past had washed away like a sandcastle overrun by the surf.

To punish me, I suspect, she sent me to federal court where I had to pore over a zillion files searching for a tidbit of information on a local politician we were investigating.

When the long, tedious day was over at last, my body wanted badly to soak in the tub, then relax on the couch, my feet on the coffee table while I ate a frozen dinner with a glass of wine, my kitty on my lap, watching an old movie. But I needed to thank Eric and see how he was doing. I also needed to talk with Jeannette and Nana about her interview with the local paper. I stopped by my apartment long enough to feed Pixie, then drove to Athens. It was heavy rain the whole way, my windshield wipers working overtime.

I called Eric to let him know I was coming. He seemed underwhelmed at the prospect. I chalked it up to fatigue and discomfort. He greeted me with a tepid hello at the door.

"Are you hurting?" I asked.

"Tired." He walked gingerly into the living room, flinching as he stretched out on the couch.

"Probably from working on that translation. It was awfully good of you, considering all that happened."

He rubbed his hand over his face like he hadn't had much sleep.

"That was my last translation, Kathryn."

Which was so totally out of left field, I didn't know what to say.

He laced his fingers together, resting his hands on his chest. "My boss stopped by today. I thought he came to see how I was doing. But he'd seen the newspaper article this morning."

"Ah."

"Yeah, he was pissed. He told me the department doesn't want its reputation sullied by that type of negative publicity."

"Yeah, my boss talked with me too."

"He said if I'm not careful, I could easily become a laughingstock. He said funding can be impacted for faculty members perceived as clowns. His words."

"But you didn't do anything."

"The rumor mill is already grinding," he said. "I've gotten several half-joking messages asking if I was cooking meth in the woods. It comes across as a very fishy story, especially since I can't tell anyone the truth."

I'd remained standing, but sank into a chair like a tire going flat.

"I'm sorry," he said.

Questions filled my mind. Who would I get to finish the translation? How could I help Amadahy? What about my relationship with Eric?

"There's something else," he said. "We took that scum of the earth five gold nuggets. Suddenly, he has financial assets. Which *we* provided him. No doubt, we changed history by letting him get his filthy hands on that gold."

"But..."

"Yeah, I know, it was my brilliant idea. And, yeah, our intentions were noble." He pulled himself up to a sitting position. "But even if we'd succeeded in that half-baked plan to trick him into running off to the gold fields, we would've been meddling with the past. Just because Jonah was an asshole doesn't give us the right to..."

"An abusive, violent, dictatorial asshole!"

"There've been plenty of those down through the centuries."

"Are you saying you're okay with leaving Amadahy to..."

"Live her life? Yes, that's what I'm saying."

"I can't stand by and let her suffer. She's already suffered enough. Her people were forced from their homes, ordered to march west! She was cheated out of her family's land. Then Jonah murdered Isham and claimed the farm. She has a horrible, shitty life that was forced on her!"

"What about Ginny and all the rest of the slaves? They had horrible, shitty lives that were forced on them too! The injustice and brutality that's been inflicted in the past – and continues to be inflicted – is mind-boggling! If you want to right some wrongs, there's plenty of causes to choose from in the here and now!"

"I thought you..."

"I think I got sucked into a time travel fantasy. We can't go back to 1840 and play God."

"Excuse me? Sucked into a fantasy?" I jumped to my feet. "You're not a child. You joined me because you wanted to, as I recall, not because I tricked you! And, as you yourself pointed out, you're the one who first mentioned gold!"

"Partly because I was falling for you. And partly it was so ridiculously fantastical that I..."

"It was never a game to me!"

"I didn't say it was a..."

"You..."

"They're all dead, Kathryn! They've been dead a long, long time."

My jaw clenched so hard, my teeth hurt.

I stormed out, slamming the door behind me, and stalked to my car in the pouring rain, jumped in and backed out of the parking space. Pounding the steering wheel as I pulled out of the complex, I fishtailed and nearly ran into an oncoming car.

Then the tears welled up. Which ticked me off. If there's one thing that makes me really mad, it's when stupid tears fall when I'm angry!

"Sissy!" I shouted, hitting the steering wheel again and hurting my hand. "You're a spineless sissy, Eric Murray!"

How could he abandon Amadahy because his department chair threatened to withdraw funding? Really?

It only took me a few minutes to get to Nana's house, which was a good thing because driving while blowing off steam might possibly be even more dangerous than driving under the influence. Especially during a thunderstorm. The only problem – I was so steamed, it would be challenging to talk with Nana and Jeannette. I parked further down the street in front of a neighbor's house.

Eight o'clock at night in the summertime normally means there's still plenty of light. But with rain coming down in sheets, it looked more like midnight.

When the urge to slap the steering wheel finally abated, I wiped my eyes and blew my nose before doing a U-turn and heading back to Nana's house.

"What are you doing here on a stormy Monday night?" Jeannette said as soon as she saw my face.

I stepped inside, considering how to answer.

"Kathryn, you're soaked!" Nana cried. "I'll get you a towel." She rushed down the hallway.

"Have you eaten supper?" Jeannette asked.

"No, actually."

"Sit down and I'll pop a frozen dinner in the microwave." She gestured at the kitchen table. "You want spaghetti or chicken tetrazzini?" she said, staring into the freezer.

"Spaghetti would be great."

"Here you go, sweetie," Nana said, hurrying back into the kitchen with a large towel, wrapping it around me and giving me a hug. "Goodness, did you lose your umbrella?"

"Forgot it." Which was funny since I had three umbrellas in my car.

As the microwave hummed and Jeannette set a napkin and silverware in front of me, Nana retrieved three wine glasses from the cabinet and a bottle of her favorite Cabernet. She poured us all a glass without even asking, then set a box of chocolate cookies on the table, reminding me of a teenager excited about camping out with her girlfriends.

I toweled my hair lightly and wiped my arms, then wrapped the towel around me like a shawl, realizing my wet clothes were making me cold in the air conditioning. But the spaghetti and wine warmed me up.

"You look tired," Nana said. "You've even got dark circles under your eyes."

"Long day."

Jeannette watched me closely as though she were waiting for the other shoe to drop.

When I finished my meal she broached the subject I was here to discuss.

"Saw the story in the paper this morning," she said, twirling her glass between her fingers.

"I did too!" Nana said. "Did you see it, Kathryn? They did a good job covering the story, I think. I really hope the police follow up and do something about that evil man. I don't care if he *is* her husband!"

"Listen, Nana..."

"And how is what's-his-name? Is he doing all right?" she said.

"Eric is fine. He's taking it easy at home."

"What luck a bullet didn't lodge somewhere inside his body," she said.

"I still don't understand," Jeannette said. "Did the bullet graze him?"

"Something like that," I replied, quickly turning my attention back to my grandmother. "Listen, Nana, I know you meant well when you called the police and did the interview with the newspaper, but I sure would appreciate it if you'd let me handle the situation."

She straightened her glasses, shifting in her chair to face me.

"I believe I gave you plenty of chances to handle the situation, as you put it, and you did nothing, as far as I could tell. I know you look upon yourself as my caretaker, Kathryn, but I've been taking care of myself longer than you've been alive. I've got sweaters older than you are! And if you and Jeannette think I don't see you rolling your eyes like some of my grey matter leaked out of my ear while I was sleeping, you're sadly mistaken."

"Nana, I..."

"Don't interrupt." Her tone was all business, and I could suddenly envision her as a capable young woman used to traveling the world or handling a classroom full of rambunctious students. "I'll call the police if I think it's warranted. I certainly don't need your permission. And I can talk to a reporter if I see fit."

She steepled her fingers like a teacher having a come-to-Jesus with a naughty student.

"I'm sorry, Nana. Truly, I am. I never meant to…"

"One day, if you're lucky, you'll be old like me," she said. "And when that time comes, I believe you'll understand."

"I didn't mean to hurt your feelings. I love you very much. I guess I've gotten a little protective."

"A little?" she said.

"It's only natural. Because of how much I care."

She grunted softly.

"Edie," Jeannette said, "I want to apologize too. When I first came, I never dreamed you'd become like a sister to me. And I guess I've been overprotective too. Like Kathryn, I've done it out of love and concern. Please forgive me."

She reached across the table and took Nana's hand in hers. I laid my hand on top of theirs.

"I used to help my grandmother when I was a little girl," she said, her usual warm tone of voice returning. "Grandma's the one who told me about my Cherokee heritage. She became a little dotty in her old age, but it didn't slow her down much. She said she'd heard stories about one of her great-grandpas beating his wife. She told me 'don't ever let a man hit you, Edie.' She said 'you need to get to know a man real good before you marry him.' I took her advice. Bob was the best husband a woman could have."

She grew misty-eyed. So did I.

"Amen," Jeannette said, emptying her wine glass.

"I was waiting to tell you both when we were all together," Nana said, "that I hired a genealogist to research my family tree. I got tired of waiting for *someone else* to do it." She gave me a look. "I told her I want to find out if all the family stories about having Cherokee blood are true."

I sensed Jeannette forcing herself not to roll her eyes. But considering all I'd learned about Amadahy, Nana's stories no longer seemed like tall tales.

~13~

My mood matched the weather the rest of the week – grey and rainy. Stuck doing tedious research on court cases at work and searching for a new translator in my off hours, I felt as though I'd been cast aside. The only one who wanted to keep me company was Pixie, who wasn't troubled in the least by hanging out with a social pariah.

I did find someone to finish translating the diary – a native speaker who lived in North Carolina. It was strictly business. No face-to-face meeting. She asked me to scan the pages and email them. I doubled her usual fee for a rush job.

A lightbulb also came on in my brain as I was treating two blisters on my toes from wearing those nineteenth century women's boots. I searched online until I found a guy who did orthopedic shoe builds. When I took the right shoe to his shop on my lunch hour and told him to add a four-inch sole, he looked more than a little skeptical.

"The patient should come in for a fitting," he said.

"She can't possibly come in. If it's not quite right, I'll bring it back and pay extra for a second try."

I convinced him to get a move on and told him I'd pick it up first thing Saturday morning. Frustrated about my awkward efforts to save Amadahy from that half-witted white male supremacist, the least I could do was make it easier for her to walk. I honestly didn't know how she endured her daily chores, much less surviving a pregnancy and motherhood. I'd seen her cringe in pain. Hopefully, I could provide some relief. And, just maybe, give her the ability to run away, if it came to that.

Friday afternoon, as we were driving back to the station in the satellite truck, my phone dinged. It was an email with an attachment from Nancy Smith, my new translator. Although I was anxious to read the new pages, I tucked the phone back in my bag.

"Is that your boyfriend asking you out this weekend?" Mallory said from her spot in the back seat.

The way she stressed the word boyfriend, with that judgmental lilt in her voice, stuck in my craw. Bad enough she sent suspicious vibes my way every day, scoping out my face and arms, obviously looking for bruises.

I refused to respond. Brandon, our camera man, glanced over at me from the driver's seat.

"Who's the boyfriend?" he asked.

It was an innocent question so I didn't give him any grief over it. I shook my head, letting him know Mallory was baiting me. He took the hint. Mallory didn't.

"Where's he taking you?" she said.

"Mallory…" I almost let her have it, but managed to dial my temper back a notch. "I don't have a date this weekend."

No way I was telling her we'd broken up. God, she'd probably want to have me X-rayed for bone fractures.

"Guess that's good news, considering."

I really did try to put myself in her shoes. If I suspected *her* boyfriend was hitting *her*, what would I do? But it was hard to imagine. She wouldn't tolerate it any more than I would.

As soon as I got home that evening, I tossed my work clothes in the hamper, sweaty from a day on assignment in the heat. I took a cool shower, then slipped into a sleeveless aqua beach shift. I needed to start calling it a house shift since I never went to the beach anymore.

I poured Pixie's favorite kitty food in her bowl, fixed myself a salad, waiting till I sat down at the table with my supper before opening the attachment on Nancy's email.

Amadahy's Journal – Part 5 Planting Month (May) 1840

When Ginny returned after two days' time, she carried a small basket of early peaches. She chased after Betsey who crawled on the ground while I washed clothes and spread them on bushes to dry. My baby's new skills became a worry to me – how to keep my little daughter from triggering Jonah's anger.

Ginny held Betsey's hands up high, letting her small feet touch the riverbank, speaking to her in a special baby language I did not understand.

"She gonna be walking real soon," Ginny said. "Then you in trouble."

She continued talking to me as I worked.

"How long you been married to Mister Jonah?"

"We visited the judge in winter."

"Here it is, the month of May! How come you ain't pregnant yet?"

"I am nursing Betsey."

"I expect you gonna be nursing her for a good while." She laughed a knowing laugh.

Jonah returned when the sun was high, sitting in the house and filling his plate with bread and meat I prepared.

"Where's your slave friend?" he said.

"She is with Betsey by the river."

"Tell her I wanna see her."

I moved toward the door.

"Alone," he said.

Pausing in the doorway, I turned to regard his face. He ignored me, spearing a hunk of venison with his knife. A small piece fell into his beard as he lifted the meat to his mouth.

When I reached the river, Ginny was singing Betsey to sleep, strapped onto her cradle board as I had instructed.

"Jonah would speak with you," I said.

She raised one brow in question.

"I do not know," I replied, careful to say nothing more.

When she entered the house, I followed quietly, standing beside the open window that faced the river to hear their voices.

"Silas says he's gonna put you on the auction block," Jonah said. "Told him I might be interested. But I gotta know if you're sound of body before I make an offer."

She did not speak.

"You had any babies?"

"No sir."

"Come over here."

There were soft footsteps.

"Don't want no damaged goods," he said, a sly tone in his voice.

My eyes closed in anger.

"Take off your dress."

"Yessir." Her voice trembled.

There was a rustle of fabric.

"Drop it on the floor and come stand by me."

I ran toward the river as fast as my feet would take me, my ungainly stride slowing me when I needed swiftness. Reaching the bank where my baby slept, I picked up three rocks and threw them one by one into the water. Then I screamed.

At once, Jonah rushed from the house, his musket in hand, the door standing open behind him. I removed Betsey from the cradle board as she cried, holding her in my arms.

Jonah held his long gun in front of him, looking in every direction as he drew near.

"What in hell's going on out here?" he shouted.

"A bear threatened the baby," I said, filling my voice with alarm.

"Where'd it go?"

"Downriver," I said, spying Ginny in the doorway smoothing her dress.

"What kind of bear?" he said, scanning the riverbank.

"Black bear." I silently asked black bears to forgive me for blaming one of their kind.

Betsey continued to cry, startled by my screaming and Jonah's yelling. I bounced her in my arms, speaking soothing words in Tsalagi.

After striding up and down the river's edge, he satisfied himself the bear was gone. Seeking to distract him, I showed him the fresh peaches, offering him one.

"Need to finish talking with Ginny," he said.

"She must leave for home," I spoke up so my voice would carry. "She is needed there to pick more fruit."

"Then give me one a them peaches."

Betsey quieted herself, so I set her on the ground and washed the fruit. I saw Ginny walking across the yard toward the trail. I handed Jonah the peach, then lifted the baby to my hip, carrying another peach as I hurried after Ginny.

"To eat on your way home." I spoke loudly as I presented it to her.

"Thank you, Missus," she said, her eyes fixed on mine.

I knew what she was thanking me for. It was not the peach.

"He has no money," I whispered.

When I returned to the riverbank, Jonah's face was sticky with peach juice.

"I seen what you done," he said, taking the last bite of the fruit, his eyes like those of a wild dog about to pounce. "Strap the baby on the papoose board."

I squatted to lay Betsey on her cradle board, wrapping her snugly. I told her I would return soon and for her not to cry, speaking with my eyes as well as my mouth. Then I turned the board toward the river so she could not see Jonah use me in place of Ginny. I willed myself not to cry out, wishing to deny him his triumph."

"That stinking pile of monkey vomit," I said, looking at Pixie. "I'm sure you agree I can't sit on my hands and do nothing."

She flicked her tail in agreement.

This time, I didn't have to park by the road. Instead, I pulled up in front of the cottage, leaving my car in the driveway since Nana and Jeannette were staying in Athens. I let myself in, set my backpack on the coffee table and pulled out Amadahy's shoes. Not stylish exactly. But I felt good about adding a lift to the right one, hoping it would give her some relief.

Besides being hot, it was also humid. I was dripping with sweat by the time I reached the riverbank.

Standing by the magical fig bush, I took a long pull from my water bottle before tucking the shoes under my arm. I plucked a fig from the bush and deposited it in my mouth. I thought of the beads, bones, feathers and river rocks, steeling myself as I stepped through the portal.

If I thought the hut had been sweltering before, it was positively stifling now. I felt like bread dough sliding into a room-sized oven. That, despite wearing shorts and a camisole top with my hair in a pony tail.

The hut was empty but there was a rhythmic sound in the distance. My plan was to stay put and wait for Amadahy. I wanted to give her the shoes, but I also needed to talk with her. One thing I didn't want was to risk being seen by Jonah. Nothing good could come of that.

Careful not to touch anything in the cramped space, I sat on the blanket, pulling my knees up in front of me. I hoped she would come soon. At least I had water, deciding at the last minute that if I were discovered, my water bottle would be the least of my worries.

I waited for over an hour, taking small sips so I wouldn't get dehydrated. How many times had I watched pro basketball players, amazed at the sweat pouring from their bodies. That's what I felt like sitting in that sauna, a headache building.

Finally, I heard a voice near the shack. The door opened and Ginny stared, wide-eyed, as though she'd stumbled upon an alien from another planet.

14

Putting my finger to my lips, I silently begged her not to reveal my presence.

It was my first time meeting her in person. Although I felt like I already knew her from reading the journal. Amadahy's description didn't do her justice, though. She was pretty, with almond-shaped eyes, her hair pulled back into a small bun. The spunk in her eyes made me like her right away.

"Who're you and what you doing indecent like that?" she whispered as though my appearance was an affront to her dignity.

"Please, Ginny, I need to speak with Amadahy."

"How you know my name?"

"Please? I'm her friend."

"Look like you escaped from a bawdy house."

"Please?"

She took in my bare arms and legs, retrieving a basket from the corner and taking it with her as she backed out the door. I hoped she would deliver my request.

After several moments I heard footsteps and the door swung open. This time, it was Amadahy, Ginny behind her carrying the baby.

"You must come outside," Amadahy said. "It is too warm now in the hut."

"But what about…"

"He is not here. He will return in one or two days."

She gestured for me to follow and we made our way to the riverbank. Amadahy had Ginny stop by the house to get a dress for me to wear.

"You must cover yourself," she said when Ginny handed it to me.

I set the shoes down, slipping the dress on before taking a seat on a rock, facing them.

"Who is she?" Ginny asked Amadahy.

"I'm a friend," I answered.

Ginny squinted one eye at me.

"She speaks the truth," Amadahy said, then turned to me. "Jonah does not know I helped you and Mr. Murray escape. I put sleeping medicine in his whiskey. If he sees you…"

"I know. But I wanted to return your boots."

I presented them to her and sat down again. She inspected the elevated shoe with intense interest.

"I borrowed them last time I was here and, in our rush to leave, I forgot to take them off," I explained. "It turned out to be a good thing because I found a man who adds these thick soles so people who have one leg shorter than the other can walk more easily."

She held the special boot, examining it from all angles. "Where you live, people are misshapen like me?"

"Sometimes. There are different causes for leg length discrepancy. Sometimes corrective surgery can be done."

It appeared both of them were struggling to translate my strange words.

"And where you come from, people wear such shoes?"

"Yes, if they need them."

"Try 'em on!" Ginny cried.

Amadahy replaced her moccasins with the high-top boots, taking time to lace them carefully. When she tried to stand, she reached for Ginny's arm. She took one tentative step, holding onto Ginny for balance. Then, another. She looked at me, amazement in her eyes.

"You'll probably have to practice to get the hang of it," I said.

Although the built-up sole appeared to be a bit shorter than what she needed, it was close enough to allow her a more natural gait. She continued taking baby steps, holding tight to Ginny's arm.

Then a hint of a smile appeared on Amadahy's face, the first I'd ever seen there. Suddenly, she looked much younger, more like her actual age. I had to remind myself that this determined young woman before me was only eighteen years old. But then, as quickly as it materialized, it was gone, as though a dark cloud had cast a deep shadow over her.

She sat roughly on the ground and unlaced the boots, sliding them off her feet, replacing them with her moccasins.

"Why you take 'em off?" Ginny said, picking Betsey up and parking the chubby baby on her hip.

"I cannot wear them in front of..." and she looked from Ginny to me.

"I didn't think of that," I admitted, imagining Jonah's reaction. He would, no doubt, be suspicious. And he would most likely not want her to be able to walk better. "I'm sorry."

"I will hide them in a secret place. When he is not here, I will teach myself."

"And then one day you'll be able to walk away from that stinking turd," I blurted.

Ginny snickered.

Amadahy replied by giving her a silent gesture. It was apparently a polite request for privacy because Ginny took Betsey's hands, helping her to toddle along the riverbank, her roly-poly legs unsteady beneath her.

"You and Betsey deserve much better," I said.

Although it was a perfect summer day, the mood had turned somber.

"Tell me of your place," she said.

Interesting, it never occurred to me she might be as fascinated with me as I was with her.

I checked to see that Ginny and the baby had moved a short distance downstream.

"It's the same place," I said. "But a different time."

Her eyes became unfocused and I could almost see her brain processing my words. Then she blinked.

"Many, many moons from now," she said.

"Yes."

Betsey's little voice babbled in the distance as the river rushed past us, drawn inexorably to the ocean.

"I don't understand how it works," I said. "I came here by accident. But now that I've met you and read some of your..."

She suddenly raised her hand, signaling me to be silent. She listened intently.

"Come quickly," she said.

She carried the black boots, hurrying across the yard. She called out to Ginny not to speak of my visit as I followed behind her, watching her painful lopsided walk.

Once inside the hut, she quickly lifted the blanket from the floor, swept aside the pine straw and retrieved the leather pouch from the heavy box, thrusting it into my hands. "Now go!"

"But..."

"Go!"

The front door creaked open an inch, causing us both to jump. It was Ginny, with Betsey on her hip.

"He's here!" she whispered, then closed the door again.

Amadahy placed the shoes inside the box where the pouch had been. Then she looked up at me, alarm in her eyes that I was still there, pointing at the back door.

"Woman?" Jonah shouted, his voice much too close.

I tucked the pouch under my arm, grabbed a fig from the bush outside the door, stepped inside long enough to pop it in my mouth and escape through the time gate.

Steadying myself until the dizziness subsided, I realized I was still wearing Amadahy's dress. It was a faded brown and red calico. I would have to return it.

As I hiked up the path, I opened the pouch she'd given me. Inside were my ruined black flats wrapped in a piece of cloth and a stack of loose diary pages. They were the empty pages she'd torn from the back of the book when she first shoved it into my hands, now filled with her words.

Once inside the cottage, I powered up my phone, finding two missed calls – one from Nana and one from my mother. There was one text from Eric and emails from Nana, Mom and Nancy, my new translator. Hers had an attachment, which made me want to sit right down and dive into the latest translation. But first, I read Eric's text.

"Kathryn, I miss you. We need to get together so I can apologize. What say?"

"What say?" I cried. "I say you can't retract your words once they're spoken, Doctor Murray of the very brown nose!" I deleted the text. "That's what I say!"

I opened my mother's email next.

"Wanted to let you know I'll be there tomorrow. Can you pick me up at the airport at 11:30 and drive me to Athens? I need to spend a little time with Mother."

Did I miss something? Was there another message from her saying she was coming? I'd asked her to come. Several times, in fact. And she'd promised she would when she had time. But I didn't remember her saying she was actually coming. A little notice might've been nice.

Then I moved on to Nana's email. She didn't send messages very often and my curiosity was piqued.

"I tried to call you but you didn't answer. I got the genealogist's report back. She dropped it off right after you left. So give me a call when you get a minute!"

After mulling it over, I decided to head straight there to let her show me the report. That way I could also find out more about Mom's visit. The new translated pages would have to wait.

I jumped in the shower, put on a pair of capris and a top and called Nana as I climbed into my car, suggesting we all go out to my favorite Athens vegetarian restaurant for supper. She thought that was a grand idea.

—

"Isn't this fascinating?" Nana gushed. "She was able to get all this information from Census reports and tax records."

We sat side by side on her teal sofa, the genealogy report spread across our laps.

"I told you I was descended from Cherokee Indians!" she said. "But you! Little Miss Skeptical Journalist!"

My stomach was doing somersaults.

"It says here," she went on, "that a woman named Amadahy – what a lovely name – and her husband Jonah Barnes had four children – three girls and one boy. The oldest child's name was Betsey."

Thank goodness Nana only knew the names Forest Water and Butterfly and didn't realize who the genealogist was talking about. I did my best to sound enthusiastic, but it grieved me imagining Amadahy forced to stay with Jonah all those years, bearing children for him to use as farm workers. Although, as it turned out, they only had one son. There was no mention of Isham being Betsey's father.

"And look!" she continued. "One of their daughters was named Edith! I must be descended from her."

Nana placed her hand over her heart, truly moved by the revelation.

Amadahy was Nana's great-great-great-grandmother, and, thus, my fifth great-grandmother. And although she was full Cherokee, it would be pure speculation trying to figure the percentage of Native American blood we had. It would depend on all those other names on that big family tree.

Nana was as chatty as a talking baby doll on the drive to the restaurant, going on and on about her Cherokee heritage and about how she always knew her grandmother wasn't exaggerating.

"Just out of curiosity," I said, "how did you end up with the land?"

"My grandma left it to all six of us grandchildren," she said from the back seat. "But the others didn't want anything to do with it. They were only too happy when Bob and I bought them out years ago."

The Grit was an Athens landmark, known for its good vegetarian cuisine. Nothing fancy. Just good food and a college town vibe. We sat at a table near the front.

"Mom sent me an email saying she's flying in tomorrow morning for a visit," I said.

"It's all your fault." Nana gave me a mock evil eye.

"She sent me an email too," Jeannette said.

"You mean you didn't know either?"

Jeannette shook her head.

"She's a very busy woman," Nana said. "Always focused on the future."

Which was an accurate assessment. Mom had never been interested in the past. She'd never cared one whit who she was descended from. Maybe I'd absorbed her attitude, a possible explanation for why I'd been so dismissive of Nana's claims over the years.

As our waitress was taking our order, I sensed someone watching me. Glancing toward the front door, I spotted Eric, a sheepish look on his face like he'd been caught parking in a handicapped parking space. Standing next to him was an athletic young woman with short brown hair, leaning into him.

I took a sip of water and tried to focus on Nana. But my maneuver didn't achieve the desired result. Eric and his lady friend came straight to our table.

"Kathryn," he said as they approached.

I stifled a groan.

"Is this your grandmother?"

"Yes," I replied, reluctantly doing my duty. "Nana, this is Eric Murray. Eric, this is Edie Crawford. And this is our good friend Jeannette Hightower."

"Wonderful to meet you both," he said. "And this is Kelsey Beck. She's visiting our department, considering doing her PhD here. Decided to bring her to my favorite Athens vegetarian restaurant."

"Nice to meet you. Enjoy your lunch." She touched Eric's arm, obviously in a hurry to follow the hostess.

As soon as they were out of earshot, Nana was the first to speak.

"Why did that feel so awkward?"

Jeannette patted her mouth with her napkin, hiding a surreptitious smile.

The first thing I did when I got home, besides feeding my hungry cat, was to scan the new pages Amadahy had given me and email them to Nancy. Only then did I sit down and read the latest translation she'd sent me.

Amadahy's Journal – Part 6 Planting Month (May) 1840

When the blackberries began to ripen, I picked a small basketful. As I rose to return to the house carrying Little Butterfly on my back, I felt eyes watching me. Without moving my head, I searched the forest, but saw no one. Then came the song of a wood thrush that I knew well. It was not a bird.

Moving slowly toward the trees, I continued plucking berries, placing them in my basket.

His voice spoke to me from behind a tangle of blackberry bushes. It was the same voice I knew from my childhood.

"I have news," said Old Noon Day, speaking in the language of the Aniyunwiya. "It is sorrowful news of your family."

I closed my eyes.

"My brother's son returned from beyond the Great River," he continued. "He says your mother, your sisters and your brother died before they reached the territory of the Darkening Land. Your Aunt Rising Fawn told him they were buried beside the trail. She and your Aunt Wild Rose survived."

The sting of tears blinded me.

"Degataga shared your story with me. You should marry him and join us. Your mother would approve."

"Mother said marrying Isham Barnes meant our Ancestral Land was returned to me as his wife. She said I should not part with it."

"Your mother is gone. You are the mother now."

"I will consider your words."

"Degataga will come in three days' time."

Betsey wiggled and squealed for attention. Then, as quietly as he arrived, Old Noon Day stole away.

Waiting until Bad Brother went into town the next day, I performed the mourning rituals. I cried in lamentation the names of my dead family as I stood in the shallows of the river, submerging myself seven times, facing east, then west. I could not bury their bones, so I buried smooth river stones and bird feathers behind the menstrual hut. I did not share my sad news with Jonah upon his return.

When Standing Together arrived, he spoke only Tsalagi, as before. I translated. He offered to build a fence around the garden and repair the chicken coop. Jonah said he would pay him two bits. I knew Degataga did these things for me, not for the money. He knew Jonah would never lighten my burden.

Degataga bided his time until the second day. Betsey was wrapped snug on my back while I picked squash and beans.

"My heart is sad upon the loss of your family," he said, speaking in our tongue as he prepared to pound another post into the ground. "So many have died. Our people have suffered much at the hands of the white man."

My voice caught in my throat. We worked in silence for a time before he spoke again.

"Old Noon Day says your mind is firm, that you wish to remain here."

"That is my wish."

"The savage white man who calls himself your husband does not know I understand his words. But I have heard him spew venom to you and your small daughter. I know he violates you. He has no respect for the ways of the Principal People." He looked deeply into my eyes with the intense look I remembered from before. "I want you to share my bed, Forest Water, and build a family with me." His eyes softened, revealing his emotion.

Approaching footsteps silenced our conversation. Degataga pounded the fence post as I set two more squash in my basket.

"Miss Amadahy," Ginny called out as she rounded the corner of the house. "Oh, you got company."

"This is my cousin, Degataga – Standing Together," I said, gesturing at the man trying to convince me to marry him. "This is Ginny."

"Pleased to meet you," Ginny said, then turned her attention to me. "I can put a fresh rag on Betsey and take her for a walk. Your back must be plumb wore out."

She helped me unwrap the baby from my body.

"Do not walk her by the river," I said.

Understanding that is where Bad Brother would be, she talked to Little Butterfly as they headed to the house. Betsey responded in her small babbling voice.

"I see she is now your family," Degataga said, once again revealing his wisdom. "She can travel with us to the mountains. We will adopt her as a member of the Aniyunwiya. She will be your kinswoman, a member of the Paint Clan."

I admired his face, so full of Cherokee dignity and grace.

He set the large rock aside that he used for striking the post, then moved swiftly to sit beside me in the row, taking my soiled hand in his.

"I love you, Forest Water."

His words echoed inside me.

"I will be a good husband. You will be a good wife. It is fated."

Warmth filled my body. But before I could respond, there was a woman's shriek, then Betsey's wail and Jonah's angry shout. I pulled myself up and hobbled toward the noise, Degataga running ahead of me.

Rounding the corner of the house, we saw Ginny lying on the ground, Betsey still in her arms. Bad Brother towered over them like a large rattlesnake ready to strike, a whiskey bottle in his hand.

"I said make that baby shut up!" he shouted.

"Yessir," Ginny said, setting my daughter on her lap. "Hush, little one," she said, her voice quivering.

Betsey cried louder, causing Jonah to threaten them with the back of his hand.

I touched Degataga's arm so he would not rush forward.

"It is my fault," I cried.

Jonah swung around and flashed his snake eyes at me. "I'm gonna give that baby something to cry about if she don't shut her mouth!"

I hurried closer, lifting Betsey into my arms, rubbing her back and speaking soothing words in my language. "Do not be afraid, Little Butterfly. Mother is here now."

She hiccupped and sniffled, her small body losing its stiffness as she leaned against my shoulder.

Degataga returned to his fence building, hiding the anger burning in his eyes.

"Ginny," I said, "you may continue picking squash and beans."

She put her hand to her mouth, wiping a trickle of blood as she hurried to the garden. Moving as fast as I could, I carried Betsey to the hickory tree where I often nursed her, sitting on the ground, facing away from the house. She calmed as I opened my dress.

Out of the corner of my eye, I watched Bad Brother glare about him as though his prey had escaped. Then he drained the last of the spirits, heaving the empty bottle toward the river.

When I returned to the garden, the bruise on Ginny's face was plain. Her eyes were troubled but she said nothing. I sent her home with a piece of cornbread heavy with beans.

When she was gone, Degataga spoke quietly but with passion, not looking up from his work.

"I will kill him."

~15~

There was no way I'd be able to sleep after reading the latest entry. Degataga loved Amadahy. Who could blame him for threatening to kill Jonah? Especially since she refused to leave the bastard.

But now, thanks to Nana, I knew Amadahy bore three babies with that walking bowel movement. Murdering him would kill off generations of their offspring, including me! What if Degataga made good on his threat? How many people would never be born?

My brain felt like the ball in a vintage pinball machine, getting whacked by paddles over and over, bouncing from bell to bell.

Pixie watched me frantically pacing circles around the living room.

"You should be worried too," I told her. "What if I disappear? What if I'm never born? Where will you be?"

She flicked her tail at me.

I stopped in my tracks, a light bulb switching on in my brain.

"We're not going to disappear! Degataga didn't murder Jonah. Sure, he *wanted* to kill him. But just because he said it doesn't mean he did it. Obviously, he didn't because I'm still here. And so are Nana, my mother and hundreds of distant cousins. That family tree the genealogist created proves all those people were born."

She meowed.

"Yeah. I've said things like that, myself. 'I'm gonna kill him.' Saying it doesn't mean I'd ever do it. Not in a million years. I realize it wasn't an idle threat when Degataga said it. He really meant it. But Amadahy must've talked him out of it. Or he came to his senses and realized he couldn't murder the guy even if he was a despicable dickbrain! Or..." I whirled around, practically shouting, "...or Jonah killed Degataga first!"

Pixie cowered in fear.

"Sorry," I whispered, sitting down on the sofa and stroking her fur. "But I can't bear the thought of Jonah murdering the man who truly loves her."

An urge to call Eric flitted through my mind. Who else could I talk to about Amadahy? No one.

I snuffed out my little flicker of longing, climbing the stairs to get my hamper. Laundry beckoned. Along with some other chores I'd been neglecting. I needed to do something to occupy my mind. Consumed with Amadahy's plight, it was sometimes hard for me to focus on my own life. Including my social life. It might help if I spent time with friends.

But who would I call for a night out? Let's see, there was Stacey, my old high school girlfriend. But she was married now and recently had a baby. She had "the hubs," as she called him, and always had to find a babysitter. There was Kara, a fellow J-School student from my days at UGA. But she liked to party hardy and the heavy drinking made me feel like I was still in college. Ryan might be an option. But the last time I saw him, he thought I was coming onto him. I wasn't. We were supposed to be buddies, not friends with benefits. There was a time when Mallory and I had gone out together. But she was a bigshot reporter now and I was her producer – her flunky, in her eyes.

There was always Pixie. She had the same taste in movies and TV shows. Plus, she never accused me of anything.

Although when I sat down beside her, my mind wandered, and instead of being satisfied cuddling with my cat, I imagined snuggling in Eric's arms. But he'd revealed his true colors. Better that it happened sooner than later, I guess. Besides, he'd already moved on, judging by our unexpected encounter at The Grit.

My mother waved at me as she stepped off the escalator in the baggage claim area. Amazing how young she looked despite being in her mid-fifties. She had that sophisticated world traveler look in narrow black slacks, a cream blouse and a short layered haircut with silver highlights.

She gave me a brief hug. "I almost ordered a limo but I like to multi-task and thought I could use the travel time more wisely – catching up with you on the drive to Athens."

"You're so sentimental," I said.

Which caused her to smile.

"So you have concerns about Nana?" she said as we arrived at the baggage carousel.

I gave her a feigned look of exasperation.

"I'm doing pretty well," I said. "Thanks for asking. How about you?"

"You're too clever for your own good, you know," she said. "Start wherever you like. I'm all ears."

"To be honest, I've relaxed about Nana over the last couple of weeks. I got worked up earlier this summer. I still think she should be tested. They have meds to help slow the progression of the disease."

"Couldn't hurt," she said.

"I think with Jeannette and you and me to look out for her, she'll be okay. As long as we're aware she's having these issues."

Her bags appeared and we stepped forward, each of us grabbing one.

We had plenty of time to talk on the drive to Athens. Time enough for me to tell her we should hire a second companion so Jeannette could have more time off. And to talk about educating ourselves about Alzheimer's.

Then she shifted gears, taking an interest in my life. Although not in the way I would've preferred.

"Mother told me what happened to you and your history professor boyfriend," she said. "She told me there was a newspaper article. I found it online. I must say, it was a strange story. Neither you nor Dr. Murray came across in the best light. That's the kind of thing that could tarnish your reputation, you know."

"It's no big deal, really."

Nana was thrilled Mom had come, thanking her again and again for taking time from her high-powered life to travel all the way to little old Athens, Georgia to see her unimportant, inconsequential, elderly mother. Not her words exactly, but that's the gist of it. I had to bite my tongue not to express my true feelings – that she should come more often than one measly time a year.

Still, at least she was here. And it was a relief.

Jeannette left in her own vehicle to visit her family as Mom cranked Nana's car to drive them to the cottage. Leaving me some time to myself. Checking my phone, I found a voice message from Eric.

"Kathryn, I sure would like to see you. I need to tell you in person how sorry I am. Please, please call me back. Or send me a teeny-tiny text message telling me when and where to meet you so I can grovel at your feet. How about Jittery Joe's? I miss you."

But his comment about getting sucked into a time travel fantasy was still ricocheting around my brain. Every time I thought about his words, it ticked me off all over again. Condescending. That's how he'd sounded. Judgmental and condescending. Judgmental, uncaring and condescending. Make that judgmental, uncaring, self-centered and condescending.

I deleted the message and drove home, stopping to pick up a couple of tacos on the way. As soon as I walked in the door, my phone rang. I thought it might be Eric, but it was Nana.

"Hi sweetie! We thought we'd go to Harold's Home Cooking for supper. Can you meet us at six-thirty?"

"I was planning on joining you tomorrow evening for supper."

"Sharon's flying to New York tomorrow," she said.

"You're kidding."

"A limousine is picking her up right after lunch to take her to the airport."

The black cat clock Nana gave me when I moved into my apartment said it was four forty-five. If I walked right back out the door, I could make it to the restaurant in Royston by six-thirty. I was way too tired to drive all that way and then drive home to sleep before getting up and going to work in the morning.

"It's really thoughtful of you to invite me, Nana. But I'm already back in Atlanta. I think I'll let you two have some quality mother-daughter time."

I stuffed my phone into my back pocket after we hung up, remembering the fall I started college when my mother put our house on the market, taking her first overseas job. She said she needed a change of scenery, that she was tired of being depressed. Which, admittedly, was her normal state after my dad died. At the time, I thought it was an excellent idea, figuring the adventure was exactly what she needed. I didn't know she'd hardly ever come home again.

⁓

Controversy erupted Monday morning. The Watchdog Team, along with the Channel Seven news department, was being accused of airing "prurient" video shot by the sleazebag drama teacher. Mallory and I were called into the news director's office.

"We've received more than a dozen emails complaining about our reporting," Ray told us.

"Orchestrated, no doubt," Mallory said.

"No doubt," he replied. "One of the complaints is from a religious group, accusing us of doing the story for the specific purpose of boosting ratings."

"It's not the first time we've been attacked over a story," she said, unimpressed.

"Nor the last," he said. "But they're picketing our station tomorrow on the sidewalk out front, and they've notified every media outlet in town."

"I'd say they're doing us a favor," she said. "I'll bet people out there who missed the story will be searching for it online."

"We took it down."

"We what?"

"As you know, we consulted our lawyers before airing the reports. And we were careful to use only short sections of the video that were deemed clean enough for a family audience. But even with our viewer discretion advisory beforehand, the footage could be seen as soft porn if it's out of context."

"Jesus, Ray!" Mallory cried, jumping up and leaning on his desk. "Are you saying the bigwigs don't stand behind us?"

"No..."

"It sure sounds like it!" She spun around to leave.

"And another thing," he said, raising his voice. "Someone apparently told our neck and neck competition about your concerns that Kathryn might be in an abusive relationship. And now the religious group organizing the protest is also accusing us of condoning domestic violence aimed at one of our producers. Apparently, the Channel Thirteen reporter's brother goes to the same church as the leader of the religious group."

Mallory stopped in her tracks.

"Any idea who told Channel Thirteen?" Ray said, a mocking tone in his voice.

Mallory chewed her lip as she turned around.

"How could you?" I snapped.

She stared at the ceiling.

The stony silence was broken when Ray cleared his throat.

"On your immediate to-do list, Mallory – tell your friend at Channel Thirteen that you were wrong about Kathryn's situation. Also on the to-do list for both of you – figure out how to deal with this. There's a lot to be said for a cohesive team that gets along and looks out for each other. The protest is scheduled for tomorrow afternoon. I want you both gone by noon. Don't want to risk having any kind of run-in. Which gives you an extra half-day off leading up to July fourth. You're welcome."

As we returned to our office, it was all I could do not to let her have it. I was pissed. And she knew it. As soon as we walked in the door, she closed it behind us and apologized as Brandon scrolled on his phone, trying to be invisible.

"I'm sorry, Kathryn. I was talking with..." She paused, pinching the bridge of her nose. "Doesn't matter who I was talking with. We were on assignment, chatting about that county commissioner... anyway, I won't do it again."

"The damage is done." I was in no mood to forgive.

Despite the boss's suggestion, that's as far as we got toward ironing out the kinks in our relationship.

165

The next installment of Amadahy's diary hit my inbox right before lunch. I went to a sandwich shop, opened the document and read as I ate, reminding myself that, so far, at least, the events she was describing occurred before Nana showed up.

Amadahy's Journal – Part 7 (May 1840)

"If you kill Jonah," I said, my eyes on Degataga, "I will be torn from my family's land. White leaders will not allow a Cherokee woman to own a farm. It must be a white man who owns the land. If you kill him, I will also suffer."

"If I do not kill him, you will suffer as the fawn suffers when the mountain lion attacks. I will adopt Isham Barnes into the Wolf Clan and avenge his death."

His eyes were like a bolt of lightning thrown by the Great Thunder.

I did not reveal that I could feel Isham's ghost wandering the farm, that I knew his spirit could not rest. I also did not tell him I feared if he killed Jonah, the sheriff would hang him from a tree.

"Degataga, I also feel a bond between us. But we must not stumble and fall into a ravine from which there is no escape."

"You have clung to this land, hoping your family would one day return. But they will not return." He shook his head. "I offer you love and a home on Aniyunwiya land."

I looked down at my dirty hands. He returned to his work and did not speak again.

He fixed the chicken coop and completed the fence enclosing the garden by the time darkness fell. The next morning he was gone when I rose to do my early chores. I was alone again with Little Butterfly and Bad Brother.

After nursing the baby, feeding the chickens, gathering eggs, cooking corn and bean bread over the fire pit and roasting squash for the day, I moved to the river to wash clothes. With Betsey strapped to her cradle board. I tried to warm my spirit by singing a traditional chant. I was startled when a woman's voice spoke behind me. Even more so when I looked upon her.

"I'm picking some figs," she said. "I hope you don't mind."

She spoke English, but it was not the kind of English I was accustomed to, even when I attended Mission school with the Methodists. She stood erect but she was very old, her silver hair cut short like a white man's. She also wore pants like a man and a shirt. But the shirt was the color of a sunflower.

"My goodness," she said. "You're doing laundry in the river? You don't have running water in your house?"

When I did not answer, she continued talking.

"My name is Edie. I live up the hill."

She waited for me to speak. But words would not come.

"Welcome to the neighborhood," she said, her voice like the sparkling burble of a mountain stream.

I watched for a sign that she was a spirit. She did not seem of my world. Or the white man's world. If Bad Brother saw her, I feared what he would do.

"Oh, dear. It appears you don't speak English," she said.

If she was a spirit, I decided she was a good spirit, not a bad one. And I knew how she traveled to my home.

"I speak English," I said, peering around her toward the house.

She looked over her shoulder as she spoke again, more softly. "You look like a mommy who's worried the noisy neighbor might wake up someone who's taking a nap. I'll keep my voice down."

She squatted on the riverbank and talked to Betsey.

"Hi there, little one. What's your name?"

My daughter responded with her baby words.

"Her Cherokee name is Kamama, which means Butterfly," I said.

She clapped her hands together like a small child when she learned we were Cherokee.

I lifted my daughter into my arms.

"We will walk you to the doorway, Old Grandmother, so you may return to your home."

When we stepped into the hut, she cast her eyes about uncertainly.

"This is the door that leads you back where you came from," I explained.

"But you didn't tell me your name."

"I am Forest Water."

I opened the small back door, plucking a fig from the bush, then handed it to her.

"You want me to eat it?" she said.

"That is what my own grandmother did, chewing the fig as she passed through the doorway."

She touched Betsey's cheek, gave her a small wave, and placed the fig between her teeth.

Betsey cooed, looking for Old Grandmother as she dissolved like salt in a boiling pot of beans. I stepped outside, searching the yard and the woods. She was gone.

I thought of my own grandmother who was known as a powerful Medicine Woman who knew all the incantations and *potions, how to heal a wound and decipher dreams. She shared much with me when I was a child. She told me how she fed strong medicine to her fig tree so it would have Special Powers. She called it Going Back Medicine. She did this to prepare for when the white man took our land, saying she wished to return to the time before the invaders. She fed the soil beneath the tree with her secret potions, burying animal bones and other totems in the earth. Until one day during the Drying Up Moon, she hugged me close, ate a ripe fig, walked through the door and vanished.*

That was the last of the pages she'd given me the first time I visited and was written only days before I arrived. The next translation from Nancy would be the new pages from the pouch.

It amazed me that she thought Nana was a spirit. Then again, that made as much sense as time travel. I ached for her and her innocent baby, the children who would be born of that disgraceful union. For Degataga and Ginny, whose lives also hung in the balance.

As I got in my car for the drive back to the station, I decided, despite my misgivings, I had to try to make Jonah a better man. I slid my phone out and clicked on the psychologist's number to leave him a message. I was taken by surprise when he answered.

"Dr. Vargas?"

"Yes."

"This is Kathryn Spears from the Channel Seven Watchdog Team."

"How can I help you, Ms. Spears?"

He sounded skeptical when I told him I'd pay for his advice on how to counsel an abuser.

"Ms. Spears..."

"It's not a ploy. This really is a friend's husband. She refuses to leave him and I've got to help her. I'm going to talk with him myself. I could use some guidance and I'd appreciate your expert advice. I'll pay your usual fee. I'm not looking for a freebie."

"I'm leaving on vacation tomorrow, spending the fourth at the beach."

"Can you spare half an hour today?"

Silence.

"Please," I said.

"Come by my office at five-thirty. But I have to tell you, I don't like it."

After a long afternoon as Mallory and I avoided each other, I broke away promptly at five. But the atmosphere at the psychologist's office wasn't any more welcoming.

We sat facing each other, both of us in arm chairs, a pad and pen on the table beside him.

Now that I thought about it, my outfit was perfect for the occasion – a V-neck, sleeveless top and skirt. He could see there were no bruises on my arms, my legs or my neck. Perhaps subconsciously, I was making sure Mallory and Ray noticed that too.

"Thanks for your time," I began, since it was obvious he was keen on putting this meeting behind him. "First off, I'm not in any kind of abusive relationship. Never have been. Never will be. I told you recently about this friend I'm worried about. I've tried to get her to leave her husband, but she

170

refuses. She's afraid she'll end up with nothing if she runs away. So, I've decided to try to make him see the light, you might say. What I need are some talking points, some strategies."

"The best strategy would be to convince him to meet with a counselor. If not me, then someone with training and experience dealing with domestic violence."

"He won't do that."

"Do you have any indication he wants to change?"

"No."

"It's kind of like trying to force a smoker to quit. If he doesn't want to quit, it's not going to happen. That is, unless you lock him up and throw away the key until he's completely withdrawn from the nicotine and the oral gratification. Even then, as soon as you let him go, chances are extremely high he'll resume smoking first chance he gets."

"Still, I have to try."

"Let me ask you this," he said. "Is your friend's life in danger?"

"Well..."

"Is the baby's life in danger? Is she or the baby at risk of severe injury? Think hard about those questions. It's possible the time has come to call the police."

Picturing Amadahy talking with the local sheriff about Jonah beating her was beyond absurd.

"A word of caution," he said, giving me a fatherly look. "You need to consider whether your friend's husband might react violently to your intervention. That's not out of the realm of possibility."

We talked about counseling approaches and he gave me a stack of literature as I left.

Sprawled across the bed that evening with Pixie beside me, I skimmed the brochures Dr. Vargas gave me, realizing the enormity of what I was proposing. It would be like trying to transform the devil into an angel.

~16~

Mid-morning the next day the boss stopped by our office reminding us to clear out before the protesters arrived. The unexpected afternoon off gave me time to swing by the local Salvation Army store to find some more pseudo nineteenth century clothing. I left with a passable outfit that made me look like an extra in a Jane Eyre movie.

On my way home, I picked up cat food and a few other items. After parking the car in front of my apartment, I was about to hoist the bag from the trunk when a familiar voice called out.

"Let me get that for you."

It was Eric. He carried the bag to my door, me trailing behind, feeling trapped.

"I tried to reach you at the TV station but they said you were off this afternoon," he said, following me inside and setting the cat food on the floor of the pantry.

I put the smaller bags on the counter and was trying to think what to say when Pixie flounced into the kitchen, meowing loudly to announce her arrival.

"I haven't met your roommate yet," Eric said.

"This is Pixie." I scooped her up.

He stepped close and scratched her behind her ears. She purred like she was in kitty heaven. But I needed to put some distance between me and Eric. I set her down and unloaded the groceries, turning my back on both of them.

"Okay, here goes," he said. "You have every right to be angry with me. I shouldn't have spouted off like I did. If I could rewind the tape, that's what I'd do. Either that, or turn back the clock. Funny, those are both out-of-date technology expressions."

I finished stashing my few items and folded the reusable bags.

"I have to admit," he continued, "having a bullet chase me through the time portal scared the hell out of me. Being attacked and held prisoner by that nineteenth century Neanderthal shook me up. I'm used to thinking of myself as an athlete. But I didn't understand what a modern-day milquetoast I am until I came face to face with the gritty, smelly summer of 1840. And then, as my mind was coming to terms with our dangerous – and futile – time-travel caper, I took it out on you."

My eyes were glued to Pixie as she stepped on Eric's sandal, rubbing against his ankle.

"I hope you can forgive me," he said. "Because I'm sorrier than I've ever been about anything. Except possibly the time I intentionally ran my sister into the carport wall on the wagon.

I got a spanking for that and fortunately she wasn't scarred. So, all things considered, I guess I *am* sorrier about what I said to you."

He was hoping I'd laugh. I sighed instead. Our brief romance had felt so good, so right. But it really bothered me that he dismissed my deep concerns about Amadahy and accused me of being frivolous.

"I accept your apology." It sounded stiff, but I couldn't help it. "And I apologize for putting you in a dangerous situation, for not fully realizing what I was asking of you."

"Kathryn..."

He closed the distance between us and was about to wrap his arms around me. But I stepped back, pivoting toward the pantry. I ripped the cat food bag open and scooped a cup of dry food into Pixie's dish. Then I opened a can of Fancy Feast and spooned it on top, like ice cream on a slice of apple pie. She rushed the bowl before I finished.

I could feel his eyes on me as I washed my hands.

The thing is, there was no way I could be close to Eric if I couldn't share my passion for helping Amadahy. If I could never talk openly about my visits to the past, I'd be hiding an important part of myself. Plus, it was a huge disappointment that he was perfectly comfortable abandoning her.

I met his gaze, taking in the frown. There was a touch of surprise in his eyes, like he'd expected to charm me into taking him back with a shallow apology and a joke.

"I can work on the translation again as long as I..." he said.

"No need. I hired another translator. She's fast, plus she's a native speaker."

There was an awkward silence before he spoke again.

"So you don't need me professionally and you don't want me personally."

"We can be friends," I said, struggling to remain cool on the outside.

"Right." He pulled on his earlobe.

He stood there as if considering what to say, then strode from the kitchen, through the living room and out the front door.

I dashed to the living room window in time to see his car exit the parking lot. Pixie meowed behind me.

"I know I told you I liked him, but it's over," I said, wiping my eyes.

Why was I having mixed feelings? I reminded myself how he caved when his boss threatened to cut his funding the moment our names appeared in that silly newspaper story. How he chastised me for trying to save Amadahy from Jonah's clutches – like I should chop down the fig bush and turn my back on her. And now he was calling it a time travel caper! I marveled at how cavalier he was about her life. Screw him!

⁓

My mom called as I microwaved a veggie burger for supper.

"Where are you?" I asked.

"New York. Meetings to attend, hobnobbing to do. I've got a big Fourth of July party I'm attending tomorrow night." She chuckled lightly. "Listen, I'm sorry I didn't get to see you again. Mother was supposed to tell you about having dinner with us. I thought she had."

"More important for the two of you to have time together."

"We did. Had a fun dinner at Harold's. That place hasn't changed a bit in twenty-five years! Still has the best fried chicken and mashed potatoes. And we spent some time at the cottage. She took me down to the river to introduce me to her new neighbors, but I think we went the wrong way. She says the woman is a Cherokee Indian, which, I have to admit, I found hard to believe. There was no house there. But I didn't let on. Anyway, we did find some fig bushes."

I held my breath.

"We picked some figs so Mother and Jeannette can make some preserves. She went on and on about how her grandmother used to make them when she was a little girl. About how she's been dreaming of her grandma lately."

"Yeah, she told me about that."

Mom spoke to someone else for a moment, then returned to the phone.

"Where was I? Oh yes – I agree with you, she's becoming more forgetful. But she seems happy overall. Except for not being able to spend more time at the cottage. I'll contact the agency that found Jeannette for us and hire a second companion to relieve Jeannette more often. We can work up a schedule to give her regular time off. Then the new companion can drive her to the cottage. I did mention to Mother that I'd like for her to be tested for Alzheimer's."

"What'd she say?"

"She dismissed the whole idea. I'll let it simmer a bit, then talk with her again. I also mentioned that Jeannette could take her to visit her former neighbor who lives in an assisted living home in Athens. You remember Louise Johnston?"

"Sure."

"I've read it's a good idea to get someone with dementia ready bit by bit before you make any dramatic changes. Like visiting a facility so they'll see how nice it is."

I agreed, but without enthusiasm. Mom didn't notice. She had to get on with her hobnobbing.

It was past midnight when I finally lay down, hoping sleep would deliver me from my frustrations. But my eyes wouldn't close, focusing instead on strange shadows on the ceiling. When I heard my phone vibrate, I found another translation from Nancy – the first from the new pages I sent her. She said she'd be with family at the beach for a couple of days for the fourth and not to expect another translation right away. I opened the attachment immediately.

Amadahy's Journal – Part 8 (June 1840)

Before the time of Bad Brother, rain was a gift that quenched the thirst of our crops so there would be plenty to eat. Now, dark clouds made me dread the raindrops, knowing that when Jonah was forced inside he became like a trapped animal, snarling and biting.

It was during a rainstorm in the Green Corn Moon that he kicked me as he would kick a dog, using his heavy shoe to strike my good leg.

"You hear me?" he shouted.

"Yes." I rubbed my thigh to ease the pain.

"Shelling them beans can wait. They're laughing at me in the saloon."

"I must bathe myself."

"Be quick about it!"

My injury forced me to move slowly as I took Betsey with me to the hut where I kept my herbs and elixirs. I did not mind the rain, which cooled my skin.

After preparing myself, I crept into the smokehouse for the secret bottle of whiskey I hid there – whiskey I stole in small portions from bottles Bad Brother did not finish before blacking out. Upon entering the house, I fetched his mug from the shelf, but he greedily snatched the bottle from me, taking a long drink as he sat down on the bed.

"Where'd you get this?" he said.

"I found it under the hammock."

He did not reply, lifting the bottle to his mouth again.

"I will feed her so she will sleep," I said, then moved to the baby's blanket on the floor. Sitting down with her on my lap, I bared my breast for her to nurse, knowing Jonah watched me. As Betsey drank, he did also. I let her suckle for a long time, sitting so he would see as I lifted my other swollen breast from my dress. By the time her thirst was quenched, Jonah had drunk half the bottle and his eyes were closing.

On my hands and knees, I gently lay Betsey down, facing away from Bad Brother. The pain in my thigh made me wince, but I remained silent except for my soothing whispers to my daughter. When, at last, I stood to present myself to him, he had passed out on the bed, only the bottle standing tall between his legs.

Ginny spoke her mind when she greeted me the next morning, which is her way.

"He done kicked you, ain't he?"

I did not answer.

"I see you can't hardly walk. Mister Jonah is Satan's seed, for sure."

"You must not speak those words," I said, fearing Bad Brother was nearby.

"He's snoring up a storm by the river while you do all the chores."

"I must pick beans," I said, bringing her dangerous talk to an end.

"Your mama need to rest her body, Little Butterfly," she said to Betsey. "Come on with Aunt Ginny." And she wrapped my daughter onto her own back as she spoke to me like a sister. "You can finish weaving that new basket you been working on while me and the baby pick them beans."

~17~

Jeanette spent Independence Day with her family, so it was just Nana and me hanging out together. I thought she'd enjoy the neighborhood cook-out and pool party. But she only recognized one person – the woman who lived across the street whose name she couldn't remember. I told everyone who paused long enough to speak with us that she and my grandfather bought their house when the neighborhood was brand new. Which seemed to impress them for about fifteen seconds.

Thursday and Friday were slow as snails at work, mainly grunt work with a skeleton crew in the newsroom while everyone else was having fun at the beach. For once, I didn't mind the hours dragging because the prospect of facing Jonah again filled me with apprehension.

When Saturday morning arrived, my stomach felt like I'd eaten eggshells instead of eggs for breakfast. Dr. Vargas might be right that I was asking for trouble.

But this time I was prepared. I had a pocket-sized can of pepper spray hidden in my dress.

It was sprinkling when I headed toward Athens. Me and the windshield wipers had something in common – we were both intermittent, off and on. One moment I wanted to turn around and go home, the next, I was anxious to get there faster. The sky grew darker as I traveled up Highway 316. By the time I reached the Athens loop, it was raining cats and dogs, as though Mother Nature was trying to send me a warning. I sipped coffee from my thermos, hoping caffeine would give me courage.

Opening my umbrella, I made a dash for the cottage. Jeannette said Nana wasn't pushing her to spend time here, knowing my mother would hire another companion soon. Thus, the cottage was empty.

Once I'd donned my long dress, I rummaged in Nana's hall closet to retrieve her giant UGA golf umbrella – red and black with the Georgia bulldog emblazoned on it. Nana's blue-flowered gardening boots were in their usual spot on the back porch. I slipped them on, tucking my black shoes under my arm. Before stepping off the porch, I gathered my long skirt in my free hand, lifting it above my knees so it wouldn't drag in the mud, and set off down the path.

The rain pummeled the huge umbrella, filling my ears with a pounding that reminded me, for an instant, of Indian drums. I breathed in the earthy scent of decaying leaves and pine needles underfoot. As I got closer, I caught a whiff of the Broad River.

There was a tightness in my chest as I approached the time portal. Before I chickened out, I pulled a fig from the bush, put it in my mouth, closed the umbrella, tossing it on the ground, and entered the invisible doorway.

The noise of the cloudburst was replaced with the usual buzzing in my ears. Instinct told me right away I was not alone. Three pairs of eyes gaped at the colorful rubber boots I'd forgotten to take off. There sat Amadahy, Ginny and little Betsey.

I let my skirt fall around my ankles.

"I came to speak with Mr. Barnes."

"You the one brought them gold pieces," Ginny said with a look that suggested she thought I was rich. "Mister Jonah fetched one to Master Wheeler so he signed my bill of sale. Then he rode into town and gambled the others away in a poker game. Came home stinking drunk, swinging his fists at anyone who got in his way." She turned her cheek, showing me a fresh bruise.

"I'm so sorry," I said.

Betsey crawled closer to her mother, then plopped down on her bottom again, looking at me uncertainly.

"Mister Jonah says one of my jobs is having babies," Ginny added. "But there's only one man on this here farm."

Amadahy's expression betrayed her discomfort.

"I want to help," I said. "Is Mr. Barnes here?"

"It is not safe for you to speak with him." Amadahy lifted Betsey onto her lap, smoothing her fine, dark hair with her fingers.

"I have to try."

"Where is your husband?" she said.

"He was wounded."

She blinked, but made no move to stand.

I slipped off the wet garden boots and put my shoes on, then fluffed my skirt as I stepped around them and into the yard.

Late morning sun filtered through the trees in the distance. But the sun was already hot in the clearing. Halfway to the house, I was damp with sweat, partly from the heat, partly from dread.

"Believe you must be one a them women that likes a rough hand, Miz Murray." It was Jonah calling out to me as he hiked his suspenders up emerging from the outhouse. "My wife likes that too." A vile grin spread across his face.

My hands patted my skirt, feeling for the pocket where I'd deposited the can of Mace.

"Why you here?" he said.

"I'd like to talk with you, Mr. Barnes."

"About what?"

"Can we sit down?"

"Too hot inside."

"By the river."

I continued along the path, rounding the house and making a beeline for the riverbank. He followed, carrying a ladderback chair.

"Your husband ain't with you?" he asked, turning the chair backwards and straddling it, his legs splayed wide, elbows on the top rung.

"Not today."

"He don't keep very good track a his wife." He looked me up and down before continuing. "What's on your mind?"

"I want to talk about how you can become a good husband and father."

He guffawed like I'd told a sidesplitting joke.

"You with the church?" he said when his laughter trailed off.

"No, I..."

"You one a them temperance nags."

"No, but there's something to be said for cutting back on drinking. It's been proven too much alcohol leads to..."

"Nobody tells me how much to drink."

"Believe me, I'm not trying to do that. It's just that men who drink a lot often lose control so they aren't considerate of their wives and children."

"Considerate?"

"You know, gentle and understanding."

"That's a woman's job."

"It's a man's job too."

"I ain't got time for this horse shit," he said, getting to his feet.

"Please, Mr. Barnes. Give me a few minutes."

He looked at me like I was crazy – and I had to admit he might be right – but I pressed on.

"Drinking can also cause a man to have financial problems because he spends too much money on alcohol and he's not able to work."

"You must be a Yankee."

"Mr. Barnes, alcohol can make a man lose control and hit his wife."

"A man rules over his wife. Says so in the Bible."

I caught myself as I was about to lose my temper. "Don't you want your wife to love you?"

"I want her to spread her legs when I..."

"That's not love!"

"And cook my food and wash my clothes."

"Were you beaten as a child?" My voice rose a couple of notches.

"Spare the rod, spoil the child," he spat. "That's in the Bible too. Believe someone should'a whupped you when you was a young'un."

"One day, when you have children of your own, don't you want them to love and respect you?"

"They'll respect me, all right. I don't take no backtalk from nobody. Now I ain't listening to no more of your preaching."

He charged me, grabbing my arm before I could react.

"Let me go!" I cried.

"Your husband ain't got a lick a sense letting you come back here. If you snuck behind his back, then you're the one who's slow in the head. Cause now I'm gonna finish my business deal with Johnny. He was right peevish after riding all the way out here and finding you was gone last time."

He twisted my arm up behind my back, nearly pulling it out of the socket.

"I'm not done talking yet!" I shouted. "The least you can do is hear me out!"

He hustled me into the smokehouse, the stench of his body filling my nostrils.

"You don't really want to be an evil man, do you? You don't want your family to hate you!"

"Don't make me no nevermind."

I squirmed, trying to free one of my arms, but his hands were like a vise grip. I gasped in pain. So much for the Mace.

"Mr. Barnes, I can pay you more than Johnny can."

He shoved me onto the dirt floor.

"You got more gold?" he said.

"I don't have it on me, but I can get some."

"How many nuggets?"

"Two."

"Four!"

"I might be able to get three."

He paced in circles around me.

Although by now I didn't hold out much hope for my original mission, I decided to keep trying.

"I hope you'll reconsider how you treat your family, Mr. Barnes. Would you treat a friend like you treat Amadahy?"

"My wife ain't my friend!"

"Your wife should be your best friend. Nobody respects you if you beat your wife. Tenderness doesn't make a man weak."

His answer came in the form of a shove with his stinking shoe. I toppled over, landing on my injured shoulder.

"You talk too damn much," he said. "Must be why your husband left you."

He continued pacing as I struggled to right myself.

"You bring me four gold nuggets, I'll let you go."

I actually dithered a few seconds, then realized what an idiot I was. Like I should argue with him when he was on the verge of giving me to a man planning on making a sex slave out of me.

"All right," I whispered.

"I'll go with you to get 'em."

"That's not possible."

"The hell it ain't!"

"Honestly, Mr. Barnes, if you come with me, there's no way I can get the gold."

He stopped in front of me, the toe of his shoe almost touching my nose. This close, it smelled like he spent too much time in that outhouse.

"If you ain't back with the gold in one week, my squaw or my slave might have a bad accident. Ain't decided which one yet. You take my meaning?"

"Yes, but, Mr. Barnes, I'd like to remind you of the Golden Rule. I'm sure you're familiar with it."

Silence.

"Do unto others," I said, "as you would have them do unto you. Straight from the Bible."

"Make sure you come alone." He adjusted his pants and sauntered out the door.

A deep and abiding loathing welled up inside me.

⁓

Back in my own time, I tried, but failed, to dodge the puddles on the sodden forest floor. The dark clouds seemed angry as they bombarded the earth with more rain than the ground could stand. I was angry too, tucking Nana's oversized umbrella under my arm, hoping the raindrops would purge the disgust from my body. As water soaked my shoes I realized I'd made such a hasty exit that I forgot the gardening boots. But, no way was I going back to get them.

It was conceivable that Eric was right. The past was gone. All those people were dead. Who was I to play God, as he put it. Or *try* to play God. Every time I went back to their time, I botched something. And now what had I done? I'd promised to bring Jonah more gold! And if I didn't deliver? I didn't want to contemplate what he might do if I broke my promise.

Plodding through the woods, rain blurred my vision. I felt like a little girl wearing ten-pound ankle weights. But it was more than physical. I was weighed down with uncertainty, with feelings of inadequacy and self-doubt.

Was it even possible to turn a raging, unrepentant asshole into a decent human being? I was ninety-nine percent certain an average TV news producer like myself would never achieve anything approaching the transformation of Mr. Hyde into Dr. Jekyll.

I stood on the back porch of the cottage for several minutes, letting the water drip, forming a puddle on the floor. Opening the umbrella to let it dry, a stabbing pain shot down my right bicep. It hurt to turn the key in the back door. Peeling the dress from my wet body was a painstaking process. My shower consisted mostly of letting the warm water pound my body.

After wrapping the dress and shoes in a trash bag, I dashed to my car, holding my small umbrella over my head. I wanted nothing more than to be at home with a heating pad.

No way would I go to the hospital where Eric was treated for his sorta-kinda gunshot wound. Some local reporter might write a story about me! I used my left hand to drive back to Atlanta.

First stop was an urgent care clinic. When the doctor asked how I was injured, I concocted my latest lie, telling her I fell off a ladder and caught myself with my right arm. She said I might have a torn rotator cuff but I'd need an MRI to confirm. She advised me to follow up with my doctor and suggested I take something for pain, use ice packs and go easy with my right arm in the meantime.

Needless to say, I was in a blue funk when I got home.

Pixie rubbed against my legs, nearly tripping me as she meowed for her supper. Once I filled her dish, I took a couple of pain pills and fixed myself a bowl of cereal, collapsing at the kitchen table. The two of us ate in silence while I scanned messages and emails.

There was a brief email from Nancy, saying she'd had time to translate a bit more of the diary. I hesitated clicking on the attachment. What good would it do?

Pixie meowed.

"I know," I said. "I can't abandon her."

I opened the document.

Amadahy's Journal – Part 9 (June 1840)

Degataga noticed my painful walking upon his return. When Ginny revealed how I had been kicked, the aura surrounding him was like fire consuming the forest, forcing the animals to flee.

He hid his fury when he met with Bad Brother.

Jonah was the taller of the two, but he puffed out his chest like a bear standing on his hind legs to appear larger. He agreed to pay Standing Together to repair the hole in the roof where rain poured in and small creatures sometimes entered.

After eating two plates of food, Jonah rode into town. With his departure, calm descended upon the farm like a soft breeze after a violent storm.

That evening, as I washed Little Butterfly along the riverbank, Degataga approached. He squatted beside me, watching her as she splashed the water playfully. Then he turned to me.

"I will find a way," he said.

He moved closer, speaking to me without words, sharing his love. Then he put his lips on mine, touching my cheek with his hand.

"You must be mine," he said. "And I must be yours. I cannot let you or your daughter suffer."

I imagined living as man and wife, a deep desire for love and tenderness burning within me.

Closing the document, I couldn't help but think that perhaps Jonah did deserve to die. Still, I couldn't condone murder even if he did kill Isham. But it made me feel guilty that part of my opposition stemmed from an urge for self-preservation.

"I don't want to save that good-for-nothing's life," I said, looking down to where Pixie sat staring at me.

She jumped on my lap, purring as I stroked her soft fur.

"Degataga wouldn't believe me if I tried to explain."

She meowed again.

"I hope you have a brilliant suggestion because I'm fresh out of ideas. Telling Amadahy to run away didn't work. Trying to lure Jonah away with gold was a waste of my hard-earned money and nearly got Eric killed. Trying to teach him to be a caring person was downright stupid. God, it pains me to think I've got to try to protect him so he can keep on abusing her! And now Ginny too! More than likely, he'll also beat his children and drink up every dime that little farm makes. Dammit!"

Pixie jumped down from my lap, dashing from the kitchen to the living room.

"I'm sorry," I called after her.

~18~

The following afternoon I received a text message from Jeannette: "Just so you'll know – Edie and I are en route to your apartment. She's irritated you didn't meet us at the assisted living place to see Louise. She's also upset about the visit. Be there in a few."

"Dang," I whispered.

So much for my laid-back Sunday, trying to rest my mind and body while icing my shoulder. I'd been moving in slow motion all day. I did manage to go online and order the blasted gold pieces, dreading my return trip to 1840 with every fiber of my being.

I picked up my lunch plate and glass from the coffee table and carried them into the kitchen, loaded the dishwasher and wiped the counter. The doorbell rang as I hung a fresh towel in the downstairs bathroom

"You're not even dressed."

That was the first thing out of Nana's mouth. Not like her at all.

"It's comfy to wear around the apartment," I replied, aiming for a perky tone.

She was more than irritated or upset. As she swept past me, she reminded me of a hornet whose nest has been knocked to the ground by a smart-aleck kid with a broom.

Jeannette raised her hands in surrender, following her into the kitchen.

"Would you like a cup of tea? I asked, trailing after them.

"I'd like a glass of wine and some crackers and peanut butter," Nana replied, her tone defiant.

I set a bottle of Cabernet on the table, along with a wine glass.

"Cup of tea, Jeannette?" I said.

"Love one."

Thankfully, Nana poured the wine. I wasn't sure I could pull the cork out with my right hand. As I microwaved two cups of water and got the tea bags, crackers and peanut butter, Nana charged ahead.

"I called you Friday and asked you to meet us at the retirement home at one-thirty. Where were you?"

"I'm sorry, Nana. I don't remember being invited."

The microwave dinged and I busied myself setting everything on the table. I knew they'd planned to visit her former next-door neighbor, but didn't know when.

"I'm sure I called you," she said.

Jeannette and I dropped tea bags into our mugs, both of us fighting the urge to exchange a glance while Nana sipped her wine.

"I guess Mrs. Johnston was glad to see you," I said, bracing myself.

"Poor pitiful Louise," she said, putting several crackers on her plate. "I don't think she even knew who I was. She didn't remember living next door to me for thirty years. It was so sad."

She spread peanut butter on a cracker and took a bite.

"I think she recognized you after we'd been there a few minutes," Jeannette said. "She laughed like she always did when the two of you were together. She seemed in good spirits to me. And what a lovely apartment she has!"

"What's it like?" I said.

"It's only one room, divided into a bedroom and a little sitting area by a Japanese screen," said Nana.

"It's decorated so nicely," Jeannette said. "It looks like her living room used to look, filled with those pretty Japanese figurines in that black lacquer curio cabinet."

"But it's not a house," Nana complained, taking another drink.

"True," Jeannette said, "but she doesn't have any house-work to do and she never has to cook or do dishes. On nice days she can sit outside in the garden, right by the fish pond if she wants to and visit with some of the other ladies."

Nana wrinkled her nose in disapproval.

"I know she appreciated your visit," I said.

"Well, I wouldn't want to live there."

"Mrs. Johnston's daughter said they moved her there and sold the house after she accidentally caused a couple of kitchen fires," I reminded her. "And they were afraid she'd wander off."

"I didn't know that."

Which wasn't true. We discussed all that when Mrs. Johnston moved away. But I wasn't going to bring that up now.

"I don't like Alzheimer's one bit!" And she slapped her hand on the table.

"Me neither," said Jeannette.

"Likewise," I agreed.

"If I get like that," Nana said, "just shoot me!"

"Nana!"

"I'm serious. I don't want to start kitchen fires and have to move to... what's the name of that place?"

"Rosewood Manor," Jeannette said.

"I don't want to move to Rosewood Manor and sit there in the lobby staring into space.

"Louise isn't like that," Jeannette said.

"Louise isn't really Louise anymore! And once you're not yourself anymore, what's the point?" She frowned as she spread another cracker with peanut butter.

I walked around behind her and hugged her and kissed her cheek. "I'm sorry the visit upset you, Nana. I love you."

So much for Mom's plan to gradually get her used to the idea of moving into assisted living. And so much for my nagging Mom to come for a visit and make some decisions. As a meddler, I was an abject failure, both with Nana and with Amadahy.

As they walked to the front door after their short visit, Jeannette told me the new companion would spend time with them over the next couple of days, before going solo.

"It won't be the same without you," Nana said to Jeannette, sounding like a little girl.

"I think you'll like Sofia," Jeannette replied. "She's got a great sense of humor."

When I got to work the next morning, I did my best not to let anyone know I was hurting. It occurred to me that any kind of injury might raise eyebrows. Especially Mallory's perfectly tweezed and gelled eyebrows. As it turned out, she was way too distracted to notice I was using my left hand for everything from holding my coffee to opening doors.

She was on her phone when I got there, in full argument mode.

"Listen, Jack, our report was tastefully done, carefully vetted and served an important service to our viewing audience. That's all I'm going to say about it. You can speak with the news director."

There were sparks in her eyes when she hung up.

"Prick!" she snarled at her phone.

"Who was that?" I sat down at my work station across from hers.

"A pushy stringer for a tabloid entertainment website who's bound and determined to do a story on our reports about that X-rated teacher." She snorted in a very unladylike manner. "I can only guess the crank who organized the picketing outside the station is the one who called him!"

"Dang."

"And, get this, the website he works for is called *The Yellow Journalist!*"

"Why would people believe anything they write?"

"Exactly! And their reporter accuses us of hyping ratings by showing some of that video. But you know as well as I do, we chose the most harmless scenes and then blurred the images so nobody could see anything. I mean, give me a break!" She stormed from the office.

Once she briefed the boss, we spent the morning in research mode, prepping for our afternoon meeting on new story ideas. We gathered in Ray's office after lunch, along with Antonio, another investigative reporter, and his producer, Sandy. Everyone tossed a couple of ideas into the hat, except for me. Which didn't sit well with Mallory.

"You're like a sixth grader on summer break," she said. "What's with?"

"I've actually been thinking about doing a story on who owns the land stolen from the Cherokee and Creek Indians in Georgia."

"You're kidding."

"That's where my mind has been lately."

"I don't think we can spend the Watchdog Team's time and resources on a history lesson," she said.

Ray tapped his pen on his desk several times before weighing in.

"I like the story about the school board chairman who's got a bunch of relatives on the payroll. Mallory, your team can delve into that. Antonio, your team can dig into that judicial appointee with the phony law degree. Meeting over, except for you two." And he pointed at me and Mallory.

As the others cleared out, I had a feeling of déjà vu.

"Okay, ladies. The shit's about to hit the fan. *The Yellow Journalist* is a website that other sites follow, and I fully expect this story to pop up all over."

"Unbelievable," Mallory said.

"I know for a fact you've been briefed more than once," he said, giving Mallory a look of exasperation. "You cannot – I repeat – cannot speak with anyone doing a story on our reporters or about any story we broadcast. Zero interviews. Understood?"

She responded with a chastened look

"You are not to let someone goad you into giving any kind of statement, even a ten-second answer referring him to me," he continued. "Do I make myself clear?"

"Got it."

"Now, Kathryn," he went on, turning to me, "the reporter who called me this morning also accused us of being two-faced – airing a story about a man taking advantage of young women, while employing a producer who's the victim of domestic violence. He's trying to dig up some evidence to that effect." He rolled his head around like he had a stiff neck. "Is it possible he'll find...?"

"Of course not," I replied without a moment's hesitation.

"Good. Because if he finds any police reports, for example, indicating your boyfriend beat you up, that would..."

"The only police report was when Mallory called the cops because I had a bruise on my face!" I wrinkled my nose at her. It still pissed me off.

"Tell your boyfriend we'd appreciate it if he didn't talk with any reporters who might contact him," he said.

"We broke up."

"On friendly terms, I hope."

"Yes."

"Then call him and ask him very nicely not to talk with any reporters who come sniffing around. Or if he does, if he could keep it short and sweet."

I gave him a thumbs up, although I was confident Eric wouldn't say anything to cause problems.

"All right. Get to work!"

Mallory headed for the door, but I did not.

"You know what, Ray?" I said. "If that website does the story, then so be it. There's nothing we can do to stop them. Instead of trying to hide – which is impossible – why don't we milk it for all it's worth? Do a follow-up on how prosecutors in other cities are now investigating the teacher?"

"I like it," Mallory said. "Better to be bold than act like a wimp. That's what I always say."

Ray contemplated me over the top of his reading glasses.

"How many other jurisdictions are investigating him?" he said.

"Three that we know of," I replied.

He drummed the desk with his pen.

"The reporter who called me says their story will be posted within the next couple of days," he said. "You guys have your report ready to air during the seven o'clock show Wednesday morning, with two other versions for later in the day. Mallory, I know you don't usually do live shots during morning drive, but I want you standing in front of that guy's home for your live shot."

"Yes sir," she said.

"I'll alert the legal team," he said.

We worked our tail feathers off the rest of the day and all day Tuesday, calling district attorneys in cities where Hobbs worked before moving to Atlanta. Which tipped me to his job-hopping history. He only stayed at a job a couple of years before moving to another city. I managed to set up Skype interviews with two assistant DAs. We updated the status of the case in our own jurisdiction and finished writing our scripts by Tuesday afternoon – in time for the station legal team to check them over. Mallory recorded several standups in front of the school where Hobbs taught and recorded her voice overs. We were ready.

It was nearly nine o'clock by the time I got home that night. Pixie demanded food – loudly. While I was tired, I was glad we were fighting back. I didn't like the idea of being pushed around by some clickbait website.

That's when I remembered Ray's order to call Eric.

He answered on the first ring.

"Kathryn!"

"Just got home from work. Need to tell you something. I hope I'm not interrupting anything."

He hesitated a few seconds before answering.

"Actually, I'm heading out the door. A rather urgent errand. Can I call you back in about an hour?"

"Sure. Talk to you then."

Which made me think I really had interrupted something. He might be with that attractive, vegan PhD candidate.

But it gave me time to shower and change into my comfy beach dress, then nuke a frozen lasagna and sit down at the kitchen table. I realized how good it was to hear his voice again. His rich, intelligent, thoughtful, witty, wise-cracking voice. Which matched the ever-present glint in his eyes. I was suddenly overcome with longing.

Funny, now that I'd been humbled time and again by my well-meaning ineptitude, I could better understand his point of view, even if I didn't agree with how he delivered it.

I checked my phone several times, waiting for it to ring.

At a quarter after ten, I was still waiting, wondering if he'd given me the brush-off with no intention of calling me back. If he didn't want to talk to me, then I'd have to send him a text to give him a heads-up about the web reporter. I'd begun typing a message when my doorbell chimed.

Quickly, I double-checked that my security system was on, then took stock of my appearance. I was barefoot and braless beneath my shift, without a speck of makeup on. Plus, my hair was still damp. Not exactly presentable. I tip-toed to the front door to get a look-see through the peephole before deciding whether I should run upstairs and get a robe or maybe call the police. It was Eric.

I deactivated the security system and opened the door.

"God, you look beautiful," he said, his voice catching in his throat.

Which, although patently untrue, made me go all misty. I opened my mouth to speak, but didn't know what to say.

He stepped inside, immediately closing the door and locking it. Then he invaded my personal space so completely that we were nose to nose.

"You were right not to turn your back on her," he said, his voice husky.

I could see tears welling in his eyes, which took me by surprise and softened my heart.

"And you were right," he continued, "about me kissing my boss's ass when he turned all pompous and judgmental on me."

"Eric," I whispered.

"I really need for you to forgive me because..."

"Eric..."

"Because I love you, Kathryn."

He waited for me to push him away and when I didn't, he kissed me softly.

"I hope you won't be offended," he said, "when I admit I also crave you."

He wrapped me in his arms and put his mouth on mine, demonstrating in the most persuasive language possible how much he wanted me. I returned his passion, pressing myself against him. We made love on the sofa like two teenagers, panting and moaning, me doing my best not to hurt my injured shoulder.

Afterwards, we clung to each other as though some unseen force might separate us if we didn't bind ourselves together.

"I'm hoping you feel something approaching the depth of my ardor," he said, his mouth on my ear.

Which caused me to chuckle.

"Only an academic," I whispered.

"You shouldn't laugh at a man as besotted as I am."

My chuckle turned into a giggle.

"I can't help it," he said, "if I desire sexual congress with such a comely wench."

Which caused my giggle to escalate into laughter.

Pulling back, his eyes locked onto mine, searching for my reply.

"Yes," I conceded, feeling slightly dizzy, "I share the depth of your ardor. It seems I am besotted as well."

The passionate kiss that followed whetted my desire for more.

～

My alarm went off at five the next morning. Which was a killer since we hadn't gotten to sleep until late. He had to drive to Athens to teach a class. I had to help Mallory with her live shot and grind out the second and third versions of our report.

I kissed him good-bye at the front door and watched as he trotted down the steps toward the parking lot. But then he returned like he'd forgotten his shoes or something, enveloping me in his arms, pulling me close, breathing into my hair.

"Wanted to make sure it wasn't a dream," he said.

I closed my eyes, savoring his embrace.

"I'll be back tonight," he said.

"You will?"

"It's not just sexual congress I crave, you know. I also need conversation with the woman I love."

He kissed me, then dashed to his car. I watched him drive away, already anxious to see him again even before he was out of sight.

Closing the door, I noticed Pixie watching me.

"Yeah, I know. You told me so."

～

After doing two live shots on the morning show and another one at noon, Mallory was pumped. When *The Yellow Journalist* report hit the web, we exchanged high fives for beating the bastards to the punch. Mallory slapped my hurt shoulder in her excitement.

I tried not to flinch.

"What!" she said. "I hardly touched you."

"Just a little sore. Nothing serious."

"Pray tell."

I did my best to hide my pain and annoyance, making a quick getaway. We'd planned to wrap up early after working long hours over the last couple of days, so I didn't feel bad about clocking out. I wasn't going to hang around for another interrogation.

Late that afternoon, I had to sign for delivery of an unmarked package. I knew before opening it that those loathsome gold nuggets had arrived. I hadn't told Eric about my latest visit. He didn't know I was over a barrel the size of Stone Mountain. I hid the package in my bedroom closet.

~19~

"Yes, he's on his way over," I said to Pixie as she eyed me in the bedroom mirror. "Yes, that's why I took a shower and put on my new white shorts and my spaghetti strap top."

I turned this way and that, checking my reflection, bubbling like a glass of champagne.

"Need a touch of lipstick."

Pixie meowed her approval as I applied Plum Pretty and fluffed my hair.

My phone dinged. Thinking it might be Eric, I checked, finding instead an email from Nancy with another journal entry. I sat down on the bed and opened it.

Amadahy's Journal – Part 10 (June) 1840

Six days after her first visit, Old Grandmother returned. But her smile faded as she rounded the corner of the house in time to see Bad

Brother slap my face, knocking me to the ground. Jonah heard her cry out, turning and shouting harsh words.

"Get off my property, old hag! You ain't welcome here!"

Fear shone in her eyes, but she appeared uncertain about leaving me.

"You must stay away, Old Grandmother," I cried from where I lay. "Go home as you did before."

She saw the urgent look on my face and swiftly ran behind the house. I hoped she would remember to eat the fig.

"So, you're sneaking friends round here when you think I ain't looking," Jonah said, weaving as he moved closer. "Remember this, woman! You ain't got no friends, 'less I say so! Specially not a woman dresses like a man!"

"She is an ancient one."

"Get inside the house!"

"I must feed the baby first or she will cry."

He could not abide her crying, so he granted my request.

I carried her into the hut, speaking soothing words as we settled onto the blanket. But as she nursed, there was a strange whisper in the air and a young white woman appeared before me like a spirit, stepping from the back door. She had brown hair that fell on her shoulders and wore undergarments as though she had lost her clothing. I knew at once that, like Old Grandmother, this woman was not of my world. She had traveled through the Going Back Portal.

Before we could speak, Jonah yelled for me to come to his bed. I left the hut and told him I was still bleeding and needed to wait another day. He was angry, but allowed me to remain in my hut.

When I returned, my strange guest questioned me in a soft voice. Like the grey-haired one, she spoke the white man's language in an unfamiliar way.

She asked if an old woman had visited me. I told her I warned Old Grandmother she was not safe here. I repeated my warning to the brown-haired woman and plucked a fig for her journey.

"I have so many questions," she said.

My grandmother conjured the magic tunnel to save herself from the white man. Perhaps her portal brought these good spirits to help me. I paused to think on this before giving her my written words – the missionary teachers called such writing a diary. That way she would know me, would know my family's story, would know my oppressor and the injustice my people suffered.

Then I pushed her through the doorway and she melted like fog in the warmth of the sun.

I was shaken as I closed the document. She thought I was a good spirit too. A spirit who could save her. God.

When the doorbell rang, I rose from the bed, eyes unfocused. All this bounced around inside my brain as I trotted down the stairs. I stalled for a second to put Amadahy out of my mind. I wanted to focus on Eric.

When I opened the door, he greeted me with a kiss on the lips while the yummy smell of Chinese take-out wafted from the paper sack in his hand.

"*The Yellow Journalist* guy emailed me today," he said as we sat across from each other at the kitchen table. "Said he wanted to ask me a few questions."

"Sorry about that."

"Not your fault."

"By the way, I saw one of your reports. Well done. Mallory's good on the air."

"True."

"Even if she *is* a pain in the ass?"

We both laughed.

"She called me today," he said.

"About *The Yellow Journalist* story?"

"That's what I assumed. But she wanted to talk about your shoulder."

I could feel my blood pressure rising.

"She asked me if I did that to you," he said.

"Who does she think she is?" My hand flailed as I spoke, knocking my fork off the table. I picked it up, depositing it in the sink.

"That was my gut reaction when she first asked me. But after talking with her a few minutes, I decided she's sincere."

"Mm-hm," I muttered as I retrieved a clean fork and sat down again. "I have half a mind to call her up this very minute and chew her out good!"

"She told me you wouldn't say how you hurt it."

"Eric, she's misrepresenting our conversation, such as it was. She slapped my shoulder and I guess I yelped a little. But when she gave that accusing look, it pissed me off. I got up and left. I'd had a long day on Monday and an even longer day on Tuesday. And I was still ticked about her calling the cops on you before. For her to tell you I refused to say how I hurt my arm is preposterous!"

"Okay, how'd it happen?"

"I got up on the ladder at Nana's cottage to clean out her back gutter. It was so full of pine straw and leaves that the water was pouring over the top and causing a waterfall right on the edge of her porch. I'd finished scooping out the crud when the ladder wobbled – probably because of the soggy ground – and I fell. When I landed, I held out my right arm to break my fall. Nothing mysterious. Nothing sinister." I had cleaned out the gutters several times, so it wasn't a complete fabrication.

He took another bite of his egg roll.

"I'm not gonna stand for her giving me the third degree every time I get a paper cut!" I added.

Lying was hard. But I couldn't afford for him to know Jonah had severely manhandled me. If I told him the truth, then he'd know I was up to something and he'd try to stop me. And that might mean another quarrel. Which I really wanted to avoid. Ranting about Mallory being an overbearing buttinsky seemed to be the safest tactic under the circumstances.

"I think her intentions are good. Anyway, she and I are cool now."

Which made me groan.

"So how's your shoulder?" he asked.

"Better. Going for a follow-up with my doctor next week. By the way, you've got rice on your cheek."

"Where?"

"Right..." and I reached across the table and wiped the grain of wild rice from his face.

He caught my hand and pulled it to his mouth, kissing my palm.

"Did I mention how much I missed you?" he said.

"I missed you too."

"Looking into your eyes like this makes me oscillate at the sub-atomic level."

"You are the most romantic college professor I've ever shared Chinese take-out with."

We sat there in a trance, hands intertwined.

"It's gonna be tough living so far apart," he said.

"The drive is only a little over an hour."

"Much too far when I need to be with you every day."

The way he caressed my hand made me shiver.

"But, unlike a rutting buffalo, I *can* exercise some self-restraint," he said, withdrawing his hand.

Which made me burst out laughing, triggering an amused grin from his side of the table.

"Although I freely admit it's a challenge," he said as we resumed eating. "So, tell me the news from 1840."

"Where to begin?" I whispered. "Maybe the latest journal entries."

Retrieving my laptop, I opened it on the table and scooted my chair to sit beside him. We read the translations Nancy had completed as we finished our supper.

"That guy needs to be put behind bars," he said when we finished.

I shook my head, preferring not to mention the rather troubling outcome of locking Jonah away. Eric didn't know about the family history, didn't know Jonah was supposed to have three children with Amadahy and hundreds of descendants, including me.

"While I don't condone murder," he said, "Degataga might solve the problem if he makes good on his threat."

I didn't want to go there either.

"And Amadahy thinks you and your grandma are good spirits," he said, his voice filled with awe.

"She might've thought that at first. But not anymore."

I began wiping the table.

"I know this may be a touchy subject," he said, "but it makes me nervous thinking about you visiting them again."

"Every time I've gone back, I've made things worse."

My aim was to sound like I was giving up while not actually making any promises. I *had* to return. There was the rather significant matter of taking Jonah his blackmail payment for not hurting Amadahy or Ginny. I was also hoping against hope that I'd figure out a strategy to protect them. Besides ongoing bribes, that is, which I couldn't afford.

"An abrupt change of subject," he said. "My sister up and decided she's getting married this weekend. Kind of a last-minute decision since she and her beau have been living together for several years. I'm driving to Savannah on Friday, returning Sunday evening. I sure would love for you to come with me."

Which caused two things to happen in my body. One, my heart suddenly felt all fuzzy and warm that he wanted to take me to such an important event so he could introduce me to his family. Which spoke worlds about the depth of his feelings. And two, my brain was extremely relieved that he'd be out of town while I was on my questionable mission to 1840, since I wouldn't have to make excuses about why I couldn't spend time with him.

"Unfortunately, Nana is having a tough time right now. She got really upset Sunday when Jeannette took her to visit a former longtime neighbor with Alzheimer's Disease who's now in assisted living. She's worried about possibly having to move into one of those facilities, herself. So I really need to spend time with her this weekend."

He tried for stoicism, but his disappointment was palpable.

"I'm sorry," I said. "If Nana wasn't so upset right now, I'd love to go. I'm touched you want me to meet your family."

I leaned over and kissed his cheek.

"Speaking of touching," I said, hoping to smooth over his disappointment, "I don't suppose you'd like to give me a demonstration of a rutting buffalo coming on to the cow of his dreams?"

He liked that idea a lot.

~

Eric decided not to come over Thursday night since he had to pack all his dressy duds and be ready to hit the road first thing in the morning. So it was me and Pixie again. Which was okay. I was too nervous to be good company.

Spread out on the sofa, trying to relax while scarfing down a peanut butter sandwich, my phone dinged. It was an email from Nancy.

"This is the final translation of the pages you sent me. I can't say I enjoyed doing the work because it's a depressing story. I sure hope things turned out all right for this poor woman. One of thousands of stories of American Indians abused by the white man. No offense.

"I don't know what to make of those spirits coming through that portal she talks about. I know my Cherokee ancestors could be very mystical. Some of us still are.

"Let me know if you need my services in the future. My final bill is attached."

"Yeah, I'm with you," I whispered.

Pixie meowed.

"He's not coming tonight," I said.

She meowed again.

"Come here," I said, patting the cushion beside me.

She leaped onto the couch, burrowing between my thigh and a throw pillow as I clicked on the attachment.

Amadahy's Journal – Part 11 (June 1840)

After the young white woman and her husband brought him gold, Jonah began to watch me more closely. One day I found him inside the hut as though searching for my secrets. If he finds my written words, he cannot read them, but he would burn them to punish me and take away the box Isham gave me.

When Bad Brother bought Ginny to be his slave, he acted as a rich man. When he gambled away the other pieces of gold, his cruelty grew stronger. He directs his anger at me. And now Ginny. Sometimes even my daughter.

I cannot give up my land. It is the one part of my family still with me. Our burial ground must be preserved so our ancestors will be looked after. But I fear for our safety. I also fear Degataga will keep his word. If he kills Bad Brother, I will be driven away. The Principal People's land was stolen. I must not let the white man rob me of my family's land as well. It would be another coup for the trespassers.

I try to protect us. But sometimes I am like a rabbit, heart pounding, wishing to run away when a hunter draws near. Degataga's invitation lingers in my mind. Especially when I look into his loving eyes.

I gave my writing to the young white woman. But I no longer think she has strong medicine. She says I should run away. She does not understand. I cannot run away.

~20~

No time like the present. That's what hit me as I emerged from an anxious night's sleep Friday morning, persuading me to move my onerous mission forward a day. My presence wasn't crucial at work and Eric was on his way to Savannah. So I called in sick.

Pixie watched as I took inventory of the items I was taking with me, arranged neatly on my bed. Gold nuggets – check. Another long skirt – check. Old-fashioned three-quarter sleeve white blouse – check. A pair of comfortable black shoes that wouldn't fall apart in the rain or cause blisters on my feet – check. Amadahy's calico dress I'd borrowed – check. A purse-sized can of Mace – check.

"Meow," she said.

"Right. I'll put an extra bowl of food out for you. But don't worry, I won't be gone long."

My stomach churned all the way from Atlanta to the country cottage.

It was a hazy July morning, oppressively humid, with the mercury expected to climb into the mid nineties. Not only did I dread seeing Jonah again, the thought of wearing those hot clothes made me hanker for a tall cold one. And I wasn't even a beer drinker. How did people survive covering their bodies in the heat of summer with no air conditioning?

I changed in Nana's bedroom. This time, I removed my shorts and tank top, leaving them in my backpack, along with my sandals and phone. I fixed my hair in the usual bun on the back of my head.

Beads of perspiration bloomed as soon as I stepped off the back porch. The trees shaded me from the sun, but my blouse was damp by the time I reached the clearing.

Bracing myself by the fig bush, I patted the hidden pockets of my skirt, making sure the pepper spray and gold nuggets were in place. Then I picked a fig from the bush and ate it as I stepped forward.

Dizziness engulfed me as buzzing filled my ears. There was no one to greet me in the hut.

I listened. No voices, but there was a rhythmic sound in the distance. I set the borrowed dress on the blanket, then pushed the rough door ajar and peeked out. No one in sight. Rather than risk walking into the yard, I slipped out the small back door, leaning against the outer wall. The noise was coming from the field on the forest side of the house, away from the river.

Crouching low, I dashed for the tree line, hiding behind the trunk of a large pine. Slowly, I made my way along the edge of the woods, far enough into the trees so I couldn't be seen. As I neared the field, I could tell the sound was coming from within the corn rows. Confident it wasn't Jonah, since he never did any work around the farm, I hurried across a bare patch, hiding myself among the tall green stalks. Following the sound to the far end of the rows, I peered between the lush plants to see Amadahy digging with a spade.

She looked up, sensing my presence, but didn't make a sound. If I had to guess what she was feeling by the look on her face, I'd say it was forbearance. She had hoped I was a good spirit who traveled here using her grandmother's going back tunnel. Instead, I was a fumbling twenty-first century woman whose visits only complicated her already challenging life.

I hunched over, making my way along the row, then squatted in front of her.

"I hope he hasn't hurt you since last time I was here," I whispered.

She resumed hoeing.

"Where are Ginny and Betsey?" I said, deciding Ginny was more likely to tell me what I wanted to know.

She pointed toward the river, wiping her forehead on her sleeve.

"You should go back to your home and never return." Her voice was weary.

"But I..."

"You cannot help me."

"I have to try."

She dropped several seeds into the mound in front of her.

"Is he here?" I asked.

"Asleep in the hammock."

I took the long way around to the riverbank, then edged closer to where Ginny was doing laundry. The baby crawled on the ground nearby, babbling to herself. In the distance, in the shade of a large dogwood tree, Jonah was stretched out in the hammock.

"Ginny!" I whispered.

She spotted me in my hiding place behind a bush. I put my finger to my lips. She gave me a look like she thought I was crazy, then wrung out the shirt she was washing.

"Since the last time I was here, has he hit you or Amadahy?" I whispered.

She put her hand on her hip impatiently.

"Has he?" I whispered.

She raised her hands like the answers to my questions should be obvious even to a dimwit like me. So much for bribing him to be a good boy. If he ever had a grain of goodness in him, it had been ground to dust and left to rot in the rain.

I fingered the gold pieces in my pocket. As much as I abhorred the idea of rewarding him for unforgivable behavior, I didn't have much choice. He said if I didn't bring the gold, he would hurt one of the women. I could only guess that he was threatening a more intense level of violence. I could see this happening again and again. What was I supposed to do?

My head was in my hands when I heard movement close by. It was Ginny with Betsey on her hip. She came around to my side of the bush and sat on the ground, keeping her voice low.

"You sick?"

Answering would take too much energy.

"You don't have to trouble yourself about Mister Jonah," she whispered. "Miss Amadahy got a cousin coming back real soon to make sure Mister Jonah don't never lay a hand on nobody again."

"He can't just murder him."

"Ain't murder when the sheriff hangs a killer! And it ain't murder when Satan's seed draws his last breath after all the evil he done."

It was hard to argue with her logic. Except that he was supposed to produce a lot of offspring before he left this world for the flames of hell. I hauled myself off the ground, brushed off my skirt and forced myself to walk toward the hammock. I had to do something before Degataga showed up.

Coming to a stop about eight feet from where he lay, I felt like I was about to poke a rabid dog with a stick.

"Mister Barnes?"

He swatted his face as though a mosquito had buzzed his head.

"I brought you the gold I promised," I said, speaking a little louder.

He farted, grimacing like the light hurt his eyes.

"Mister Barnes, it's Kathryn Murray. I came to bring you the gold nuggets we talked about."

He opened his eyes, giving me a cold look. Which triggered a terrible sense of looming disaster.

"You brung the gold?" He pulled himself slowly to a sitting position.

"Have you kept your side of the bargain?" I tried my best to sound confident.

"I let you go, didn't I?" He hacked, spitting on the ground in front of me, wiping his mouth with his filthy sleeve.

"I mean about not hitting anyone."

"I done told you, a man's got a right to do what he wants with his wife. Now, where's them five gold nuggets?"

"We agreed on four."

He held out his hand, palm up, jutting his scruffy beard in my direction.

"You have to promise to be gentle with Amadahy and Ginny," I said.

He cocked his head, stretching his hand out further.

"Well?" I said, sounding like a mother interrogating her teen-age son. Then I slid my right hand into the pocket with the can of Mace, putting my finger on the trigger, ready to use it.

"Hand 'em over, goddammit!"

He pulled himself up to his full height, which was considerable.

Reluctantly, I reached into my other pocket with my left hand and withdrew four gold pieces. I slowly closed the distance between us and dropped them into his greasy hand. He looked them over, gauging their heft, then deposited them in his pocket.

"Ginny!" he hollered.

"Yessir?" she cried from the riverbank.

"Get over here!"

She was beside me in a flash, Betsey in her arms.

"Hand the baby to Miz Murray."

Which didn't make sense, but she did as she was told. It was the first time I'd held the soft, sweet baby and she was none too sure about it.

"Now, come here," he instructed Ginny.

Wariness crossed her face as she took two tentative steps toward him. Then he grabbed her, twisting her arm behind her back, holding her in front of him so she couldn't stand up. I was stunned when he pulled his knife from the waist of his pants and held it to her neck.

Ginny squealed in pain and Betsey tuned up to cry in my arms.

"Mr. Barnes," I pleaded. "Don't hurt her!"

"You see this knife? I keep it sharp for gutting fish and skinning animals. And I'm gonna use it on one of my women if you ain't back here in two days with five more pieces of gold."

"But..."

"You want me to cut her?" he said, touching the point of the blade to her skin, causing a drop of blood to trickle down her neck as she whimpered.

"All right!" I said, hugging little Betsey to me.

Then I caught sight of Amadahy limping in our direction from the field, going as fast as her legs would carry her.

"You keep your nose out of this, squaw!" he barked. "I'm working on a business deal here."

"Mr. Barnes," I said, "please let her go."

"You understand, Miz Murray?"

"Yes. Yes, I understand! Now let her go!"

He released his grip on Ginny's arms, stepping back as though nothing had happened while Ginny clamped her hand over her bleeding neck. Betsey stretched her arms out toward her mother, who rushed forward, taking the crying baby from my shaking arms. Jonah wiped the blade of the knife on his pants and slipped it back into the sheath at his waist.

"Two days," he said, then turned and walked toward the barn.

Amadahy held Betsey close, whispering in her ear, stroking her small back. Ginny glared at me.

"You ain't poison like Mister Jonah, but you sure do bring trouble," she said, then headed for the river.

"I'm sorry," I said, squeezing my eyes shut.

So it would be blackmail from here on out. Every time I returned, he would demand more gold, threatening terrible violence. My head throbbed.

"Amadahy," I said.

She waited for me to speak, but I didn't know what to say. She walked away, carrying the baby on her good hip.

I decided to return to the time portal before Jonah changed his mind and locked me up again. I hurried around the corner of the house, letting myself into the hut, then quickly stepped through the back door to pick a fig. But I didn't see one. I bent down, scanning the lower limbs. I walked around the bush, checking every branch, top to bottom. The only figs on the bush were like tiny green rocks.

I trotted around to the garden side of the shack to another bush. Thank goodness, there were figs there! I plucked one and stepped inside long enough to pop the fig in my mouth and walk through the doorway. But there was no buzzing in my ears. The hut was still there.

~21~

Hearing Betsey's little voice coming from the field, I dashed for the corn rows, finding the two of them on the far end where Amadahy had been working when I arrived.

"There aren't any figs!" I cried. "Only some little hard ones. Not edible, that's for sure."

She struggled to her feet, then lifted Betsey. I followed her down the row. As we neared the shack, Ginny approached from the river, having washed the blood off her neck.

There was a look of surprise on Amadahy's face as she pulled branches one way and another.

"The first crop is gone. There will be no more figs until the second crop ripens." She pointed at the figlets. "When animals eat them, there are leavings on the ground, but I see no sign of animals."

Ginny pushed the dirt with the toe of her worn shoe, a hangdog expression on her face.

Both of us stared at her.

"I didn't know they was s'posed to be for someone special," she said. "Only ate a few. That's all there was. But there's plenty on them other bushes."

I rubbed my temples.

"What's wrong with the other ones?" she said.

"The young figs will ripen by the Drying Up Moon," Amadahy said, ignoring her.

Not familiar with the phases of the moon in my own time, I had no clue when the Drying Up Moon would arrive. But by the look of those hard figs, it wasn't anytime soon. Sweat trickled down my back as the full weight of her words registered.

First, if I didn't bring those gold pieces to Jonah, he might actually deliver on his threat to do bodily harm to Amadahy or Ginny. Second, if I stayed here, there was a good chance he'd get in touch with his scuzzbucket pal Johnny about using me in his "business." Third, there was also the possibility that Jonah would lock me up and break my arm, or worse.

"We will make room for you," Amadahy said.

"You don't understand. He gave me two days to bring more gold."

"I will tell him you are sick and cannot travel."

I suddenly felt weak standing in the hot sun.

"Ginny, please bring water," she said, then turned to me. "Come sit and rest."

We moved into the woods, sitting in the shade. Fanning myself with my hand, I closed my eyes, trying to think. I couldn't hang around the farm for several weeks. Degataga could show up any day now, ready to mete out justice. And no telling what Jonah might do in the meantime – to me, and to the women he thought of as his property. I had to act.

Ginny returned with a gourd of water. I gladly drank, disregarding the germs. Which made me think of water bottles. Which made me think of Eric, the avid bicyclist. Which made me think of a comment he made – that Jonah should be locked up for his crimes.

"I'm going into town," I announced.

"Mister Jonah ain't gonna let you ride his horse," Ginny said.

"I'll go on foot. How far is it?"

"Bout five miles," she replied.

"I can jog that far in an hour. Well, an hour and twenty minutes."

"Jog?" she said.

"Run."

"It is not wise to travel alone," said Amadahy.

"Ironic, you keep telling me what's not wise for me to do, since you're the one risking your life staying with that thug."

It popped out of my mouth without thinking. Part of me wanted to take it back, considering the consequences of her leaving him. But the honest part of me knew I'd spoken my true feelings unencumbered by my own survival instinct.

"Just point the way," I said.

"Who do you wish to speak to?" Amadahy said.

"The sheriff."

She pursed her lips, then turned to Ginny. "Go with her."

"Yes'm."

We set off through the trees so Jonah wouldn't see us. Ginny led the way until we were far enough from the farmhouse to walk along the rutted dirt road.

"Let's jog for a bit," I said.

"Too hot."

"I need to get there as quickly as possible."

"You ever faint from the heat?"

"We'll run nice and easy for a few minutes, then we'll slow down and walk again."

"I don't run 'cept when I'm in danger."

"I'm in danger," I said.

"Danger of your own making, if you don't mind my saying so."

"You're in danger too, you know. Along with Amadahy and Betsey."

I lifted my long skirt to knee level and jogged down the road, realizing how ridiculous I must look. She reluctantly followed suit. But it didn't take more than a couple of minutes to eat humble pie. It was one thing to jog in the heat while wearing shorts and a tank top made of breathable modern fabrics, a water bottle strapped to my waist, a sun visor shading my eyes while wearing quality running shoes. Quite another to run while wearing a long skirt and blouse and ballet flats with no water.

"Okay, let's walk a while," I said, slowing my pace.

Both of us were breathing hard, sweat pouring. She gestured for me to follow her as we left the narrow road for the shade of the woods. But the underbrush hindered our progress, so once we retreated from heatstroke territory we returned to the wagon tracks.

"You got a notion the sheriff gonna put Mister Jonah in the jailhouse?" she said.

"I don't know."

"White men generally stick together."

"Not always."

"Pfft."

We walked in silence for a bit until Ginny couldn't help herself any longer.

"I don't understand 'bout them figs," she said.

"It's complicated."

"Complicated. You talk peculiar. And you act peculiar too."

"Is that so?".

"Seem like you can't do much a nothing, 'cept talk a lot."

"You're pretty good at talking, yourself," I said.

"But I know how to cook, how to work the fields, how to feed the chickens, how to mind a baby. You like some rich woman never had to lift a finger!"

"I know how to microwave a frozen dinner, how to heat up a can of soup, how to bake canned biscuits in the toaster oven, and I can make my own coffee in a Keurig machine!"

"See? That's what I'm talking 'bout. You strange."

"I'm from a different place, that's all. And I do different kind of work than you do. I'm a reporter."

"Like for a newspaper?"

"Like for a newspaper."

"Where you come from, they let a woman do that?"

"Yes, they do."

"Where you from?"

"A city called Atlanta." It was the perfect answer. In 1840, Atlanta was known simply as Terminus – the terminus of a railroad line. It wouldn't be incorporated as Atlanta for several more years.

We walked a while without speaking, the cicadas raising a ruckus all around us.

"You speak different words, but there's something else. You talk to me like I ain't a slave. Same as Miss Amadahy."

"Where I come from, you wouldn't be a slave."

"I'd be free?"

"Yes."

"Maybe I oughta go with you when you go home. But then I'd miss Amadahy something terrible."

I raised the hem of my skirt and used it to wipe my face and neck but had to quickly tidy my clothing when we heard a wagon approach. A buckboard rounded the bend in front of us, a man and woman seated behind a team of two brown horses. The man wore a hat, the woman, a large grey bonnet. We stepped aside so they could pass, but the man reined in the horses, stopping a few feet in front of us. Now we could see children in the wagon bed, along with some supplies.

"Morning," he said, touching the brim of his hat. "Don't recognize you. You new around here?"

"I'm visiting Mrs. Barnes," I replied.

"Mrs. Barnes?" the woman said, her round face suddenly filled with concern. "She doing all right?"

I considered her question carefully before answering.

"She stays busy."

The woman eyed me closely.

"Isham was my cousin," she said. "Still hurts me that he's gone."

I looked down, uncertain how to reply.

"I'm Ida Berryman. This is my husband, Eli."

"Kathryn Murray. And this is Ginny."

One of the horses whinnied and Mr. Berryman adjusted his grip on the reins.

"We need to get on home," she said. "Please give my regards to Mrs. Barnes."

When the wagon passed by, the four children dangling their legs from the rear of the bed waved at us. I waved back. It was a welcome reminder that there were decent people living nearby.

As we continued on our way, I mulled over the brief conversation with Mrs. Berryman. I wasn't sure what to make of her interest in Amadahy.

"Almost there," Ginny said, stopping in the shade of some tall pines.

By that time, I was questioning my sanity. I was lightheaded and smelled like I'd come in from a long run and desperately needed a shower. I also feared I was grasping at straws hoping the sheriff might see things my way.

The trip had taken a lot longer than I figured and my throat was parched.

"Remember," Ginny said, "if you talk to me, you gotta act proud-like."

Danielsville was nothing like my twenty-first century mind expected. We passed a dark brown, unpainted house on our right, then there was a sizable garden and another wooden structure with a hand-painted sign that said Pulliam Dry Goods, Barber & Dentist. Beyond that was Long's Saloon. No swinging doors like in a western, just a door standing open, a bar visible in the dark interior of a plain wooden building with two horses tied out front. Across the dirt road was a smaller building with a sign in the window that said Sheriff. There were two other buildings, one of them made of logs. And that was it.

Feeling anxious, I moved closer to Ginny, but she quickly stepped away, silently reminding me that in 1840 a white woman wouldn't walk with a black slave like they were bosom buddies. She followed two steps behind me as we crossed the road to the sheriff's office.

"I'll wait out here," she whispered and sat down on the wooden porch.

My hand trembled as I turned the knob.

"Can I help you?"

It was the booming voice of a wiry man in the process of putting on his hat.

"Are you the sheriff?"

He replied by patting a silver star on his breast pocket. His face was like leather, and, although he didn't stink as bad as Jonah, he did smell like he needed a bath. But then, pretty much everyone smelled like they could use a bath except for Amadahy, who must bathe every day in the river.

"My name is Mrs. Kathryn Murray. I'm not from around here so I don't know your name."

"Ezra Moon. You visiting someone? Passing through?"

"I'm a distant cousin of Mrs. Barnes."

He eyed me closely. "What can I do for you?"

"I've come to report a crime."

"That so?"

"A murder."

Which got his attention.

"Who's the victim?" he said, hanging his hat back on its hook.

He motioned for me to sit in a ladder-back chair in front of his desk while he settled into a sturdier chair behind it.

"Isham Barnes," I said.

He scratched his forehead before responding. "Isham Barnes disappeared last year. What makes you think, all of a sudden, that someone murdered him?"

"His brother killed him to get the farm."

"Miz Murray, I know for a fact Jonah ain't exactly the most upstanding citizen of Madison County. He drinks too much. He gambles too much. He's a regular customer of the less reputable ladies on the outskirts of town. And he ain't exactly well liked. But I'd be careful if I's you, calling him a murderer."

"He is a murderer! And he beats Isham's wife and the slave he bought from Mr. Wheeler."

He leaned forward, elbows on the desk. "Ain't a crime to beat your wife. And it sure ain't no crime to beat your slave." Then he stood, retrieved his hat and put it on his head, adjusting the brim. "I gotta make my rounds."

"Aren't you even going to investigate?"

"You show me some proof there's been a murder, I might consider it."

Amadahy's account of burying her husband came back to me. How she'd dragged his body on a handmade sled behind the horse. How she dug the grave herself, covering it with rocks. But telling the sheriff the body was buried in her family burial ground might implicate her, not Jonah. Isham's body would be badly decomposed by now. And even if it weren't, a bump on the head or water in the lungs wouldn't point to

Jonah. It could just as easily point to Isham's wife as the killer. Especially in a time when a white man's rights far outweighed an Indian woman's rights.

He crossed to the door.

"Jonah Barnes forced Amadahy to marry him!"

"I'm sorry Miz Murray, I don't have time for anymore of your gossip. I got…"

"It's not gossip, Sheriff! I'm telling the truth! He threatened to send her to Indian Territory in Oklahoma if she didn't marry him. And he forces her into his bed. He hits her, kicks her."

"She could leave him if she wanted."

"To go where?" I cried, keeping Degataga's offer to take her to the Great Smoky Mountains to myself. "He killed her husband to get that farm and now he forces her to do all the work!"

He ignored me, reaching for the doorknob.

Desperation got the better of me. "What if I contribute to your re-election campaign?"

Which made him pause.

"I've got a gold nugget," I said.

"And you'd give me that piece of gold so I'd…"

"So you'd at least investigate Jonah for killing his brother and stealing his farm and forcing his wife into servitude."

"Servitude? Where'd you say you was from, Miz Murray?"

"DeKalb County."

"Is that how things is done there?"

"I…"

"You got that gold nugget on you?"

It suddenly occurred to me I might've fallen down a rabbit hole I couldn't climb out of.

"The gold piece?" he said, extending his open palm.

Throwing caution to the wind, I reached into the pocket of my skirt and handed him the one nugget I'd held in reserve, in case Jonah required a little more persuasion. He put it between his teeth, biting down hard, then inspected the tooth marks.

"Even if I don't believe your story, I do believe this here is real gold." He dropped it in his vest pocket, then touched my arm with his left hand. "I'm arresting you for bribing a public official. If you'll kindly step this way."

"It wasn't a bribe!"

"If you don't cooperate, Miz Murray, I can use force."

He was well built, armed with a gun and had a dead serious expression on his face. I reined in my fight or flight instinct, deciding not to risk getting shot trying to escape. He escorted me to one of two jail cells along the back wall and locked me up.

"Sheriff Moon, it wasn't a bribe."

"What do they call it in DeKalb County when a good-looking woman tries to pay the sheriff to investigate a man she don't like?"

"But you can't lock me up like this."

"Why not?"

"I'm not from..."

"Don't matter where you're from. You break the law, you pay the price."

He put the cell key in the same pocket he'd dropped the gold into and walked out, locking the door behind him.

My hands gripped the iron bars, shaking them in an absurdly futile gesture. What I really wanted to do was scream. But I settled for a pointless wrestling match with the bars holding me prisoner. They didn't budge.

I did a quick scan of the cell, realizing there was only a small high window with bars. No hope of escape. I paced six feet one way, then six feet the other. That's all the space I had. Then I cursed. Loudly. Which is when I heard Ginny's muffled voice.

"I gotta go on home," she called out, waving at me through the blurry window at the front of the building. "I'll tell Miss Amadahy." Then she was gone.

I resumed pacing. But it was stifling inside, even with no glass in that high cell window. I was used to air conditioning and ceiling fans. This primitive jail didn't even have electricity. God, for a drink of water, I thought and collapsed on the cot.

By the time the sheriff returned, I'd drifted off to sleep. The slant of sunlight told me it was suppertime. My stomach confirmed it. But my first priority wasn't food.

"I need water," I said.

He hung up his hat before sauntering over to a keg behind his desk and lifting the lid. He filled a tin ladle, passing it between the bars. Another communal cup, but I no longer cared. I drank every last drop and asked for more.

The second ladleful I drank more slowly, leaving some to pour into my hand, so I could wipe it over my face and neck.

"Any chance I could have something to eat?" I asked, handing the ladle back.

He pulled a small parcel from his pocket, unwrapping a hunk of bread. He handed it to me and returned to his desk.

Once I consumed the hard bread and regained a bit of strength, I begged him to set me free.

"I wasn't trying to bribe you. I just want to help Amadahy because Jonah gets meaner and meaner, and I'm worried about her safety."

He didn't bother to reply.

A short time later, he put his hat on again and started for the door.

"You're not leaving me here for the night, are you?" I cried.

"Yup."

"But at least let me use the bathroom!"

He pointed to the far corner of my cell and walked out, locking the door behind him.

Turning toward the back wall, I noticed what had once been a white bowl, rather large with a lip around the top, and now stained a muddy color. Not only was there no electricity, there was also no indoor plumbing. I remembered hearing Nana talk about using a chamber pot when she was a child and realized that's what I was looking at.

⁓

When the sun rose the next morning, I was sitting on the hard bed, propped against the wall. The air in the room had finally cooled enough so I could breathe. But real sleep had eluded me, what with the heat and the mosquitoes buzzing my ears. Another modern luxury I took completely for granted – window screens.

While I waited for the sheriff, I tried to keep my mind from focusing on the insistent hunger pangs in my belly.

When he moseyed through the front door, he greeted me like I was a guest staying at his Airbnb.

"Morning, Miz Murray. Hope you slept all right."

"Unfortunately, my roommates kept me awake."

He gave me a quizzical look.

"Mosquitoes," I said.

He snickered under his breath as he brought me the ladle.

After I chugged the water and asked for more, I got right to the point.

"When will you let me out of here?"

"Don't rightly know," he said, returning the ladle to its hook. "The judge won't be here for another two weeks."

"Two weeks!"

"He's riding the circuit."

"I can't sit here in this jail cell that long!"

"Reckon you don't have any say-so in the matter."

My hands tightened on the bars. "Sheriff Moon, I'm pretty sure you've got better things to do than deal with me."

He sat down in his chair but didn't reply.

"I'm thinking you could consider that gold nugget as payment of my fine," I said. "You know, the one you dropped in your pocket?"

He gave me a quick glance out of the corner of his eye as he opened a desk drawer.

"Wouldn't paying a fine make more sense?" I said. "Much better than taxpayers having to foot the bill to keep me locked up, don't you think?"

He pulled a piece of paper from the drawer, setting it on the desktop.

"Much better than you having to turn the gold over to that judge when he shows up."

"One thing's for sure," he said. "You talk more than any woman I ever met. Except maybe my wife."

With that, he stood and retrieved his hat.

"I'm really hungry," I said.

"Well," he said, turning as he tapped the hat onto his head, "you better hope that slave girl brings you some food."

Thankfully, Ginny arrived mid-morning, a bundle under her arm. Moments later, the sheriff returned. He let her in so she could bring me the dried fish and bread wrapped in a small piece of cloth.

"What's your name, girl?" the sheriff asked her.

"Ginny."

"Who's your master?"

"Jonah Barnes."

"Ginny, I want you to go tell Mr. Barnes there's a woman in my jail who says her name is Kathryn Murray."

"Yessir."

~22~

When I heard the scrape of heavy boots that afternoon and Jonah filled the doorway, my trip to 1840 suddenly felt like a suicide mission.

"You acquainted with this woman?" the sheriff said.

"I am."

"I arrested her for trying to bribe me."

"Bribe you?"

"She wanted me to investigate a murder."

The menace in Jonah's eyes sent a chill down my spine. While the sheriff didn't specify whose murder, it was pretty clear who he was talking about.

"She says she's kin to your wife," the sheriff said.

Causing Jonah to examine me with fresh eyes.

"Anyhow," the sheriff continued, never saying a word about the gold piece in his pocket, "I decided to let her go. Too much trouble keeping her for the judge."

He unlocked the cell door, swinging it open, and gestured for me to come out.

"Mr. Barnes can take you home to your cousin," he said.

He acted like he was doing me a favor instead of feeding me to a pit viper. He had to know he was putting me in danger, so there was no point appealing to his sense of decency. Then again, if he didn't release me to Jonah, he might not release me for who knows how long. At least this way, there was a slight chance of escape. Assuming Jonah didn't kill me first.

"Good luck, Miz Murray," the sheriff said as Jonah escorted me through the door.

As soon as we were outside, he gripped my arm more firmly, correctly assuming I'd make a break for it first chance I got. I acted like it didn't bother me, not making any effort to pull away. I have to admit when he hoisted me onto the saddle and then climbed on behind me, I found it difficult to breathe with his arms around me holding the reins. He walked the horse to the edge of town then clicked his tongue and kneed the animal's flanks, spurring him to a canter. The rocking movement, with my back against Jonah's chest, his legs rubbing against mine, made me grasp the pommel for dear life. He was trying to unnerve me and doing a first-rate job.

My mind raced ahead, hoping Amadahy or Ginny could help me escape his clutches once we got to the farm. I had a bad feeling he didn't plan to lock me up this time.

But we slowed to a walk about a mile out of town, veering off the trail and into the woods. When we came to a stream, he reined in the horse, quickly dismounting and latching onto my arm to make sure I didn't take off as soon as I slid to the ground. He gripped my right arm with one hand, leading the animal to the water so he could drink.

"Distant relative?" he said, more like an accusation than a question.

"Fifth or sixth cousin."

"You don't favor that heathen."

"That's rich, you calling her a heathen, since you're the most un-Christian man I've met in my entire life."

He tightened his grip on my arm.

"You gonna be punished for telling the sheriff I killed my own brother."

"I didn't..."

"Don't know where you got that notion, but it ain't a good thing to do, waltzing into the sheriff's office and spreading lies."

I trained my eyes on the stream beyond him, watching the horse lower his head to drink, noticing the water flowing off to the right as the ground sloped toward the river.

"Who told you that lie?" he said.

"Nobody told me anything." My voice came out a whisper.

"Then why'd you tell the sheriff I done it?"

My body stiffened, waiting for the blow that was sure to come. But he didn't strike me. Instead, he grabbed my other arm and pushed me backwards until he had me pinned against a tree. It was the first time in my life I could honestly say I would've preferred being slapped in the face rather than what he had in mind.

"Let me go!"

"Been thinking about this for a while now."

His foul breath made me want to gag. But it wasn't his breath I was most concerned about as he pressed his body against mine, reaching down to hike my skirt up.

"Stop!" I screamed.

I thought of the little can of pepper spray in my right pocket but couldn't free my hand to reach for it. Then I remembered a story we'd done at the station on self-defense for women. I bent my knees and pulled myself downward. To keep his hold on me, he had to lower himself as well. I scraped my back as I slid down the rough bark, lowering myself bit by bit. He tightened his grip on my left arm and put his other hand between my legs.

"At least, let's do it lying down, not standing up!" I begged.

He yanked me away from the tree, shoving me onto the ground near the stream, then unhitched his suspenders and unfastened his pants. I scrabbled in the brown leaves and pine straw, pushing myself toward the water, my hands searching for anything to use as a weapon. Then he placed his feet on either side of me, his trademark sneer spreading across his face.

I yanked my legs up and using every ounce of my strength, kicked with both feet as hard as I could, planting them on his left kneecap. There was a slight cracking sound and he tumbled on top of me, growling like a wounded bear. Groping about on the ground, my hand finally latched onto a stick. I used it to stab him repeatedly about the shoulders and head, struggling to shove him off.

"Goddammit!" He scrambled to deflect the blows with one hand as he fought to hold onto me with the other.

I stabbed him hard on his neck and rammed my knee in his crotch with as much force as I could muster, wishing I could reach my Mace. He was enraged and hurting. I managed to push him halfway off, struggling to extract myself from beneath him. He grabbed my neck but his grip didn't have its usual strength. I yanked my knees up to my chest, levering his body away from mine. Using the point of the stick, I speared the side of his head.

He roared in agony, putting his hand to the oozing blood – my chance to make my break.

I clambered up, rushing toward the horse, which had wandered further upstream. But he shied away, trotting off into the woods. Even though Jonah was injured, I knew I was still in grave danger. As he staggered toward me, I fumbled in the large pocket of my skirt, wrapping my fingers around the can of pepper spray. He limped closer, blood trickling down the side of his head. In his hand was the same knife he'd use to prick Ginny's neck. I was shaking as I held the little can in front of me. It took all my nerve to wait, but I steadied myself, my pulse racing. I realized at the last second that I didn't know which way the wind was blowing – whether I was upwind or downwind. Not good, since I could easily incapacitate myself instead of him.

When he was a few feet from me, I pulled the trigger, aiming at his face, continuing to spray and spray and spray as he faltered. The knife fell to the ground as his right hand went to his eyes. He moaned, his other hand flailing in the air, trying to find me in his blindness.

My eyes stung as some of the spray floated toward me. Which was my cue to make tracks.

With the horse playing hard to get, I took off for the river, following the stream. I had bought myself some time, but I had no idea how much. I knew different people reacted differently to Mace. It took some people a couple of hours to be able to see again. Others, only fifteen minutes. Depended on how much got in their eyes and how strong the pepper spray was. If I hadn't wanted him to catch me before, I really didn't want him to get his hands on me now.

Dodging rocks and squeezing through the underbrush, I lurched down the slope so fast, I tripped and fell, landing hard on my knees. I looked frantically behind me. Nothing yet. I pulled myself to my feet and continued on my way.

It was much farther to the river than I'd hoped and I was tiring. If I didn't reach it soon, there was a very real chance he would overtake me. A combination of terror and dehydration made it hard to swallow.

I needed to put some distance between myself and the little stream. That's where he would look when he could see again. Even if I'd succeeded in breaking his knee, I had no doubt he'd hoist himself into the saddle and give chase. So I swerved off to the right, far enough so I could still see the creek but he might not see me before I heard him coming.

Minutes later, as I finally detected the smell of the river and heard the distant sound of water flowing, I also heard a noise behind me that made the hairs on my neck stand up. I hunched over, keeping low, trying to maintain my speed. The footing was becoming more challenging and I stumbled and nearly fell again, but managed to right myself.

Definitely hoofbeats behind me. I clawed my way through a thicket of blackberry bushes, the thorns scratching my arms and body. I had to get to the river! But I realized the hoofbeats had slowed, which meant Jonah could probably hear me thrashing through the bushes. I stopped, squatting close to the ground and tried to slow my breathing.

There was a whinny as the horse moved in my direction. If he found me, I wouldn't stand a chance.

I got to my feet again, staying low as I moved toward my right, trying to bypass the thicket so I'd have an easier path. Then I stepped on a fallen branch.

He must've heard the sound because he moved forward quickly, apparently trying to get between me and the river.

"Come on out," he called.

What were my odds if I hauled ass to the river, trying to zigzag so he might not catch me? Not good. Not good at all. But I had to do something. Slowly, I stood up.

When our eyes met, I knew he was going to kill me. But I was pretty sure he would want payback and would make me suffer first. I gripped the empty Mace can tight in my hand, thinking I might be able to throw it at him, if nothing else. He withdrew his knife from his waistband.

It was obvious his eyes stung. He kept squinting and sniffing. Blood was smeared along the side of his face. If he had to dismount, I was pretty sure he wouldn't be able to chase me down after what I'd done to his knee. But he might be able to throw that knife in my back.

As long as he was in the saddle, he was in charge. I needed to level the playing field.

Little by little, I emerged from my hiding place until there was nothing between us. He was about fifteen feet from me, sitting on his high horse, quite literally, and seething. I edged forward, my face toward the ground, but my eyes looking beyond him toward the river, which was close enough to see between the trees.

"Now that it don't make no difference," he said, "I'll tell you a secret. I did kill Isham. How'd you know?"

"I didn't," I lied, taking another half step closer. "I figured that's what happened, you being the sadistic asshole that you are."

He chuckled, but pain lined his face.

"Why'd you do it?" I said.

"Didn't have no money. Lost my horse in a poker game. Needed me a farm. Wasn't never gonna get one no other way."

"And that's the reason you married Amadahy – in case the judge might let her keep it."

He gave a slight shrug.

"Plus," I said, "you probably realized no woman in her right mind would accept you voluntarily, you being a foul-smelling, depraved excuse for a man."

He rotated the knife, holding the blade instead of the handle. A throwing grip. My time was up.

"If you kill me too, the sheriff might ask questions." I took another baby step forward, hiding my hand in the folds of my skirt as I adjusted my grip on the small can, realizing there was a good chance I was about to die.

"Nah. I'll tell him you went back home. Nobody'll miss you round these parts."

I had gradually moved forward, positioning myself about ten feet from the horse's muzzle.

And that's when all hell broke loose. As Jonah cocked his hand back, I lunged forward, screaming like a banshee as I raised the Mace in front of me. I squeezed the trigger, hoping there was something left in the tiny can. The combination of the spray hitting the horse in the muzzle and my screeching caused the poor animal to rear. Jonah struggled to hang on, but was thrown to the ground, landing in a heap.

I rushed for the river, making a running dive when I reached the bank. Holding my breath as the current swept me downstream, I barely dodged a large rock and tumbled down a series of small rapids. The river saved me last time I ran from Jonah, but this was obviously not the same section of river, the current churning along at a much faster pace. I hoped it wouldn't do me in this time.

At the bottom of the rapids, I plunged into a deep blue pool that whirled in a circular motion, dragging me down, my legs tangled in my long skirt. I kicked and paddled furiously, jabbing pains killing my injured shoulder, desperate for a breath of air. Not fair that I managed to escape from that monster, only to drown in the river!

With my right arm about to give out, I finally broke the surface just in time for the surging water to dump me into yet another eddy. But, thank God, this one turned out to be a calmer stretch. Exhausted, I aimed for the bank, barely able to swim. When, at last, I made it to shore, I dragged myself onto the muddy bank.

Crawling on all fours till I reached a patch of weeds, I collapsed on my back, chest heaving. For a moment, I let myself feel victorious that I was alive, having survived Jonah's attack and the wild ride downriver. It was a fleeting moment.

The peaceful blue sky above me made me wish I could close my eyes and sleep. But there was too much at stake. Jonah's body might be battered, but that would only make him more vicious. It wasn't just my life hanging in the balance. There was Amadahy, Ginny and little Betsey. And there was even Jonah's life to consider.

Feeling an obligation to protect him galled me. But what was I supposed to do? Ginny was right – he was Satan's seed. Amadahy was right – he was the Bad Brother. It was maddening that he should be protected! Especially if I was the one doing the protecting.

Was I supposed to take Degataga aside and explain that future generations depended on him letting Jonah live? That I, myself, was one of the descendants who would never be born if he carried out his threat? Right. I could picture the skepticism on his face. And if he didn't believe me, deciding I was a crazy white woman poking her nose in where it didn't belong, then what? Was I supposed to take Degataga out of the equation? No way I could ever hurt the man who loved Amadahy. It made me want to scream.

Thankfully, the only noise I made was inside my head. Because there were voices nearby. I lay still, trying to determine which direction they were coming from. Holding my breath, I realized it was two men talking, their voices coming from the river.

Were they searching for me? It was hard to believe Jonah could've climbed back on his horse, ridden somewhere to meet up with someone and launched a boat in such a short time. Still, I couldn't help but fear it might be him and his low-life friend, Johnny.

I crawled a few feet further into the woods, then got to my feet, crouching as I moved away from the water. If I followed the gradual incline of the land, I should eventually come to the road. Staying hidden in the trees, I could follow the road back to Amadahy's house and... well, I wasn't exactly sure how things would play out, but I knew that's where I had to go.

Sprinting through the trees as I listened for voices behind me, I didn't hear what was in front of me until it was too late – a full-grown black bear.

It stood on its hind legs, its brown eyes trained on me. My mind went into overdrive, trying to retrieve information. July. Mating season. Shy animals that won't mess with you if you don't mess with them, according to the wildlife management people my TV station interviewed when black bears were sighted in the Atlanta suburbs. That didn't calm me one bit.

"Nice bear," I whispered as I backed away.

It gaped at me like I was the interloper. Which was true. I retreated a little further, then ran toward the river with my heart in my throat. I was running so fast, I didn't see the two men until I was right on them.

They carried a wooden fishing boat above their heads, which they immediately lowered to the ground. The man I'd nearly crashed into took a threatening step toward me, a deep scowl on his face.

"Who're you?" he barked.

He was a beefy white man in overalls, wearing a farmer's hat with a fishing basket hanging from his shoulder.

Before I could answer, the other man who'd been carrying the rear of the boat stepped forward. It was Mr. Berryman, the man Ginny and I met on our way to town. He didn't look as friendly now.

"The question," Mr. Berryman said, "is what're you doing on my land?"

Suspicion was plain in his eyes. I realized I must look a fright. My skirt and blouse were drenched and torn, my hair was plastered to my neck, my arms were scratched, and I was pretty sure my face was too. Panic and exhaustion must've been plain by the way I trembled.

"I... I fell into the river," I said.

Mr. Berryman examined me more closely.

"This way," he said, heading into the woods, the other man behind me, leaving the boat on the riverbank.

"I saw a black bear a moment ago," I said.

They seemed unconcerned, not bothering to reply.

It took about twenty minutes for us to emerge from the trees into a green pasture surrounded by a primitive rail fence. A dozen cows grazed in the distance. Mr. Berryman helped me climb over the rails and we made our way to an unpainted wooden home.

"Mind your step," he said, pointing to a cowpie.

As we neared the house, I recognized a smell that reminded me of the pot roast Nana used to cook. Children's voices greeted us as we walked into the yard, two little boys calling out "Pa!" as they ran to their father.

"Who's she?" the little one said, giving me a curious look.

"That's the lady we saw on the road," the other boy said.

"Run along," Mr. Berryman said, ruffling their hair as he led the way to the kitchen.

Mrs. Berryman stood in front of a large fireplace, using a long spoon to stir something in a black pot hanging above the flames. Her long brown hair was pulled into a large bun at the nape of her neck. She turned, wiping her forehead with the back of her hand, a jolt of surprise transforming her face.

"Miz Murray!" she cried, setting the spoon down on a big wooden table in the center of the room. "Good Lord! What happened to you?"

I don't know why, exactly, but her reaction made tears well up. I didn't dare open my mouth. I knew I'd cry.

"She says she fell in the river," Mr. Berryman said, doubt coloring his voice.

She shooed her husband and his buddy outside, telling them she'd call them when supper was ready.

"What in God's name happened?" she said, her voice soft and her forehead pinched as she led me to the table. "Rest yourself."

She took a rag, dipped it in a bucket near the fireplace and blotted my face.

"Can you talk?" she said, filling a gourd with water.

She handed it to me and waited patiently as I drank.

"If Isham was your cousin," I said, "then Jonah is your cousin too."

"No. Isham's mama and my mama were sisters. Jonah had a different mother. When she died, his daddy married my Aunt Betsey."

Yes, I remembered Amadahy's daughter was named for Isham's mother.

"Believe you need some vittles," she said.

She called her two daughters to help set the food out. There was a flurry of activity as they arranged utensils and cups of water on the table. Mrs. Berryman scooped meat and potatoes onto tin plates, which the girls dutifully served. Then she slid a round loaf of cornbread from a skillet onto another plate and placed it in the center, telling her daughters to call the family.

The two girls and one of the boys sat beside me on one bench. The other son took a seat on the opposite bench between his mother and the man who'd come with us from the river. Mr. Berryman sat in the only chair at the head of the table.

I was about to pick up my fork when they bowed their heads for Mr. Berryman to say grace. Only when he was finished did we begin eating.

Noticeably absent were any introductions. The Berrymans never told me their friend's name, nor he, mine, and they didn't explain to the children who I was. The two men talked about fishing spots they frequented downstream, the children remained quiet and Mrs. Berryman asked the men if they wanted seconds. They did, and she served.

Once we finished eating, she directed the girls to scrape the few leavings into the slop bucket for the pigs and to wash the dishes in a tub outside.

When we were alone again, she sat across from me.

"Sometimes it's good to share your burden," she said.

Could I trust her? Even if I did, there was nothing she could do to help me.

"Did Jonah hurt you?" she said.

The more I thought about it, the more I decided she might make things worse if she tried to intervene. If worse was even a possibility.

"There was a misunderstanding," I said.

She considered my reply. "Are you sure?"

"Yes. I really appreciate your kindness. And the food. But I need to be going now. I feel much stronger."

I smoothed my damp skirt.

"You don't look strong. I'll get Eli to hitch the wagon."

"No!" My voice sounded panicked so I toned it down before continuing. "Thanks for the offer but it would be better if I walked."

Concern was written all over her face as I stood to go.

"It's good to know there are kind people like you in this place." I almost said "in this time," but realized how weird it would sound.

"Wait!" She hurried across the room to the hearth, returning with a small knife. "Take this!"

"Why would I..."

"I saw Martha Wheeler in town last week," she explained. "She told me her slave Ginny, who now belongs to Mr. Barnes, says he beats his poor crippled wife. And I have a notion you're not telling me everything."

"Wouldn't do for me to have a knife. I can't even slice a tomato. But, thank you."

At the door, I turned to face her again.

"It would be better if Jonah didn't know I was here," I said.

It was clear from her expression she knew that already.

The sun was setting by the time I reached the road. While I didn't relish the idea of being on the move by myself in the dark, I couldn't put Mrs. Berryman and her family at risk. So I trudged along among the trees parallel to the wagon ruts, keeping about twenty paces from the trail in case someone suddenly appeared around a bend. I also kept my eyes peeled and my ears open for the bear.

As the light dimmed, I found it more difficult to navigate the woods as underbrush caught my skirt, roots and fallen branches causing me to stumble. When it was full dark, I moved onto the road, finishing the last half mile with the moon and stars my only source of light. Nighttime out in the country in 1840 was darker than anything I'd ever experienced in my own time.

The turnoff to the Barnes' farmstead was marked by a massive oak tree. During the day, you could cool off beneath its broad branches. I sat with my back against the enormous trunk considering my options. Deciding this was as good a place as any to sleep, I scooted around to the back side of the tree and curled up on the ground, ordering myself to wake up before dawn.

Using my good arm as a pillow, I scanned the darkness surrounding me, thinking of Eric. The wedding was this evening. He would still be celebrating in Savannah, toasting his sister and her new husband. I missed him. A lot. What if I never saw him again? What if I never felt his arms around me again? God, I couldn't dwell on that right now.

It took a while, but exhaustion eventually won out, a chorus of crickets gradually lulling me to sleep.

I was awakened by a cacophony of shrieks and whistles. I couldn't imagine how so many boisterous birds got into my apartment. Pixie must be going nuts trying to catch them. Then my eyes opened and I remembered where I was.

Dawn was breaking. I rubbed my eyes, listening to the birds above me sending messages to each other.

I stretched my sore body before heading cautiously down the trail toward the river. In the dim light, the shadows were so deep, I felt as though I disappeared inside them.

All was quiet when I arrived. Easing into the trees near the garden, I took one step, then paused and listened before taking another. The sky lightened a bit as I tip-toed to a large pine with bushes hugging its trunk. This would be my hiding place.

Once ensconced, the birds nearby resumed their concert, the beauty of their songs at odds with the ugliness that hung like a suffocating blanket over the little farm.

At the same moment I caught a glimpse of a bright red cardinal perched on a low branch, I heard a small crunching noise behind me like someone stepping on a twig. Twisting in slow motion, I spied a black bear not twenty feet away. I felt around on the ground for something to throw, resisting the instinct to let loose with a scream that would announce my arrival. Before I could take any action, a large hand clamped over my mouth, accompanied by a man's voice whispering in my ear.

"The danger comes from man, not beast."

His voice was calm, but strong. It exuded the confidence of a man at home in the wilderness. His speech pattern reminded me of Amadahy. My body stilled as the bear ambled away.

"My people believe the black bear is a spirit guide," he said.

He lifted his hand from my mouth and moved away so I could see him.

"I am called Standing Together."

"Degataga," I whispered, causing a momentary look of surprise to cross his face.

My mental image from Amadahy's description didn't do justice to the man crouching before me. His face was striking, with strong lines and penetrating eyes. His thick black hair hung on his shoulders. And, although he was dressed in regular pants and shirt, it was obvious he was nothing like the men I'd seen in town.

"You are the white woman from faraway. Do you bring strong medicine?"

"I don't have any medicine, strong or otherwise."

"Why do you travel here?"

"I want to help Amadahy, but I can't figure out how."

"Why on this day of the Ripe Corn Moon?" He gestured toward the farmhouse and my hiding place.

"I came, hoping to save Jonah's life."

His friendly countenance vanished, replaced by suspicion.

"Not that I think he's worth saving, mind you," I said. "But he's my great-great-great-great-great-grandfather."

His eyes widened then.

"I come here from the future," I explained.

If I'd said that to a white man of this time, he would've concluded I was out of my mind. Not Degataga. He peered deeply into my eyes as though searching for the truth, recalling whatever Amadahy had told him, evaluating the possibilities through the lens of a Cherokee man of the early nineteenth century. If there was one thing I'd learned, it's that the Cherokees of this time held onto their traditional beliefs even while working hard to adapt to the white man's ways as a means of self-preservation.

At length, he lifted his chin, looking down his nose at me. "You wish to save yourself."

"And many others. Amadahy and Jonah are destined to have three children together. And those three children have many offspring, including me."

A steely look hardened his features. "I no longer believe in destiny."

The crowing of a rooster drew our attention to the house. We watched Amadahy emerge, the baby strapped to her back and a bucket in each hand. She walked to the river where she filled the buckets, then changed and washed Betsey. She stopped on the way back to feed the chickens, then returned to the house.

As soon as she went inside, Jonah's unmistakable voice shattered the quiet of the early morning.

"Goddammit, I'm sleeping!"

She hurried out, Betsey still on her back, Ginny behind her. They moved to the far side of the house where we couldn't see them. Within minutes we saw smoke rising from the outdoor cooking fire. A short time later the smell of cornbread filled the morning air.

So close beside me, Degataga startled me with an insistent croaking noise. He paused, then croaked louder.

Before long, Amadahy meandered toward us, the baby no longer strapped to her back. She squatted at the edge of the garden. I could tell by the tension in her body that she was listening.

Degataga croaked again and she moved in our direction.

When she was near enough, he spoke softly in their language. She responded, also in Cherokee. Then she spoke in English.

"Degataga tells me you are here, Kathryn." It was the first time she'd called me by name. "Bad Brother says he will kill you."

"As much as that terrifies me," I said, "I also fear Degataga will keep his word and kill Jonah."

She looked toward the house.

"The thing is," I continued, "if he kills Jonah, terrible things will happen. I know he's a hateful man. And I know when I first came, I tried to convince you to leave him. But now I've learned more about who he is. And if you leave him, or Degataga kills him, Jonah's children will never be born. And his children's children. And his children's children's children."

"That is the natural way."

"Yes, but do you have any idea who I am?"

She pulled an ear of corn from the stalk beside her.

"I'm one of your descendants," I said. "You're my great-great-great-great-great-grandmother. And Jonah is my fifth great-grandfather."

She listened intently as I continued.

"Jonah is supposed to have three children with you. And they all have children, and so on down the line, all the way to my generation. Which is really awful, I know. It makes me sick that you have to tolerate his cruelty. And I cringe at the thought of being related to him."

"I would not have children with Bad Brother," she said.

"I understand you wouldn't want to."

She picked another ear of corn.

"Sometimes I wish I'd never discovered the time portal," I said. "Because now I really care about you as a person. I don't want you to suffer. I don't want Betsey to suffer. I don't want your future children to suffer."

I closed my eyes, wishing there was some kind of magic to un-do what had already happened. Including Isham's death.

Degataga said something in Cherokee and she replied, an obvious strain in her voice.

But they were interrupted by a scream. As one, we turned to see flames engulfing the hut. Ginny bounded through the door, Betsey in her arms, running right into Jonah, who stood in her way with a torch in his hand. He pitched the torch onto the hut's thatched roof and grabbed hold of Ginny. She screamed again and the baby cried out in fear.

Degataga leapt to his feet and raced toward them, pulling a knife from the sheath at his waist. I dashed after him, Amadahy bringing up the rear.

"Don't come any closer, Injun!" Jonah bellowed, pulling his own knife and holding it to Ginny's throat.

The three of us came to a halt in the yard, causing Betsey to stretch her arms out for her mother. Ginny's eyes were filled with desperation as Jonah dragged her to the front of the house and through the door. He was barely able to walk with his injured knee.

"You better get your crooked self in here right now, squaw!" he shouted.

Degataga spoke urgently to Amadahy in Cherokee as she hurried away. She replied in their language, her tone sharp.

There was a sudden loud thud as though something had landed against the wall.

Degataga set his jaw, training his eyes on Amadahy who walked as fast as she could, swaying with every step.

As she disappeared inside, there was another crash.

"You're the reason I'm laid up!" he yelled. "That woman claims she's your kin! She's gonna pay for what she done to me. She like to broke my goddam knee! All 'cause a you, you heathen!"

There was a sudden noise followed by a woman's scream. Then the baby screeched in terror.

Degataga barreled toward the house, me right behind him.

Half of me wanted him to stab Jonah to death. The other half was terrified at what would happen if he did.

~24~

Degataga came to an abrupt halt at the door, causing me to plow into him. Inside, I could see Jonah standing by the bed, Amadahy sprawled on the floor in front of him, blood on the sleeve of her dress. When Jonah saw us, he tightened his grip on Ginny, the squalling baby still in her arms. Blood dripped from the blade of his knife as he held it to Ginny's throat.

"You tell your Injun cousin this ain't none a his business," Jonah barked at Amadahy. "If he don't hightail it outta here right now, I'm gonna do a lot more than cut a gash in someone's arm."

"Please let Ginny and Betsey go," she said, slowly pulling herself to a sitting position, pressing her hand over her wounded arm. "I will stand with you."

"I'm done with you, squaw," he said. "Gonna find me a white woman who'll be nice to me and give me sons."

"My cousin can take my baby and me away from the farm to make room for your new wife," she replied, her voice amazingly calm under the circumstances.

"Believe I'll turn you in for a reward." He gave her a cocky look, watching her struggle to her feet. "I hear tell the government's still looking for Cherokees to march 'em west."

Betsey's wailing grew even louder.

"I'm sick of that screaming baby! Make her shut up!"

Amadahy spoke softly to her daughter in Cherokee as she had done many times before. After a moment, the crying turned to whimpering, Betsey eyeing her mother longingly.

"Now tie Miz Murray up," he commanded. "On the bed. And tell your cousin to put that goddam knife away and get off my land!"

Amadahy looked hard at Degataga as she said something in their language.

"Mr. Barnes," I said, "please…"

"I got a score to settle with you," he butted in, glaring at me.

The thought of him touching me made me weak, especially considering the knife in his hand. I forced myself to step around Degataga and into the house. Amadahy reached into a trunk at the foot of the bed and withdrew a piece of cloth, quickly ripping it into strips. Jonah gestured for me to lie down on the lumpy mattress so she could tie my wrists to the headrail.

"Her feet too!" he snapped.

She followed his instructions, tying my ankles to the railing at the foot of the bed.

With her back turned to Jonah, she widened her eyes at me, trying to send me a message. A message I couldn't decipher.

Jonah checked my wrists and ankles to make sure I was bound securely before turning his attention to Degataga.

"Move out into the yard so I can see you through the door. Understand?"

Jonah looked at Amadahy, indicating she should translate.

She said something to Degataga in their language and he slowly backed out the door.

"You next," Jonah said, jutting his ragged whiskers in her direction.

Once they were both outside, he dragged Ginny and the baby backwards to the corner where his musket leaned against the wall. In an instant, he released her, tucked the knife in his waistband and swung the big gun up in front of him so it was aimed directly at her. Then he cocked it and smiled.

He motioned with the barrel for Ginny to join the others. She held the baby close, kissing her cheek as she followed them, Jonah hobbling along behind her.

Lying there shackled to the bed, I tried to tamp down the panic spreading through my bloodstream. It didn't work. Especially with the air in the house turning hazy. Twisting around, I could see smoke seeping in along the back wall. I yanked my arms and kicked my legs in a vain effort to free myself.

I felt like I'd been zipped up in a down-filled parka on the hottest day of the year. And now I was coughing from the smoke. Not only did I have to free myself to avoid whatever

Jonah planned to do to me, I also had to get out of here before the house caught fire. Not to mention, trying to stop him from killing someone with that long rifle of his.

What message had Amadahy tried to send me with her eyes? What was she trying to tell me? I swiveled slightly, struggling to see my wrists, then lifted my head to check my feet. The strips of cloth binding me to the bed were the color of wheat but I had no way of knowing what kind of material it was. I renewed my yanking and pulling, to no avail.

It must be the fabric itself, I thought. I used my fingers to investigate. The fabric wasn't as thick as it looked and the edges were frayed. I pulled threads along the margins. After a few seconds, I succeeded in unraveling several threads. That had to be it. Amadahy's unspoken message.

I clawed and pulled until the strip of cloth was narrower than when I started. I tore at the fibers, separating them from the fabric, deconstructing it bit by bit.

As I continued my painstaking task, there was more shouting. They had moved to the side of the house and I couldn't hear the words, but Jonah's voice was filled with bile. Time was running out. I worked my fingers as fast as I could. Finally, finally, I felt the cloth give. Yanking my arms as hard as I could, I tore it in two, sending a jolt of pain through my right shoulder. I hissed, trying not to cry out as I sat up and untied my ankles.

Hurrying to the door, I listened intently.

"Are you deaf? I said drop your knife, Injun! If he don't understand me, squaw, you better translate right quick before I blow him to kingdom come!"

Amadahy spoke in Cherokee. Degataga replied. Were they waiting for me to do something? To distract Jonah so Degataga might overpower him?

"I can shoot that little crybaby too! So you better do like I say!"

I edged out the door and along the front wall, peeking around the corner just as Degataga tossed his knife on the ground.

"Bring it here!" Jonah barked.

Amadahy strained to bend down and pick up the blade, dropping it several feet in front of him. Then she returned to Degataga's side, holding her bloody arm.

"I know he ain't your cousin," Jonah sneered.

He shoved Ginny away from him, causing her to stumble and fall to her knees. Betsey slipped from her arms and landed on the ground, which prompted a new wave of crying. As Amadahy took a step toward her baby, Jonah pointed his musket directly at Degataga, his finger moving to the trigger.

"No!" I screamed, rushing from my hiding place.

Jonah looked in my direction, but a crashing noise drew everyone's attention to the hut. The thatched roof had already been incinerated and now we watched as the walls collapsed outward. As they pancaked onto the ground, Nana materialized from the smoke like a magician performing an illusion, squinting in the morning sunshine. A second later Mallory appeared behind her, mouth agape.

Nana stepped over the burning planks, glancing at them as though mildly interested in what caused the mess. She hurried forward, a quart jar in each hand.

"I brought you some fig preserves!" she called out, holding the jars up as she smiled at Amadahy. "My daughter helped me pick them when she was here and my friend Jeannette helped me cook them."

"Get off my property, old hag!" Jonah screamed, his face contorted with rage. "You got till the count of three. And if you ain't gone..."

"There's no call to be rude, young man," Nana said, advancing toward us, seemingly unaware of the danger.

"Nana!" I cried.

She looked from me to Amadahy to Degataga to Ginny and the baby, then briefly focused on Jonah, dried blood visible on the side of his head, his rifle aimed at Degataga's chest.

"I only want to give my lovely neighbor these fig preserves," she said, giving him a friendly nod. "I used my grandmother's recipe. Which means I put extra sugar in them. I think you'll like them."

"Nana," I said, stepping forward.

Jonah tightened his grip on the gun. He was about to pull the trigger. No more thinking about what all this would mean for the future.

Darting forward, I flung myself between Jonah and Degataga as a deafening gunshot echoed through the air. At that very instant, Nana did the same thing from the opposite side. We crashed into each other and fell in a tangle, Nana still clutching the fig jars.

I thought Jonah would continue firing, but he heaved the musket at his adversary as Degataga rushed him. The weapon ricocheted off his body and fell to the ground. With lightning speed, Degataga retrieved his knife from the dirt while Jonah pulled his own from his waistband. So haughty a moment before, he now had no human shield, no rifle to protect him. He backed away, his knee injury from our fight the day before taking its toll. Then he cocked his arm, preparing to throw his blade. But before he could release it, Degataga dived at his enemy, knocking the weapon from his hand. Then he plunged his knife deep into Jonah's belly.

Shock filled Jonah's eyes as he dropped to his knees. Shock was replaced by a look of agony as he teetered and fell in slow motion, face down on the ground.

"Shit," Mallory mumbled.

There was a flurry of activity as Amadahy rushed to lift Betsey from the ground, Ginny hurried to collect Jonah's rifle and knife, and Degataga checked to see that Jonah was dead.

I turned my attention to Nana, easing her off of me, gently laying her down as she relaxed her grip on the jars. I was confused, seeing blood on both of us. But I felt no pain.

She smiled up at me, her glasses slightly askew.

"I saved them from that monster," she said. "Who is that young man?"

"That's Degataga, the man Amadahy, I mean, Forest Water..." but I choked up, realizing she'd taken the bullet – that she'd thrown herself between Jonah and me as I rushed forward.

"The man she loves," she said. "I'm so happy."

Scanning her body, I discovered the side of her blue shirt soaked with blood.

"Oh, Nana!" I whispered.

Tears overflowed as I fought to keep a sob from rising in my throat.

"Don't cry, sweetie." She spoke haltingly, her voice as thin as a blade of grass. "My grandpa was bedridden and senile – that's what we used to call it. I don't want to follow in his footsteps… but I've felt it coming." She coughed and I heard a gurgle in her throat.

"We need to get you to a hospital," I said, noticing the sudden pallor of her skin. "But there aren't any figs on…"

"This is how I want to go. Like a gutsy old woman. Saving my Cherokee neighbor." She winced, her eyes fluttering. "Wait till I tell Bob."

There was an obvious crackling in her throat as she breathed. Some long-forgotten memory told me that's what people used to call the death rattle.

Amadahy knelt beside us, her daughter in her arms.

"Thank you, Old Grandmother," she said, laying her hand on Nana's cheek. "You showed great courage."

Nana looked from Amadahy to Betsey, contentment obvious on her wrinkled face.

I kissed her forehead and held her hand. "I love you, Nana."

"I love you too," she whispered, so soft, I could barely hear the words.

A blissful smile spread across her face as she gazed into my eyes. And then her eyes focused somewhere beyond me. Somewhere far beyond me.

My body was racked with sobs as I held her in my arms. My wonderful Nana was gone.

I cradled her body, rocking slowly to and fro, tears rolling down my cheeks as I tried to process all that had happened.

Not only did she save Degataga and Amadahy, she also saved me. Which weighed me down with guilt. Then again, she was overjoyed that she'd died doing something meaningful. My emotions were so conflicted.

Hearing another familiar voice, I looked up to see Eric trotting toward me, the terrible scene reflected in his expression. He dropped to his knees beside me, wrapping his arm around my shoulder. Taking one look at Nana's vacant stare, he reached across me and with great tenderness removed her glasses and closed her eyes as I continued to cradle her in my arms.

"Are you wounded?" he whispered, noticing blood on my blouse.

Unable to speak, I shook my head.

Gradually, I became aware that Amadahy and Degataga were talking quietly. At length, she addressed the group.

"We must bury the dead without delay." Then she turned to Ginny. "The knife and gun should be wiped clean."

Degataga took hold of Jonah's ankles and dragged him to the front of the house, leaving a blood stain on the ground. Ginny carried Jonah's weapons to the river. With the baby still on her hip, Amadahy crossed the yard to the edge of the garden, retrieving her spade. She set Betsey on the ground and dug into the stained soil where Jonah died, turning the dirt over so the blood was no longer visible. When she was satisfied, she picked up her daughter and came to stand before me, looking down with sorrow in her eyes.

"I did not know Old Grandmother would give her life for my family. She had strong medicine. Let it be said that she was a Beloved Woman of the Aniyunwiya."

"There's no way to take her home," I said, speaking through my tears. "Even if there were figs, she can't..." and I faltered.

Amadahy considered that. "It is fitting that Old Grandmother be laid to rest in my family burial ground."

Eric followed her directions, carrying Nana's body to the river while Amadahy ducked into the house. As he lay the body on the riverbank, we saw Degataga ride away, Jonah's corpse draped over the horse behind him, covered by a blanket. The musket and a shovel were tucked into the saddle.

Ginny followed Amadahy to the river, carrying Betsey, Mallory trailing behind like a lost child.

Amadahy took a moment to wash the knife wound in her arm – the last abuse Jonah would ever inflict on her – then wrap it in a strip of clean cloth. Then she turned her attention to undressing my grandmother.

Eric asked for Mallory's assistance hauling water to wet the back of the house to make sure no sparks would smolder.

We laid Nana on a blanket, then Amadahy lovingly washed her body. I helped dress her in a shift she'd brought from the house. I finger-combed Nana's hair into place, surprised at how natural the whole process felt.

A short time later, Degataga returned, having completed his unpleasant task. He made quick work of constructing a drag sled, letting the horse drink from the river as he worked. Then he attached it to the saddle and Eric helped him lift Nana's body onto the cross-hatched branches between the poles.

Degataga hoisted Amadahy onto the saddle. He walked on one side of the horse while I walked on the other as we headed off through the woods, leaving the others behind.

The burial ground was a quiet place, secluded by several large boulders and a row of tall pines and shorter scrub oaks.

Degataga dug the grave while Amadahy meticulously wrapped the blanket around Nana's body, creating a burial shroud. Then, holding the ends of the blanket, we lifted her from the litter and lowered her into the ground, careful to position her facing west toward the Darkening Land.

Once we finished piling a mound of rocks atop the grave, Amadahy lifted her voice in song. I sensed the sadness even though I didn't understand the words. It was a song of lamentation, half chanting, half singing. I closed my eyes, swaying to the doleful tune, and thought of Nana, remembering her love, remembering her cheerful voice, remembering her laugh.

When Amadahy finished, it was so quiet, I was acutely aware of birds singing their own song above us. There was a rustling of leaves as a light breeze whispered through the branches, lifting my hair, cooling my skin. I looked around me, trying to memorize that peaceful scene.

On our way back to the homestead, Degataga played his flute as we walked beside Amadahy on the horse, the melancholy notes resonating deep within me.

As soon as we arrived at the farm, Amadahy led me to the river. Holding hands, we waded fully clothed into the current.

"It is Cherokee custom," she said, referring to the ritual we performed.

Remembering her narrative after Isham's death, I followed her lead as we submerged our bodies in the water seven times, each time, facing east, then west, calling out Nana's name. Edie, Edie, Edie. Edie. Edie. Edie. Edie.

Nana would be honored to know we performed the traditional funeral rites for her – she, who always believed she was part Cherokee.

Degataga held Amadahy's hand as she stepped from the water, pulling her gently into his arms. I averted my gaze, focusing instead on the high wispy clouds that streaked the blue sky, reminding me of Nana's soft white hair. With the current flowing around me and the sun warming my face, my burden of grief and sorrow eased enough so I could breathe normally again.

But once I approached the house, it hit me. Not only was I stuck in the past. Now Eric and Mallory were trapped too.

25

Eric had been caring, yet respectful, allowing me space to grieve and bury my grandmother. When we reached the stoop, he held me close.

Upon entering the house, Ginny jumped up, handing blankets to Amadahy and me to wrap ourselves in, our dresses still soaked from the funeral ritual. Then she placed three tin plates on the table, motioning for us to sit down and eat. It was a simple meal – cold cornbread filled with beans.

Giving us time to put some food in our stomachs first, Eric broke the silence from his spot beside me.

"We wet the back of the house to make sure there weren't any hot embers. And we poured buckets of water on what's left of the hut. Which isn't much. But at least the fire is out."

Degataga gave him a nod of thanks before Eric continued.

"But we discovered a rather significant problem. The fig bush was burned to a crisp along with the hut."

"The bush is dead?" I whispered.

"It will grow back one day," Amadahy said.

"But how long will that take?"

"Two or three years. Longer until it once again produces fruit."

"What's the big deal about that particular fig bush?" Mallory asked. "I saw some others out there."

"That is the only one with going back magic," Amadahy explained.

I pushed my plate away.

"You know, I didn't believe Eric when he told me we'd time traveled," Mallory said. "While you were gone, I actually walked all the way up the hill looking for your grandmother's cottage and my car before I was convinced. And as fascinating as it is sitting around the table together in the past, I seriously need to get out of here. Now you tell me the time travel thing only works when you eat figs from one special bush that no longer exists?"

"That's the gist of it," Eric replied.

"You mean we're stuck here?" she said, jumping up and pacing about the room like a caged animal.

"There were no ripe figs on the bush anyway," I said. "That's why I was trapped here waiting for a second crop." Which caused Ginny to avert her eyes.

Lord, what would become of us? We were all so ignorant. No skills we could use in this era. Even Eric, with his PhD, might find it hard to survive. He couldn't prove he had a doctorate. And Mallory – she might be in the greatest danger of all. 1840 was not a good time to be a black woman in the deep south.

Amadahy must've read my mind.

"We will help you," she said.

Our voices woke Betsey who'd been napping on the bed. She looked around in alarm, calming down once she saw her mother sitting across from me at the table. Ginny hurried to gather her up, delivering her to Amadahy's arms.

As I watched the loving mother and daughter, my eyes came to rest on the two jars of fig preserves sitting on the sideboard behind them, visible now because Mallory had left the table.

"What was it Nana said about those fig preserves when she got here?" I said.

"She said her daughter helped pick 'em," Ginny replied.

I turned to Mallory. "Tell me how it came about that you and Nana arrived here together. Everything that happened."

"It started when you showed up at work with that sore shoulder. I happen to know from my sister that's a sign of a man yanking a woman's arms behind her back, you know." And she gave me a look. "When you called in sick on Friday, I was pissed, thinking you were hiding a black eye or something. I tried to call you, but you never answered, never called me back, didn't respond to my texts or emails. I was about to call the cops but then I remembered you were close to your grandmother. I looked up that article where she was quoted about that weird shooting to get her name, then found her address online. I drove to her house in Athens and told her about my suspicions. She said no, your boyfriend was a nice guy. Which I didn't believe for one minute. But she said you'd been trying to help her new neighbor who had a violent husband. So I drove her to the cabin. When we went inside, she found your clothes and your phone in a backpack in her bedroom. She got really concerned then. We left by the back door but she stopped and said she forgot something. It was those two jars of figs. We hiked through the woods till we came to the river. Then she picked two figs off a huge bush. She said I should eat mine and follow her. I wasn't keen on putting that yucky brown thing in my mouth, but I played along. And presto, we arrived here just in time to see that caveman waving his big gun around."

Ginny grabbed the jars and quickly set them on the table in front of me. I mouthed "thank you," which drew a self-conscious smile.

"You think?" Eric said.

"Would the figs still work if they were cooked?" I asked Amadahy.

She stroked Betsey's hair, lost in thought. "I do not know."

Eric unscrewed the ring, but the cap beneath it wouldn't budge.

"Vacuum packed," he said.

Degataga slid his knife across the table, which Eric eyed warily. It was the same one that had killed Jonah.

"It is clean," Degataga said. "Washed in the river."

Eric carefully pried the cap loose.

"Can I have a fork?" Mallory said.

Ginny handed her a three-tined fork which she used to lift a large, gooey brown fig from the jar. She started to put it in her mouth, dripping syrup on the table.

"Wait!" I cried. "You have to eat it as you..."

"Right," she said, promptly walking out the door, leaving a trail of fig syrup behind her.

"Mallory!" I said, jumping up to follow her. "I need to talk with you first."

"Make it quick," she said.

"You know you can't tell anyone about this, right?" I said, hurrying after her.

She didn't reply until we reached the charred remains of the hut.

"I get it, I get it!" she said, whirling around to face me.

"Do you?"

The baby babbled contentedly behind us, the others having followed as well.

"You want me to swear on a stack of Bibles?" she said.

"I'd like for you to think long and hard about the damage that could be done if you talk about this. For one thing, your career might suddenly come to a screeching halt when everyone decides you've lost your mind. But, more importantly, traveling to the past could really screw up the future. I may have already caused a slew of people in our time to disappear."

"What're you talking about?"

"That guy you called a caveman was my fifth great-grandfather."

Her eyes were like saucers.

"I'm not sure what'll happen if I go back through the doorway," I said.

"You mean you might go... poof?"

"Kathryn," Eric said, stepping forward, "I think if Jonah really was your ancestor, it would've happened already."

"I don't know. It's not like we have an instruction manual. I mean, here in 1840, I haven't been born yet, but I exist. What if it happens when I return to my own time?"

No one spoke for a moment, all of us lost in our own thoughts.

"So you might stay here?" Mallory asked.

A small lift of the shoulders was all I could manage.

"Jesus," she whispered, then gave me a long hug. "First things first." She blinked back tears. "I'll be the guinea pig. That way, at least we'll know if these cooked figs do the trick. Because no way, no how am I staying in a time when slavery still exists."

"Before you go..." Eric said, touching her arm. "Can you let me add my parents' number to your contacts?"

She responded with a confused look.

"In case I don't come back," he said.

Her expression softened as it dawned on her what he was suggesting. She handed him the phone and, without a moment's hesitation, he took off for the river.

"Hey!" Mallory cried. "What the hell?"

He reached the riverbank before she figured out what was going on and watched as he heaved her smartphone into the water.

"Are you freaking crazy? That's my phone!" She kicked one of the charred boards at her feet, causing it to crumble.

"I saw you taking pictures and shooting video," he called out, trotting toward us again.

"Damn you! All my contacts are in there. Important contacts."

"You'll survive," he said.

She seemed on the verge of a serious rant, but as she looked from Eric to me, and then the others, it was like she realized how insignificant it was in the great scheme of things.

Then she stepped carefully around the debris until she reached the spot where she'd arrived in the past.

"Is this the doorway?" she said.

"It is," Amadahy replied.

"Okay," she said. "Hopefully, I'll see you guys on the other side. You, because it would be way too much trouble to train a new producer." Then she shifted her attention to Eric. "And you, so I can kick your ass!" Turning to Amadahy and Degataga, her voice softened. "I wish both of you the best of luck." And then she offered her new friend some parting advice. "Ginny, remember, freedom is coming. Don't give up hope. But it's still a couple of decades away and it'll take a long war between the north and the south to make it happen. So, whatever you do, stay out of harm's way."

"Yes ma'am," Ginny said.

"And it's not gonna be pretty," Mallory muttered under her breath.

Then she put the soft fig in her mouth, tossing the fork on the ground behind her. As I held my breath, she stepped forward through the space where the back door used to be and vanished into the ether.

Ginny gasped. So did I.

⁂

Eric tried to take my hand as we strolled along the riverbank but I pulled away.

"You can't be serious?" I said.

"Ah, but you're mistaken," he replied.

280

He had offered to stay in the past with me if I decided it was too risky to follow Mallory back to our own time. But he had a life, a career, a bright future ahead of him.

"I won't let you sacrifice yourself," I said.

Although, truth be told, the selfish part of me wanted desperately for him to stay. The thought of being separated from him for the rest of my life was unbearable.

"You don't really think I'm leaving without you." He stopped in his tracks, taking my hand in his. "I love you, Kathryn. And, as I think I made abundantly clear, you're the only comely wench I ever want to have sexual congress with for the rest of my life, regardless of whether we're in the twenty-first century or the nineteenth."

"But…"

"And it's not only the sexual congress I'm worried about," he continued. "It's the eyes too. I'd be lost without your skeptical, know-it-all eyes looking into mine. And the melodious voice."

"You are so full of it."

"You do have a melodious voice. Although it does occasionally veer towards a high-pitched security alarm going off." He laughed, pulling me into his arms. "If you stay, I stay. We'll move to the big city of… let's see, what's a big city right now? Savannah. Charleston. Although maybe we should move up north so we don't get caught up in the Civil War. How about Philadelphia? I'll become a teacher and you can be a newspaperwoman."

"This is serious, Eric," I said.

"Believe me, I know."

He kissed me, a kiss that was full of love and commitment.

"You once said you loved me too," he whispered. "You haven't changed your mind, I hope."

"No, I haven't changed my mind. I do love you. Rather a lot, in fact. It's just that..."

He kissed me again.

Relief washed over me. But it was short-lived as I realized the enormity of our situation. It was one thing for him to volunteer to stay with me in the heat of emotion; quite another to live the life he'd have to live in the eighteen hundreds. If he thought there was prejudice and injustice in our own time, the depth and breadth of discrimination and oppression in this time was mind-boggling. Living in a world where slavery existed would, no doubt, try our souls. Even after it was abolished, the intense racism of the nineteenth century would be impossible to accept. Not to mention the pathetic state of women's rights.

We were quiet on the way back to the house. Like me, he was probably imagining what life would be like without running water, electricity, air conditioning, telephones, computers – the list went on and on. There was also the challenge of making a living and figuring out how to accomplish the most basic life skills – building a fire, cooking, taking care of ourselves. And then there was the challenge of birth control. Having a baby in the nineteenth century was out of the question. Medicine was primitive. Childbirth was downright dangerous. Besides, I couldn't quite figure out what it might do to the timeline and my family tree.

My words to Mallory came back to me. It was true, staying here in the past meant there was a risk of changing history. What if our very presence screwed things up? Every interaction we had with other people caused changes, some of them rather significant, like Jonah's death. God, it was exhausting to think about!

We found Degataga and Amadahy seated at the table, Betsey on her mother's lap. Ginny stood by the window, a dreamy look on her face. It was obvious they, too, had been discussing the future. They were as vulnerable as we were.

We sat across from them.

"You have decided your plan?" said Amadahy.

"If Kathryn stays, I stay with her," Eric announced.

"We welcome you to live with us," she said.

"We can teach you," Degataga said, his eyes fixed on Eric.

Betsey slapped the table with her hands, smiling at her mother. She spoke as though she were actually saying something in her baby talk. Amadahy gave her a kiss, then turned to me.

"I see the echo of her father's kind spirit in Little Butterfly's eyes. When I look into your eyes, I also see a warm spirit. I do not believe you are descended from Bad Brother. I would feel it here." She placed her hand over her heart. "I also believe if you were Bad Brother's granddaughter, you would never be born."

But good people did come from bad people, and bad from good. So I didn't put too much stock in her words about my warm spirit being proof I didn't descend from Jonah. But the more I thought about her other comment, the more I agreed. If Jonah had really been my fifth great-grandfather, his death would've already rippled through time. And I reached my decision.

"You need to get rid of his horse, weapons, clothes, razor and any other personal stuff like that," I said. "If anyone comes searching for him, it should look like he packed up and left town."

"Yes," Degataga said.

"I'll write Sheriff Moon telling him Jonah went out west to prospect for gold," I said. "You have anything I could write a short letter on?"

Amadahy brought me a rough sheet of paper, a small bottle of ink and a quill.

"I'm used to a different kind of pen," I said. "Can you write down what I say?"

She sat at the table, opened the ink, dipped the tip of the quill and waited for me to speak.

"Sheriff Moon," I began, and Amadahy scratched out my words. "I shall never forgive you for releasing me to Jonah Barnes." I waited as she wrote. "After he beat me into revealing where another gold nugget was hidden, he stole it from me." I paused. "He also forced me to tell him exactly where my brother-in-law is panning for gold in California." Again, I waited. "I wish him the worst luck possible as a prospector. He is a wicked man. I am returning to my home and hope never to see you or your jail again. Sincerely, Kathryn Murray."

"How do you spell your name?" she asked.

I told her and she signed my name in her distinctive handwriting, blowing on the ink.

"It might be a nice touch if the letter is delivered to the sheriff by U.S. Mail from another town," I suggested. "If anyone comes around asking about him, you could say he decided he'd had enough of the farmer's life and left for California to look for gold."

"I like it," Eric said.

I stood, picked up the open jar of figs and gestured for Eric to accompany me to the portal. The others followed us outside.

"I hope your lives are happy," I said, looking at each of them as I tried to keep my voice from breaking. "That's all I ever wanted."

"You and Old Grandmother will not be forgotten," Amadahy said.

Handing the jar to Eric, I wrapped my arms around her, giving her a hug that took her by surprise. Once more, I had to remind myself she was only eighteen years old. Amazing, considering all she'd been through.

"You won't be forgotten either," I said, tears threatening to fall. "You're truly an inspiration to me. I hope with all my heart that your bad times are over."

I kissed little Betsey on the cheek and embraced Ginny.

"I wish you the best, Ginny."

"You too, Miss Kathryn."

Then I turned to Degataga. "Thank you, Standing Together. Your name is fitting. You are a loyal, honorable man."

If Jonah wasn't my fifth great-grandfather, then Degataga must be. I remembered Nana being delighted when she found out from the family history that one of Amadahy's daughters was named Edith. Which might mean she and I were descended from that child.

"I believe you're my fifth great-grandfather," I said, trying to memorize his features and the warmth of his dark eyes.

"I would be proud to call you granddaughter," he said.

Eric reached out to shake Degataga's hand.

"I will write more in my diary," Amadahy said. "You will find it in my hiding place."

Blinking furiously, I pulled Eric with me to the portal. Using our fingers, each of us extracted a wet fig from the jar.

"I'll go first," I said.

Eric grinned. "I'll be right behind you."

But what if Amadahy was wrong? What if I ceased to exist when I crossed the portal? My hand shaking, I placed the syrupy fig in my mouth. But I couldn't bring myself to lift my foot.

Living here in this time might not be so awful. I could learn how to gut a fish. And sew by hand. I could adjust to using an outhouse and a chamber pot. Amadahy and Degataga would let us live here on the farm and teach us how to survive. And then maybe we could move somewhere so we could make a living.

But surely she was right. If I was descended from Jonah, when he died, my existence and Nana's existence would've been erased. We would never have been born and I wouldn't be standing here. I would never have met Eric, so he wouldn't be here either. But he was! He was right behind me, patiently waiting for me to cross through the time gate back to where we belonged.

So I bit down on the sweet fig and crossed the threshold where the back door of the hut used to be.

~26~

The familiar buzzing filled my ears and dizziness almost made me fall, but I steadied myself, then spun around in time to watch Eric emerge, fig juice dripping down his chin because his smile was so big.

"Kathryn!" he whispered. "Thank God!"

He drew me into a fierce embrace, nearly squeezing the air from my lungs. When he pulled back to look at me, there were tears on his face. He hugged me again and we rocked gently back and forth. His calm, reassuring demeanor had been a bluff. It was obvious now he'd been as scared as I was. It was only when he wiped the tears from my cheeks that I realized I was crying too.

"We're quite a pair," I said.

"Of gonads," he said, laughing.

"Gonads?"

"You've gotta admit, we've got balls, the both of us."

I slapped him playfully on the shoulder. "I don't have balls!"

He swooped me up like a prince carrying a princess. "And for that, I'm very grateful," he whispered and then kissed me.

When he set me down, I looked around the now empty clearing, thinking of our last moments on the farm.

"Amadahy's diary!" I cried. "She was going to write more in her diary!"

I almost crossed through the space where the time gate was, but, nervous about accidentally returning to 1840, I walked around to the other side, entering from where the front of the shack had been. I got to my knees where I remembered her lifting the book out on my first visit, set the jar of figs down that I'd accidentally brought with me, and swept the leaves and pine straw aside with my hands. Together, we brushed away a layer of dirt until we came to the remains of the blanket, now mostly disintegrated. Below that, we discovered more dirt. We scraped until our fingers touched something that was hard as rock. But it wasn't a rock. It was a flat surface made of rusted iron.

It was the same strong box I'd seen in the past. Eric grunted as he lifted it from its hiding place, setting it on the ground beside the hole.

"It's gotta weigh fifty pounds," he said, sweeping dirt from the lid, then wiping his hands on his pants.

"Is it locked?"

"No lock." He slowly lifted the lid.

Inside was a blanket, tattered and faded.

I clapped my hands together, then wiped them repeatedly on my skirt. As I reached inside, he stopped me.

"We should wait till we get home," he said. "The pages might crumble."

"You think?"

"You brought the original diary with you so the paper wasn't that old. This paper has been stored underground all these years."

He dragged the heavy box as I tramped through the woods behind him, my mind flitting from one thought to another.

"I never thought to ask why you came looking for me," I said.

"If you want to know the truth, I was a little suspicious when you told me you couldn't come to the wedding. All that stuff about your grandmother. I tried to reach you over and over yesterday before the ceremony, and then during the reception last night. When you didn't answer, I knew something was wrong. So I drove through the night. Stopped at your apartment, saw your car wasn't there. Headed over here. Found your car by the cottage, along with a vehicle I didn't recognize, and ran all the way to the river."

"Mallory's car," I said.

He set the box down to take a breather.

"I should've guessed that's why you didn't come to Savannah," he said.

As we resumed walking, another question occurred to me.

"Jonah only fired one shot. Then he threw his rifle at Degataga. Why didn't he keep shooting?"

"Repeating rifles weren't invented until a couple of decades later."

"Ah."

We were quiet as we continued up the hill. I was relieved Amadahy and Degataga were together. And I truly hoped they would be happy. But guilt weighed heavily on me.

When we reached the cottage, my grief for Nana hit me hard. It was unimaginable that she was really gone. It dawned on me then that I had to tell Mom. And Jeannette. I had no idea what to say.

When I retrieved my bag from Nana's bedroom, I found five voice messages from Jeannette on my phone, frantic about Nana's whereabouts. She said Nana left the house while Sofia, the new companion, was in the shower.

Despite wanting more than anything to know what Amadahy had written, I had to wait on that for a while and drive to Athens. I offered to meet Eric later at his condo but he said he wasn't letting me out of his sight. After changing into my own clothes and bagging up my bloodied nineteenth century clothing for the dumpster, I texted Jeannette that we were on our way. Eric followed me in his car.

"Where is she?" Jeannette said, answering the door with Gracie in her arms – a sight I'd never seen before.

"Let's sit down," I said.

Once we were seated at the kitchen table, I dialed Mom's number, using the FaceTime app. She didn't answer the first time, but on my second try, she picked up.

"It better be important if you're calling me this early," she said, her voice husky. "And I'm not doing that damn FaceTime." She was twelve hours ahead of us. The sun was coming up in Hong Kong.

"It's about Nana," I said. "You can see my face. I don't have to see yours."

Her voice changed immediately from cynical to worried. "What's wrong?"

"I have Jeannette here with me, Mom. Eric is here too."

"What's going on?" she demanded.

"I need to begin by giving you a little backstory."

"What happened?" she shouted.

"That's exactly what I'm about to tell you."

I went through my story as I'd decided I needed to tell it. I didn't start out revealing Nana was dead. I wanted them to know how it came about. Mom interrupted me several times, but I insisted I had to explain it this way. I told them about Jonah beating Amadahy and forcing her to have sex against her will, about how Jonah murdered Isham, about how Amadahy refused to leave, desperate to stay on her family's land – all that stuff. And then how I tried to intervene, but only succeeded in causing more trouble, actually getting myself locked up in the local jail.

"But when we walked down to the river," Mom said, "there was nothing there. Nobody's living on that land."

"Correct," I said. "Nobody is living on that land right now. But in 1840 there was a little farm there. That's where Amadahy lived after she married Isham, before he was killed by his half-brother. And that's where she lived with Jonah after he stole the farm."

"Excuse me," Mom said. "Why are you talking about people who lived there in the eighteen hundreds?"

"I know this is hard to understand, Mom, but we traveled back in time to when Amadahy lived along the Broad River. Me, Nana, Eric and my co-worker, Mallory."

There was silence on the phone as Jeannette shook her head in disbelief.

"Nana's the one who accidentally discovered the time gate," I continued. "But she didn't understand she'd traveled back through time and thought Amadahy was a new neighbor. She was so upset when she saw Jonah hit her and knock her down, she asked me to call the police."

"I think I've listened to enough backstory," Mom said. "Where's Mother?"

A sob was lurking in my throat and it was all I could do to tamp it down.

"Nana saved Amadahy and Degataga," I said, deciding to give her the exact details later. "Jonah was about to shoot them and Nana leaped in front of Degataga and the bullet from Jonah's gun killed Nana instead." The scab covering my grief ripped off and a deep, sorrowful sob shook my body.

Eric was by my side, wrapping his arm around me.

"Are you telling me my mother is dead?" she said.

My voice wouldn't work.

"Yes," Eric said, moving closer so Mom could see him. "Kathryn held her in her arms as she breathed her last breath. But before she went, your mother told Kathryn she was happy to die this way. Happy to die a brave old woman saving someone's life. She said it was far better than succumbing, bit by bit, to Alzheimer's disease."

I was glad I'd told Eric what Nana said because there was no way I could've shared it with my mother at that moment.

"This is insane," she muttered, sounding tired and angry. "Where's her body?"

I wiped my tears with the back of my hand. "I'll take you to the burial ground when you get here."

⁂

A warm shower never felt so good. Eric let me have the master bathroom while he took the guest bathroom. I spent half an hour washing all the dirt and sweat from my hair and body.

As the water poured over me, memories of Nana streamed through my mind. The time she rescued me when I climbed the magnolia tree in her back yard and was too afraid to climb down. Baking Christmas cookies together and letting me decorate them with red and green frosting. All the plays we saw together. The board games she let me win as I was growing up. She was so much more than my grandmother. She was my best friend.

It came to me then that Nana was my past – a past that shaped and molded me, a past I would always cherish – and Eric was my future. I clung to that thought as I dried off and slipped into the pale blue boxers and T-shirt he'd loaned me, then slipped into his bath robe. Squeezing toothpaste on my finger, I brushed my teeth, then combed the tangles out of my hair with his comb.

I found him lying on the bed, hands tucked behind his head, dressed in an identical set of boxers and T-shirt.

He hopped up, crossed the room, taking my hand in his.

"You okay?"

I gave his hand a squeeze.

We went downstairs and fixed peanut butter sandwiches, sitting side by side at the kitchen booth to eat them. Then he opened his laptop and translated the delicate pages we'd painstakingly removed from the strong box.

Amadahy's Journal – Part 12 (Sep) 1840

For many moons, I fought Bad Brother with cunning and potions to calm him and make him sleep. I used traditional Cherokee herbs to cleanse myself when he forced me to lay with him, telling him I used them to make myself more fertile. When Ginny came to live with us, I shared the knowledge learned from my mother and grandmother so we would not carry his child. But I feared one day my medicine would fail.

This allowed me to remain on our Ancient Soil. But the danger increased with the passing of time. And as his savagery grew, I feared he would abuse my daughter.

Then came the visitors through the Going Back Portal. The young white woman called Kathryn injured Bad Brother when he attacked her. Then Old Grandmother sacrificed herself to save Degataga's life when Jonah fired his long musket. So it was that Degataga avenged Isham's murder, allowing his spirit to rest. And so it was that the evil spirit ruling my family's land was defeated.

After burying Old Grandmother and watching our visitors depart, I wrapped all of Bad Brother's belongings in a flour sack and Degataga took it with him to hide the horse. Unease filled our minds. Would white men come to steal the land when they learned Jonah was gone? Would the sheriff believe he departed to search for gold?

When we heard a wagon approach as the shadows lengthened that day, Degataga put his hand on his knife, telling Ginny and me to take the baby and hide behind the house. He said we should flee if he gave the signal. Watching from our hiding place, I was surprised to see it was Mr. and Mrs. Berryman.

Degataga stiffened when we joined him in the yard, but I did not believe they meant us harm.

Her husband helped her from the wagon, her large bonnet shading her face from the afternoon sun.

"Mrs. Barnes," she said, "Eli and I wanted to make sure you're safe. And that your cousin, Miz Murray, is all right."

"We are well." I replied, uncertain why she would be worried.

"She had supper with us last night. She was right banged up, covered with scratches, her dress torn. Eli found her by the river. She said she fell in and was carried downstream. She said she had to return to your house right away. I told Eli we needed to come check on the two of you."

I could feel Degataga waiting for my words as I searched her eyes.

"She is safe," I said. "She returned home with her husband. I, too, am safe now." I cast my eyes upon Degataga, Ginny and Betsey, hoping Mrs. Berryman would understand my unspoken message. "Jonah is gone."

She regarded each of us with kindness.

"Is that Isham's baby?" she said, fixing her eyes on Little Butterfly.

"She is Isham's daughter and has his gentle spirit."

"What's her name?"

"Betsey."

She patted my daughter's hand, nodding warmly. "May I return next week to visit you?"

"You are welcome in our home."

Mr. Berryman did not speak, but I saw approval in his eyes. I hoped it was a sign we would be allowed to live in peace.

In the following days, Degataga took Jonah's horse from its hiding place and sold it to a man in Tugaloo. When he returned, he asked me to cut his hair in the white man's style. We also cleared the burned wood from the yard and built a new women's hut, being careful to include a narrow back door where the old one had been.

When Mrs. Berryman returned, we had coffee and bread with the cooked figs Old Grandmother brought. She said they were the best preserves she had eaten.

"I want to tell you something, Mrs. Barnes," she said, setting her cup down. "In private." She looked down at her lap while I asked Ginny to take the baby for a walk.

"At first, I wasn't too sure he did the right thing, marrying a young Indian girl," she said when we were alone. "But he was a happy man. I grieved when he disappeared. When Jonah moved in here so soon after, I had my suspicions. I hear Miz Murray told the sheriff that Jonah murdered Isham. When I heard that, I knew deep down it was true. Jonah was a violent, sinful man. And thinking back on how Miz Murray looked when she arrived at my house that day, I knew that Jonah..." she waved her hand, not wanting to speak the words. She touched her coffee cup before continuing. "You see, my sister, Fanny, is Sheriff Moon's wife. So the sheriff is my brother-in-law. One good thing about him – he's loyal to Fanny. He listens to what she says. I told Fanny I prayed you could live here with your family and not be troubled by anyone trying to take the farm away from you. Isham paid good money for this land and you and his child should have it. I told my sister it's the Christian thing to do. I believe she convinced Ezra to make sure folks leave you be."

Her words lifted a terrible weight, causing me to smile at this kind white woman.

"I wish to tell you something also," I said. "I did not marry Jonah. I signed a false name on the paper. But that is done. Now I will marry Degataga. He is like Isham – a good man."

When she departed, I gave her Old Grandmother's jar of figs. I had two reasons. To thank her and to remove the figs from our home so Ginny would not be tempted to pass through the portal. She did not understand the danger. Before the fig bush grows again, I will explain that the portal would take her back to the time of our ancestors, not to the time where slavery is ended.

Old Noon Day performed the marriage ritual when he arrived during the Nut Moon. I bathed in the river and put on the same gingham dress I wore when I married Isham. Degataga dressed in deerskin leggings and a blue shirt buttoned high, looking at me with powerful love in his eyes. Ginny stood beside me as my sister while Little Butterfly walked from tree to tree, chanting and singing. Degataga presented me with venison. I presented him with fresh corn and cornmeal I had ground. And we mixed our blankets together.

That night, I lay with Degataga for the first time after he closed the deer hide flaps he hung to make a private sleeping space for our bed. Ginny and Betsey slept on a thick pallet near the hearth.

Moonlight shone through the window so I could see his face in the darkness.

"You are mine, Forest Water," he whispered, stroking my unbraided hair with his fingers.

"And you are mine," I said.

"It was fated."

When his hand touched my body, I shivered. He was gentle and loving. As he held me close after our passion was spent, I thanked Selu for giving me such a man.

"There's more," Eric said. He was bleary-eyed from working too long, knowing I was desperate to read it all.

"It can wait," I said, placing my hand on his cheek. "Thank you."

"Anything for you," he whispered.

I realized how lucky I was to find him. Something that wouldn't have happened if not for some old grandmothers who had strong medicine.

"Let's get some sleep," he said, closing his laptop and leading me upstairs.

We lay facing each other, his hand resting on my waist.

Naturally, that's the moment my phone buzzed on the nightstand. I reached over to switch it to Do Not Disturb, but noticed it was Mallory, who I'd forgotten to call.

"You made it back," she said.

"Yeah. So you won't have to train a new producer."

"Eric too?"

"Mm-hm."

"You really had me scared saying all that stuff about not being born. Listen, I'm really sorry about your grandmother. I know you were close."

"Thank you."

"I understand now why you wanted to do a story about all of us living on land stolen from the Indians. I'm sure we can talk the boss into it," she said. "I'm thinking it would add a lot to the story if we could interview Amadahy and Degataga."

"Mallory..."

"We wouldn't reveal to viewers where they are. Or rather, *when* they are."

"Don't be ridiculous."

"I'm not being ridiculous. We just have to frame it right. It would make a dynamite story."

I was about to remind her again about the dangers of interfering in the past but realized that would only make her more determined.

"I'm bushed, Mallory. I'm taking a week off. Let's talk when I get back to work."

"Something's come up that can't wait till then."

"It'll have to wait."

"I got a call from the weekend producer who says the scumbag teacher has agreed to do an on-camera interview with us tomorrow."

"No kidding."

"But there's a catch," she said. "He'll only do the interview with you."

"Me?"

"Surprised me too since I'm the one who did the report. Anyway, we need you to come in tomorrow so you, me and Brandon can meet him at his house."

"Tell Mr. Hobbs I'm not available and you're doing the interview."

"Already tried that. He says no dice. Has to be you."

"Why me?"

"He must know you're the fake teenage girl who got the goods on him."

"Not gonna happen. Besides, I'm positive his attorney told him to keep his mouth shut."

"We don't care what his lawyer told him. And we really need you to come in tomorrow. We'll do all the prep and follow-up. This would be a real coup."

She was right.

"And," she continued, "you'll be interested to know eleven high school girls have now come forward in other cities where he used to work, saying Hobbs suckered them into his bedroom."

"Jeez."

"And police have intercepted offers from porn websites on his phone. That reporter from *The Yellow Journalist* is doing a story on that."

I closed my eyes, wishing I could avoid all that.

"Kathryn, I know the timing's not great, but we've got to get that interview with Hobbs. He'll shop it around to someone else if we don't play ball."

"All right, all right," I said. "I'll come in tomorrow. But I refuse to go to his house. If he wants to talk, he has to come to the station."

"But, Kathryn..."

"But nothing. Not going anywhere near that house. Period."

There was a long silence before she gave in, saying she'd talk with Hobbs and see if he'd go for it.

After wrapping up the call, I couldn't help but wonder why things hadn't changed more in the nearly two centuries since Amadahy's time. Why was preying on women still so common? I silenced my phone and turned my attention to Eric again.

He was one of the good guys. I reminded myself there were a lot of good guys. Even in Amadahy's time. Isham Barnes. Degataga. Eli Berryman.

Eric was incredulous I'd agreed to interview Ed Hobbs. He thought Mallory should've pushed harder to do it herself.

"She probably did," I said. "She likes doing the splashy interviews. I'm sure it's sticking in her craw. You'll be interested to know there's another interview she's chomping at the bit to do that has me worried."

"With who?"

"She wants to tape an interview with Amadahy and Degataga."

"Whoa."

"What if she goes over tomorrow morning and picks a fig?" Alarm bells were going off in my head.

"You think she…"

"I need to beat her there." I hopped up, looking for my clothes.

"It's pitch black out there."

"True," I conceded. "She would never hike into the woods at midnight. I don't much like the idea myself."

"Tell you what – we'll get up early, zip over there and pick every last fig before she rolls out of bed. I'll set my alarm."

Which took him about ten seconds to accomplish. Then he lifted the sheet, motioning for me to slide in beside him. We snuggled together in our matching boxers and T-shirts, falling asleep wrapped in each other's arms.

~27~

Trekking through the woods at first light reminded me of the previous morning when I'd slept under a tree and found my way to the farm. It seemed so much longer than twenty-four hours ago.

When we arrived in the clearing, we pulled out two trash bags and stripped the giant fig bush of its fruit. There weren't that many ripe ones since the first crop was fading. We also picked the small green ones, hard as hickory nuts, even though they wouldn't be edible for a few weeks. I didn't want to take a chance on Mallory finding even one that might ripen enough to navigate the portal.

Finally satisfied we'd done a thorough job of it, we washed our hands in the river, the sun's brilliant morning rays glittering on the water's surface.

"Jonah was like a malignancy," I said.

"Like the white man was a malignancy for all indigenous nations," he replied.

When we reached the cottage, I thought of Nana's fig preserves. What if there were more jars?

I used my house key to let us in. We stood inside the front door as I soaked in the colors and odors of the living room. Everything about it made me think of Nana – the aqua and white décor, the scent of cinnamon hanging in the air, the shafts of sunlight giving the room a warm glow.

The sound of her cheerful, loving voice filled my mind. I pictured her rushing to hug me when I arrived, no matter how recently I'd seen her. She told me she loved me in so many ways. I desperately hoped I'd given her that message often enough.

Eric placed his hand on my back, as though to remind me I was not alone.

"What amazes me," I said, "is that our Cherokee ancestry became invisible so quickly. Why didn't we know?"

"You've gotta remember, American Indians were classified as colored along with black people. They were persecuted and discriminated against. Considering the realities of the nineteenth and early twentieth centuries, it makes sense that many of those who lived among white people tried to blend in."

"What a travesty."

Searching the cabinets, I found two jars of fig preserves labeled in Nana's neat cursive handwriting.

"I'm going to hire a man to dig up that bush," I said.

"You sure?"

"The last thing I want is for anyone else to go back to 1840 and throw a monkey wrench into everyone's lives."

I had to go home to see about poor Pixie, hire someone to take care of the fig tree, and drive to the station for the interview Ed Hobbs had reluctantly agreed to do on our turf. Since Eric needed to go to work, we went our separate ways, him in his car, me in mine, after kissing good-bye two times.

Pixie forgave me once I petted her for a solid hour while calling around to find a handyman for my weird little job along the Broad River. I found a guy who said he could do it on Wednesday.

"What makes you think it's okay to slip a drug into a teenage girl's drink so she'll black out while you rape her?"

That was the first thing out of my mouth sitting across from Ed Hobbs in a small studio at the station. Not exactly what Mallory planned when she emailed me a list of questions. And, although she thought I was being extreme, I insisted on wearing my blonde wig and glasses again, to make it more difficult for that perv to recognize me in the future.

"Miss Spears," he replied, "I've never raped anyone in my life."

"Doctoring a girl's drink with Rohypnol to incapacitate her before having sex qualifies as rape, Mr. Hobbs. There are now more than thirty girls who've given statements to authorities about what you did to them. Prosecutors in Georgia, Alabama, South Carolina and North Carolina are lining up to file charges."

"Those girls begged me – *begged* me – to teach them. I gave them what they wanted."

"Do you really believe they wanted to be blackmailed with pornographic videos after you drugged them and molested them?"

"I don't solicit business, Miss Spears. They come to me. Obviously, they're looking for a thrill." He slouched in his chair, giving me a cocky look.

Disgust overwhelmed me. He felt no remorse.

"Does your attorney know you're talking with us today?" I asked.

"I'm representing myself."

"So your defense is that these girls *want* you to drug them and rape them?"

"Like I said, it's not rape if they come to me and give me their consent. And pay me money!"

I could see Mallory out of the corner of my eye, shaking her head as she stood beside Brandon who was shooting this disgusting interview with a handheld camera.

"Would you want your daughter to be treated this way?"

"I don't have a daughter."

"Your sister?"

"Don't have a sister either."

"You must have a mother."

"Used to, but she's gone."

"If she were still alive, would you want her to be treated like you've treated these girls?"

"No one would want my mother, Miss Spears."

"Do you really not understand that what you've been doing is abusing other human beings?" I cried.

"Miss Spears…"

"Were you abused as a child? Did your mother or father sexually molest you? Beat you? Neglect you?"

He gave me a smug look like it pleased him I was upset.

"Kathryn," Mallory said.

"I want to know!" I shouted. "Why in God's name would a boy grow up to become such a lowlife sicko using his position as a teacher to hurt young women?"

"God obviously has nothing to do with it," Mallory said, hurrying to my side and putting her hand on my arm as if to restrain me.

I yanked my arm free and threw my lavalier mic on the floor, not taking my eyes from Hobbs as I shouted at the top of my lungs.

"You, sir, are a putrid pustule on the face of humanity! I hope you rot in hell!"

I stalked from the studio, Mallory trotting after me.

"Come back, Kathryn! We've got more questions."

"That guy wants us to help prove he's crazy, hoping the court will go easy on him," I said. "He's not crazy. He's nasty."

"But we need this interview."

"I'm done."

When I pulled up in front of my apartment, Eric was leaning on his car waiting.

"I brought crackers and cheese," he said, taking my hand. "And a bottle of Merlot."

We walked inside and he wrapped me in his arms. I was grateful he showed up without my saying a word. Like he instinctively understood I would need him. His existence gave me hope.

He poured us both a glass of wine and we sat thigh to thigh on the couch, eating our crackers and cheese, Pixie curled up on the cushion beside me.

"I finished translating the last pages," he said. "You want to read them now or would you rather wait?"

"Now."

He opened his laptop, draping his arm around me as we read.

Amadahy's Journal – Part 13

The day after our marriage ceremony, Ginny ran into the house, hands in the air.

"I found two gold pieces!" she cried, holding one in each hand for us to see. "They was in the barn, up high on a shelf. I had a suspicion he might've hid some. Then, lo and behold!"

Degataga caught my eye and I knew we shared the same fear. It would be dangerous if people knew we had gold. Ginny was disappointed when we said we could not travel into town to buy sugar and cloth for new dresses, but she understood when I explained.

"There's one thing I was hoping for," she said, an aura of sadness surrounding her.

"What do you hope for?"

"I know freedom is coming one day, but I was thinking one a them nuggets might buy my freedom so I don't have to wait till my hair turns grey."

"The day Bad Brother died, you became a free woman."

"I did?"

"You are my sister."

She threw her arms around my neck and kissed my cheek and ran from the house shouting to the trees "I'm free! I'm free!"

I sent word with Degataga, asking Mrs. Berryman to return to drink coffee. When she visited, I told her about the gold.

"I heard that's why Jonah ran off," she said. "To pan for gold way out in California."

But her eyes told me she knew the truth.

"We wish to give you one piece of gold," I said, "if you will buy what we need with the other one."

"Goodness sakes. That is most generous of you."

I also told her of our wish to make Ginny free. She said her husband would help us with the proper paper.

And so it was that when Harvest Time Month arrived, Mr. Berryman drove our new wagon into the yard, pulled by two horses that now belonged to us. In the back was a bundle containing two pieces of cloth, one for Ginny and one for me, a diary for me to write in and a large bottle of ink. There was also a plow and two books Mr. Berryman bought for us as I requested. And for Ginny's happiness, we bought a sugarloaf so she could make her sweet foods.

When winter arrived, Johnny knocked at our door. He looked the same as he did the day of my hurried wedding to Isham Barnes, when he and the other white men forced my family from our home – dirty straw-colored hair, unshaven face, the same meanness in his watery blue eyes.

Degataga stood close beside me in the doorway. We did not ask him to warm himself by the fire.

"Jonah owed me one a them gold nuggets he flashed around at the poker table," he said. "I come to collect it."

"He is gone from this land," Degataga said, his tone as bitter as the cold wind racing through the trees.

"Well then, where's that white woman he promised me?"

"She returned to her home far away," I said.

He looked down his nose at me. "The colonel might be interested to know you're the little squaw that got away during the round-up."

"I am not a squaw," I replied. "My husband and I own this land."

"And you are not welcome here," Degataga said, resting his hand on his knife as he stepped forward.

Johnny's boldness melted like the last snow of spring under a blazing sun. When he rode away, we hoped he would never return.

The special shoe with the tall heel was ruined by the heat of the fire when the hut burned. Degataga made another one, carving a sole from the branch of an oak tree and attaching it with leather straps and glue to my new boot. It was good that I walked without pain because I was soon with child and Betsey lived up to her name, flitting like a butterfly from tree to tree.

During the Cold Moon, I began teaching my husband and my sister to read and write. We read from the books Mr. Berryman bought for us – "The Last of the Mohicans" and a book with Ginny's favorite story, "Rip Van Winkle."

❧

I have not written in my diary for many years. Degataga says now is a good time since our children are grown and have children of their own. I sit at the table by the fire, no longer hiding in my hut to write as I did when I was young. I still use the Cherokee Syllabary, no longer to conceal my words in fear, but because it makes me feel as one with my ancestors.

For ten years Degataga rode into town to pay our taxes. Then Mr. Berryman warned us that a man would come to find out who lived in our house as Washington City counted all the people of the country. We listened to his plan. And when the stranger came to our door, I told him my name was Amadahy Barnes.

"And this is your husband?" he said, pointing at Degataga.

"Yes."

"Jonah Barnes was listed on the 1840 Census as head of household," he said, writing in his book.

"Yes," I replied.

He asked the names and ages of our children. As he departed, I gave him venison and cornbread wrapped in cloth for his journey.

We judged that using a white name would protect us. Mr. and Mrs. Berryman told the sheriff that it should be so.

We honored Old Grandmother when we named our firstborn. I asked Mrs. Berryman and she explained that Edie was a small name for Edith. So our daughter's name is Edith. But we call her by her Cherokee name, Adsila – Blossom.

Our son is named Isham. His Cherokee name is Dustu – Spring Frog. I believe Good Husband from long ago would be pleased.

Our last child is named Kathryn after my distant grandchild who lives in a time when there are no slaves. Her Cherokee name is Ahyoka – She Brought Happiness.

We now have seven grandchildren. They keep their Cherokee names secret, saying it is better outsiders do not know they are Cherokee.

Ginny married Degataga's cousin Gawonii – He Is Speaking – who visited our farm from his home in the mountains. She told me as we sat weaving baskets one day that he had asked her to be his wife.

"I told him I want to stay here with you," she said. "Is that all right?"

"It is the natural way for the Principal People that sisters stay together. And you are my sister. You are a member of my clan."

So Gawonii cleared more trees and built a house for them on the other side of the garden. She had two sons and one daughter, who she named Maloree. Her Tsalagi name is Tohi Adedi, which means Freedom. Ginny and Gawonii have six grandchildren.

After Ginny's friend from the future spoke of the coming war, Mr. Murray told Degataga many things. His words were true ones. There was much death, hardship and hunger. Degataga learned that Johnny was killed in battle, which did not make me sad. But good men died also, including the Berrymans' oldest son. I do not wish to write of that time. It is done.

Degataga and I visit my family burial ground every year when the flowers bloom to honor our ancestors. We chant the old songs taught to us in childhood. We speak of our mothers and grandmothers, our fathers and grandfathers, our sisters and brothers, our aunts and uncles. We placed markers on the graves so our grandchildren and our grandchildren's grandchildren will know who they come from. So they will not forget Nunahi-Duna-Dlo-Hilu-I – The Trail Where They Cried. So they will not forget the Cherokee Nation's land was stolen. So they will not forget how they were marched west to the Darkening Land, too many dying along the trail.

That is why I began writing my diary. I wished my descendants to learn my story. I also hoped the story of the Aniyunwiya would not be forgotten.

When I called out after Isham died and Bad Brother forced himself into my home, it was my own grandmother I wished for – the powerful Medicine Woman who created the Going Back Portal.

But another Old Grandmother came to help me. For that, I will be grateful until I join my ancestors on the other side.

Now that our hair is grey, Degataga reads my thoughts.

"You still wait for your Faraway Granddaughter," he said yesterday as we shelled walnuts Mrs. Berryman brought us.

"She is also your granddaughter."

"But she is of your clan – the Paint Clan, the clan of strong medicine."

"I believed she might return one day," I said. "But she fears traveling through the Going Back Portal will do harm."

"She is wise."

"When she left that day, I did not say 'until we meet again.'"

"She heard your unspoken words of parting," he said, taking my hand in his.

"I hope this lifts the burden of guilt from your shoulders," Eric said. "Since you're descended from Degataga, it was apparently predestined that you would intervene."

"I think Degataga would've killed Jonah without my help."

"But without you, he would probably have been hanged for murder, assuming they caught him. Then how would Amadahy have kept the farm? And if he was forced to flee, same thing – she couldn't have kept the land. If she fled with him, she would've lost the land that way. All three scenarios would've resulted in losing the farm. Meaning you'd never have been born."

"I don't know," I said, sipping my wine.

"And those gold nuggets allowed them to buy Ginny, keeping her from being sold to a plantation."

"True."

"Plus, you made friends with the Berrymans. I mean, like Amadahy said, Mrs. Berryman interceded on their behalf with the sheriff. And they used the gold to buy the tools that allowed them to make a go of it. Plus, I bet that letter you wrote the sheriff helped grease the wheels for them to be accepted."

"Hm."

"One more thing," he said. "What you and your grandmother did when Jonah pulled the trigger may have meant the difference between Degataga murdering that son of a bitch and killing him in self-defense. Your grandmother made the ultimate sacrifice. But it was a sacrifice that allowed them to have the land *and* each other."

I took a deep breath, considering.

"You deserve a lot of credit, Kathryn."

"Well, it was a team effort. If it hadn't been for Mallory's suspicions about me being abused, she never would've driven to Athens to find Nana and take her to the river. If they hadn't shown up, I guess I would've taken that bullet."

He grunted, pulling me closer.

"Of course, it was Nana who found Amadahy in the first place," I said. "She's the one who led me to the time portal. And I wonder about those dreams she had about her Grandma cooking figs and trying to tell her something."

"Gives me chills," he said.

"And you helped too."

"Not much."

"Eric, it was you who made me risk traveling through the portal to come back to our time. I wanted you to return but I couldn't stand the thought of being without you."

Which made him tug me onto his lap for some serious kissing that led us to adjourn to the bedroom in short order.

"I think it was fate," he whispered as we lay wrapped in each other's arms.

～

Mom, Jeannette, Eric and I walked single file. Far from civilization, it was almost like we'd gone back in time again. All we could hear was the crunching of leaves and twigs beneath our feet and the chirp and trill of birds in the branches above us. We walked from the cottage to the river, then turned and traveled in the direction I remembered taking when we transported Nana's body to her final resting place.

The heat slowed us down, along with a few zigzags as I got my bearings. But finally, we reached the large boulders I remembered.

When we rounded the big rocks, I recognized the peaceful place where Amadahy had chanted the Cherokee songs of lamentation over Nana's grave. Since my last visit, more rock mounds had been added, along with small granite headstones.

Eric stood close beside me as we read the names carved into the markers, now eroded by time.

"There," he said, pointing at three mounds, all in a row.

We moved closer, squatting down so we could make out the inscriptions.

The one on the left read: Isham Barnes 1818 – 1839. The middle one was inscribed: Amadahy "Forest Water" Barnes 1822 – 1895. The engraving on the marker to the right said: Degataga "Standing Together" Barnes 1821 – 1895.

Emotionally, it was incomprehensible that they were dead. I'd just been with them. They were young and strong, their whole lives ahead of them.

"That's the most romantic sight I've ever seen," Eric whispered.

I wiped my tears.

"She was laid to rest between two good men who loved her," he said. "And, judging from the dates, it looks like Degataga and Amadahy may have died together. What more could you ask?"

I leaned my head against his shoulder.

"Which one is Mother's?" Mom said, her voice uncharacteristically quiet.

I looked around, trying to see the spot in my mind's eye where we buried Nana. Then I recalled how the large boulders looked from where I'd stood with Amadahy and Degataga. That's how I found it. I knelt down to see the timeworn marker: Edith "Edie" GoingBack Died 1840. Below that was something carved in the Cherokee Syllabary.

"It says 'Old Beloved Grandmother,'" Eric said.

I ran my fingers over the words. Mom knelt beside me, Jeannette standing behind us with Eric.

"She's really here?" Mom whispered.

"Yes," I said.

We remained still for a long time, no one wanting to break the silence. Gradually, I became aware of sweet birdsong all around us. It was as if the birds were providing music for our private memorial service. Which reminded me of Degataga's flute – the mournful Cherokee music he played as we returned to the farm after burying Nana.

Sitting cross-legged on the ground, I pulled out my phone, searched online and found what I was looking for – a Cherokee Indian musician playing a lovely song on a flute. The music enveloped us as we remembered the brave woman who saved Amadahy, Degataga and me, as well as a whole bunch of other people whose names were on that family history.

We listened until the song faded and then Jeannette spoke softly.

"I know Edie is loving this."

Mom contacted the authorities, reporting that Nana was missing and might've fallen into the river because of her dementia. Mallory convinced the boss to let us do some stories on popular areas around Atlanta that used to belong to Native Americans. Following an MRI, I did some physical therapy for my partial rotator cuff tear. But I have a feeling the ache in my right shoulder will be with me for the rest of my life.

Nana left a couple of investments to divvy up between Mom and me. She left Jeannette her beloved little dog, Gracie, along with the Athens house and enough money for taxes and upkeep. And she willed her cottage and the acreage behind it that included the old farmstead to me.

After months of driving back and forth, Eric and I began searching online for a condo to share somewhere between Atlanta and Athens. Funny how neither of us wanted to sleep alone anymore.

"There's one thing maybe we need to double check before we get too serious," I said.

"What do you mean before we get too serious? I'm already too serious. As I've said about forty-seven times now, I think we oughta get married."

"I'm deciding what kind of ceremony I want," I said.

"On the beach. You bring some fresh corn, I'll bring some liver and onions and we can mix our towels together." And he chortled at his own cleverness.

"But first," I said, "we need to double check..."

"Double check what?"

"I really hope it's not a fly in the ointment."

"What fly in what ointment?" he said, taking my hand and leading me to the bed.

"When we started dating you told me your family was from the same area of Madison County that my family is from."

"Yeah?" He pulled me down with him so I was on top.

"And you said you had some American Indian DNA and some African DNA."

"So?"

"You also told me about that family Bible saying you had a fifth great-grandmother who was half Cherokee born not long after the Trail of Tears."

"Your point is?" he said, rubbing his hands over my body.

"My point is – I'm wondering if you might be descended from Ginny and Gawonii. In which case, you and I might be related since Gawonii and Degataga were cousins."

He groaned and kissed my shoulder.

"If that's true..." I said.

"I don't wanna know," he said, his lips traveling from my shoulder to my neck.

"If it's true, then you and I would be…"

"Extremely, exceedingly, exceptionally, extraordinarily, ultra-distant cousins." He said, looking up at me.

I made a show of inspecting his eyes more closely.

"No," he said, giving me a mock serious scowl, "we do not resemble in the slightest."

I kissed his nose.

"You're curvy," he said, his hands gliding over my skin. "I'm not. You're beauteous. I'm not."

"I agree, you're not curvy. But you are one hell of a beauteous man."

The End

Review it

Thank you for reading *The Going Back Portal*. If you enjoyed it, please help spread the word by posting a brief customer review wherever you buy books. Or recommend it to your friends, in person or on social media. And I'd love for you to check out my other books!

A note from the author

Despite old family stories suggesting I have Cherokee Indian heritage, a DNA test shows not one drop of Native American blood. My knowledge of Cherokee culture comes from books and articles. Any misrepresentations or mistakes are my own.

About the author

Connie Lacy writes time travel fiction, speculative fiction, magical realism and historical fiction, all with a dollop of romance. She worked for many years in radio news as a reporter and news anchor. She and her husband live in Atlanta.

Contact/follow

Website: www.connielacy.com
Facebook: Facebook.com/ConnieLacyBooks
Twitter: @cdlacy
Goodreads: Goodreads.com/ConnieLacy
Email: connielacy@connielacy.com

Sign up for occasional author updates/get a free short story

www.connielacy.com

Also by Connie Lacy

The Time Telephone

What if you could save your mother's life by calling her in the past on a time telephone? An intriguing coming of age story about a teenager dealing with feelings of rejection and abandonment.

VisionSight: a Novel

Seeing the future is a curse, not a gift for Jenna Stevens. A heartfelt novel of secrets and unexpected love.

A Daffodil for Angie

It's 1966. Angie's got a lot on her plate – the women's rights movement, school integration, the Viet Nam War, a cocky anti-war activist and a sexy quarterback. A coming of age story that drops you right into the social upheaval of the 1960s.

The Shade Ring Trilogy
The Shade Ring, Albedo Effect & Aerosol Sky

A compelling Climate Fiction trilogy set against a backdrop of runaway global warming. A love story in a hotter, more dangerous world.